GREEN
DOT

GREEN DOT

A NOVEL

MADELEINE GRAY

HENRY HOLT AND COMPANY

NEW YORK

Henry Holt and Company
Publishers since 1866
120 Broadway
New York, New York 10271
www.henryholt.com

Henry Holt® and ⓗ® are registered trademarks of
Macmillan Publishing Group, LLC.

Distributed in Canada by Raincoast Book Distribution Limited

Library of Congress Cataloging-in-Publication Data

Names: Gray, Madeleine, 1994– author.
Title: Green dot : a novel / Madeleine Gray.
Description: First US edition. | New York : Henry Holt and Company, 2024.
Identifiers: LCCN 2023042986 (print) | LCCN 2023042987 (ebook) |
    ISBN 9781250890597 (hardcover) | ISBN 9781250890580 (ebook)
Subjects: LCGFT: Romance fiction. | Humorous fiction. | Novels.
Classification: LCC PR9619.4.G738 G74 2024 (print) | LCC PR9619.4.G738
    (ebook) | DDC 823/.92—dc23/eng/20230925
LC record available at https://lccn.loc.gov/2023042986
LC ebook record available at https://lccn.loc.gov/2023042987

Our books may be purchased in bulk for promotional, educational, or
business use. Please contact your local bookseller or the Macmillan Corporate and
Premium Sales Department at (800) 221-7945, extension 5442, or by e-mail at
MacmillanSpecialMarkets@macmillan.com.

First U.S. Edition 2024

Designed by Kelly S. Too

Printed in the United States of America

1 3 5 7 9 10 8 6 4 2

For the workers in song

I saw the best minds of my generation destroyed by madness, starving hysterical naked

Allen Ginsberg

But I've got a blank space, baby, and I'll write your name

Taylor Swift

GREEN
DOT

For some years of my twenties I was very much in love with a man who would not leave his wife. For not one moment of this relationship was I unaware of what every single popular culture representation of such an arrangement portended my fate to be.

Having done well in school but having found little scope in which to win things since then, it is possible that my dedication to this relationship was in fact a dedication to my belief in myself—that I could make a man love me so much that he would leave what he had always known, all his so-called responsibilities, purely to attain my company forever. I offered nothing but myself, you see. I was not rich; I had no assets or important connections. I did not have children or things that tied me to anywhere, really. Whereas he had all of these things—so settled into the couch of his life and just approaching middle age! I craved the stability he seemed to exude—I was intoxicated by the promise of ordinary happiness implied by his cargo shorts, by his chemist-bought sunglasses. I was besotted with the way he combined a high-powered job with the nervous shyness of someone who was bullied in primary school and has since taken on knowing timidity as an endearing personality trait. My god, how I wanted him. And I just knew that if I did enough, put in enough energy, waited long enough, was understanding enough, kind enough, funny enough, horny enough, accommodating enough, I could have him. And then I could have a life which didn't require me to make decisions anymore. I would adjust myself to snuggle in with him, into his life couch. No more anxiety about what to do or who to see or how to spend my evenings. I would be his, and that would be enough, and I could rest.

PART · ONE

In high school, my classmates would often speculate about their dream jobs, and about which degree they should pursue to attain that dream job. In our final year of school, we would sit around on the deck at lunchtime, girls from different social groups and hierarchies, girls with different skirt lengths, all of us united in filling in the blanks of this vague hypothetical time of "when school is over." As I was one of the highest achieving in our grade, the ball was inevitably lobbed my way. I was supposed to say a dream job that required a high leaving certificate mark, and an exclusive university degree, and then everyone would nod because the things that I said would have made sense.

Although I was clever, I had never conquered my times tables or evidenced any aptitude as a woman in STEM, so my options included lawyer, journalist, and academic. Lawyer: money. Journalist: exciting. Academic: worthy. I just had to pick one, I knew this, and then the conversation would flow on like a bounce pass from a wing defence to a nimble centre.

But I couldn't do it. I fobbed the pass. I intercepted my own shot. (This is something I have made quite a habit of, as you'll see.) In a condescending monotone I said, "Well I don't really want to do anything but learn or, like, read because everything else seems kind of tragically depressing and meaningless and on the way to school I see people on the bus who are going to work and they look fucking devo."

My friend Soph was on the deck with me, and I looked to her for support. She gave an encouraging grimace; I read this as her giving me the go-ahead to dig in, dig deeper.

I have a habit of scratching my neck when I am nervous to

feign casualness and what I imagine to look like cool impropriety, and I certainly did this then. Attention was on me. I was aware of my body, my pose—which I've been told can read as defensive. Holding myself in, using my arms as a cage. But what is defensiveness if not a waving hand above a drowning body? It seemed to me that surely, any day now, I would be caught out. I used my words, my wit, to deflect from my trembling fingers, to divert attention from the fact that my thighs chafed as I walked, no matter how little I ate, no matter how far I ran. Outside the school walls I struggled to retain agency—my lack of confidence in engaging with members of the opposite sex correlated to a direct deflation of my human capital out there. Inside the school walls, however, with words, and with girls, I could do it, I could direct the play.

At this moment I had not entirely lost the crowd. I could see others thinking back to their own morning commutes, I could see them reflecting on the dejected faces of those wearing skirt suits with trainers and running miserably for the bus. But then one of the boarders, sounding exasperated that she even had to explain something so simple, piped up: "Yeah but my dad says if you love your job you'll never work a day in your life."

A Greek chorus of other boarders murmured in assent. Without the support of the boarders I could not hope to win the popular vote: their numbers were simply too vast.

I knew then that I was about to be mean and I just didn't have the self-restraint to stop myself; I was powerless to resist the temptation of a clap-back barb.

"What does your dad do?"

"He's a farm manager." Arms crossed against plaid polyester, back against bench legs, territory claimed.

I looked to Soph for reassurance, to confirm that I could go on, hook the blade. Her expression was impenetrable; she'd evidently decided that she was just going to sit there, observing.

She'd watch me make a mess, like she had done many times before. Unlike me, Soph always knew when to stop.

I had one more chance to not be a dick, and I did not take it.

"Right, well your dad is either an idiot or a liar, unfortunately, and that sucks for you." And then I gave a little comic grimace, to convey that I did not relish telling her this bad news but, regrettably, someone had to.

This did not go down too well, as you might imagine. Some of the popular girls snorted laughter but most didn't, because even though what I had said was funny, it still wasn't cool to be an outright cunt. I did know this, I had gleaned this before, but my anger at the prospect of a future of remunerative labour must have briefly obscured my social self-preservation instinct. Or, perhaps more accurate, I had spied a window of opportunity in which I could confound, upset, confuse, and so I took it, because I was angry with the world and I didn't know where else to direct my anger, except at people who seemed more content with their lives than I was.

The boarder was upset; I could see that I had hurt her feelings. Soph looked at me with love and with pity. I think that's how she looked. That's how I read it, at least. It seemed to me that she was thinking, *Oh, my sweet Hera, when will you learn?*

I made a half-baked attempt to apologise to the boarder, but I hadn't yet internalised the word "systemic" and so my apology-cum-explanation lacked the rhetorical gravitas I could have given it a few years later. More to the point, I had learned self-hatred but I had not learned humility. What I actually said was that I was sorry I was right.

The moment after I said this, I regretted it, but it was too late to take it back. Then, before the next stage of the conversation could unfold, the lunch bell rang, and, physically tethered to the structured patterns of our days, drawn inexorably by the summons like plates of sushi on a train, we knew we must dissipate back to our various locker rooms to collect our folders and pen-cil cases for periods five and six. The boarder was mutely crying as she passed me, and her boarder friends gave me death stares. I averted my gaze, no longer broiling with the conviction that had directed my acidic tongue just moments before. I wanted the scene to be played out, done, and so I waited on the deck until it was.

That afternoon, however, I was walking past the school staffroom and I overheard my favourite history teacher narrat-ing a not totally inaccurate version of the exchange to a young substitute teacher, and rather than being disapproving or grave, both of them were cackling with laughter, so it was very hard for me to feel as guilty about being a bitch as I should have been. By the end of the school day the zing of my cruelty had been transfigured into an amusing anecdote among my friends. Only Soph did not join in the laughter, and I wondered how much of me she could see: I feared her recognition as much as I wanted desperately to be known.

As a teenager I presumed that in life I would encounter rooms I wanted to enter more fervently than the teachers' staffroom at lunchtime, but this has so far not proved to be the case. Each one of the teachers, even the substitutes, must have had some sort of life before coming here. And yet they had all decided that this room was it for them. I was desperate not just to impress the teachers but to know them. I wanted to know which teachers liked which other teachers, and which students were universally detested by them. I wanted access to all the schoolyard anecdotes from the perspective of those whose social lives were not determined by those anecdotes. I wanted to know why Mrs. Vale had left Ireland, and why she always had such a sadness in her eyes when she plotted our assessment marks on the whiteboard like a passive aggressive Rorschach test. I wanted to understand why Mr. Simmons was so obsessed with e e cummings—who had hurt him? I wanted them all to tell me candidly what they thought of the outside world, and whether they recommended ever entering it.

Back then, what was difficult to convey to others was that I really was not being disingenuous when I said that I had no specific career ambitions. I did not want to have a job. Obviously we would all need money to feed and house ourselves when school was over; I didn't not foresee that. Maybe for most of us this would mean having to do stuff for companies or whatever happened in business. KPIs? P&Ls? Circling back? But why were we all talking like the way we *wanted* to subsist was via indefinitely spending most of our waking hours doing something with very little relation to the formation and development of our selves, a development which, until this point, we'd been told by our teachers and parents was very important? Why would anyone dream about having a job? I felt like the world was trying to trick me. I felt like the butt of a joke I did not understand.

I'm aware that some people have terrible school experiences, and so creating a life for yourself on your own terms might seem like a really appealing prospect. But far from feeling bridled by restriction in my school uniform and my timetabled classes and the school gate that locked stragglers out at 8:45 a.m., I must admit that I enjoyed this little haven, sundered as it seemed from the rest of the world. Here, we had no obligation to anything but our own learning. Sure, the system was set so that our knowledge about Sparta would eventually transmute into a leaving certificate mark that would gain us entry into a profitable university degree, but just for now, if we experienced this chunk of our lives in the abstract, the goal was simply to learn about the hoplite phalanx and the socioeconomic stratification of ancient civilisations and metaphors in Australian poetry and the relation between Anselm Kiefer's indexical traces and the collective guilt of post-war Germany. It was a girls' school: there were no boys to distract us from our bizarre fixations and antics. It was a girls' school: we were insane and brilliant.

Disappointingly and confusingly for my guidance counsellor, who prided herself on her ability to "match" students to their perfect future careers by asking them five questions about their interests and aims, I worked hard in school because I liked learning and because I saw school as a perfect little realm of intellectual industry and competition that could act as a litmus test for my own potential. I wanted to confirm my own suspicion that if I put my mind to it, I could beat everyone I knew. I wanted direct evidence that I was not like the other people, and that if in life I did not gain money or professional accolades this was not because I was less capable than others, but because I chose not to engage in systems that presented careers as rewards.

Others would be rich, but I'd have the music, or something to that effect.

I thought that if I beat every other person my age in high school, then as the years rolled by and the disparity between their incomes and my own grew ever larger, or maybe they felt happiness and contentment and I didn't, I could comfort myself by knowing that I was smarter than all of them. Much like when I lost a tennis match (or, indeed, any game I played as a child), I totally could have won if I'd tried.

As someone who now writes this without money or my own Spotify subscription, I suppose if I were either cruel or even pragmatic I would report back to seventeen-year-old me and warn her that her logic would actually bring her neither the riches nor the music. But I am neither cruel nor pragmatic, and she'll find out soon enough, with or without help from me. It might also be helpful to tell her that "Dance Me to the End of Love" is actually about the Holocaust, so perhaps best not sing it to boys at parties like it's a seductive come-on—but no, you're right, she'll work it out.

When I first meet my married man, I have not yet worked it out. I have been through a fair bit of pain and I am aimless and sapped, despite still being in my mid-twenties, which seems young to most people but not to people in their mid-twenties. I feel like I have lived for a very long time, and the prospect of having to keep doing it until I die is exhausting. I am in Sydney, the city of my birth, and I am living in my father's house because I do not have any money on account of the choices I've made. I've spent the years since school trying to kick and scream into existence a life I care about and have a stake in protecting and cultivating. I have loved someone but not enough to want to stay with her forever, and she deserves more than that and so do I. I've finished degrees in other cities and now I have them and I don't really know what else to think about them, these degrees, these bits of paper. My degrees are the years of freedom from work that I have bought with money aka loans. Unfortunately there are only so many degrees you can do before it occurs to those around you that your passion might actually be less for study and more for not working a job. You can do one PhD, but if you do a second people tend to ask what is wrong.

After another day of being twenty-four years old and living in my father's house and listening to his records and wondering when he will be home from work because I look forward to talking to him, I decide to answer The Smiths' immortal question: soon is, in fact, now. I need to go on Seek and find myself a job, and then do that job, and then "start" a "life." I cannot think of ways to put it off any longer and I have listened to Morrissey's emphatic drawl too many times. Our dog Jude, who acknowledges my position as second-in-command when Dad is not home, follows me from the lounge room to Dad's study. I place my laptop on the desk and sit myself in Dad's chair. Jude lies down with his chin on my feet.

It is hard to convey to those who have been fortunate enough not to have been jobless and browsing Seek how truly soul-destroying the experience is. Imagine you've been in love with a person for years, and your relationship has brought you every good feeling and you find every single thing they say interesting and holding them brings you a comfort you hadn't known was possible. This person embodies everything you've ever hoped for, all the ways in which your life might mean something. Now imagine that this person is, for a totally arbitrary reason, removed from you, and instead a random stranger places a rock in your hand and says, "This rock is what you have now. You don't have your partner; you have this dirty rock."

That is kind of what it is like to scroll through Seek, except on Seek the rock is, for unclear reasons, a hot commodity that everyone wants, and you might not even get the rock. For every rock, there are two thousand other people who want the rock. And at the end of the day the one person who gets the rock . . . gets a rock.

As I have three variations of arts degree under my non-existent belt, I am vaguely competent in reading, writing, and knowing rudimentary things about a lot of different areas of the humanities. I could once have told you the three major classi-cal column types used in ancient Greece. At twenty-four, a few long years out from Introduction to Art History, I could perhaps tell you two. Sitting at my father's desk, scrolling the Seek home page, I know that Zoroastrianism is very old and has something to do with duality. I know that the trolley problem is tricky for all involved and that utilitarianism does not sit right with me, but I do not have a better or more practical alternative when asked for one. I know that content production is not my calling but at this point it looks like my options are content production or working in a call centre, and I know I can't work in a call centre because a few years ago I interviewed to work in one fielding donations for firies and I was rejected by the manager because the average Joe would find my accent a bit uppity, he thought.

Fair enough, content production it is, I say to myself as I stretch my fingers like Mr. Burns.

There are a lot of content producer jobs because, as far as I can tell, content production is pretty much just everything there is. From the job descriptions I read, I intuit that the main difference between content production and journalism is that content production pays a bit more and, unlike journalism, it actively prefers that the content produced evidence absolutely no subjective input from its creator. A content producer sources images (googles photos and then uploads them to a company website). A content producer writes engaging copy (paraphrases marketing emails and uses the word "dynamic" a lot). A content producer uses social listening to monitor audience engagement and edit content accordingly (glances at which topics are trending on Twitter and then uses those topics as SEO tags for corporate posts about optimisation).

Am I fluent in Photoshop, Seek wants to know. I reason that I know what Photoshop is and I know how to use Google, so yes. I affirm my competence in most of the "required key attributes" by the same reasoning.

Do I enjoy working in a team? "Enjoy" "working." These two words juxtaposed as if they aren't fundamentally incompatible! I do not enjoy collective work any more than I enjoy lonesome work, but I can't say this if I want to secure a position in an agile multidisciplinary team in a transformational environment. Clicking on the "further details" hyperlink for this particular job précis, it becomes apparent that "agile multidisciplinary team in a transformational environment" actually means "rural local council office."

You know when you've not slept well and it's 11 a.m. and you're at the electronic barrier at the train station and you just keep tapping your card, tapping your card, and nothing is happening and you curse technology and you curse your own life, and eventually an old woman next to you points out that the card you have been tapping with mounting frustration and audible sighs against the scanner thingy is in fact your health insurance card and might this go some way to explaining why the gate is not opening? That is how I feel writing cover letters for content production jobs, armed as I am with four facts about art history, two about religion, one about philosophy, and the ability to type with only three fingers out of the traditional ten.

However, I soon get into a rhythm. The key here, as it is for many things, is disassociation. The key is to sit at the laptop like the Buddha, if he were unemployed and on Seek. You must ease yourself into a state of Zen-like ambivalence, allowing buzz words to course through your veins and onto the blank document without ever consciously noting what it is that you are typing. Sometimes it helps to recite Virginia Woolf's great mantra as the page fills with the corporate gibberish that you yourself, apparently, are writing. I am rooted but I flow. I am rooted but I flow. I am rooted but I flow. Jesus Christ, I will kill myself. Sometimes the odd stray thought slips in but I ignore it, recite the mantra, keep typing.

My bum hurts from sitting on my father's wooden chair for so long. My posture is bad, which does not help. I've removed the clock from my home screen's taskbar, and I've placed my phone upside down and on aeroplane mode more than an arm's reach away. I must fend off all distraction.

I hear a knock at the front door, and I exhale with relief. Jude rises and barks, as is his job. I feel like Bernard Black when he doesn't want to do his taxes, so he invites the Jehovah's Witnesses in for a drink to talk about Jesus. I would invite anyone into this house right now. I would ask them about their childhood and then I would ask detailed follow-up questions. I would make them tea I would bake them a cake I would FaceTime their nana with them I would read the entire dictionary aloud in an Irish accent and then see if they wanted to hear it again with more of a northern twang.

I run downstairs to the front door, Jude at my side, and manage to catch a glimpse of the postman's disappearing posterior. The package on the doormat is addressed to my father, which makes sense as I have little currency with which to purchase packages. Deflated by the non-event, I debate the pros and cons of going to buy a takeaway coffee.

Coffee: good. Money: none.

I am twenty-four and I am scrolling Seek in order that I might find an opportunity to produce content in exchange for money so I can move out of my father's house and pay a few hundred dollars a week to live somewhere less nice and tell people that I am independent and that my life is following a recognisable bildungsroman narrative arc. I return to the desk, play a Taylor Swift song for motivation, and refresh the page. Now at the top of the screen, above the ads for a content producer for a cancer charity and a content producer for a government department for "digital transformation," sits a new, gleaming prospect.

Online community moderator. There it is!

Have I ever had any aspirations to be an online community moderator? I cannot say that I have. However, this job is advertised by a well-respected and smart-signifying media organisation, and I figure that this is likely the only way I'll ever get an interview to work in those hallowed journalistic halls, being as how I have no non-retail job experience because, as mentioned, I have never wanted a job. Compelled by a deranged masochistic impulse, like squeezing a pimple that is not ready to be popped, I think: "Perfect." I think: "This will allow me to observe how the rest of the people live, in their offices, day after day, going to after-work drinks, buying succulents on the weekend, hoping for 'promotions.' If I get this job I'll have enough money to live and I can spend my days judging those who are trying to make the system work for them more earnestly than I am."

When I google the position to see if there is a Reddit thread or a Glassdoor review that might help me to nail the cover letter, what I instead find is a widely shared opinion piece by someone who was once an online community moderator, the title of which is "I tried to kill myself after two years as an online community moderator." The rest of the article is, as one of my old teachers would say, "what it says on the tin." The writer describes how his job was to delete racist comment after racist comment, block trolls, and impotently attempt to attenuate the worst of humanity, and that after a while he thought a better alternative would be to asphyxiate himself in his Mazda, Willy Loman–style.

I see this article as a positive sign, suggesting that there will be less job competition for me, like when a murder has occurred in a house so then the house sells for less at auction. I guess in this case it is more like buying a house cheaply but with the murderer still at large in the house with no promise that he will ever leave, but no matter, who doesn't like adrenaline and saving cash dollars? I begin to construct my cover letter.

My name is Hera Stephen and I am passionate about online community moderation. As the world becomes more and more divided, it is increasingly important to facilitate the operation of discursive platforms for community members to engage in meaningful discussion and debate about the news of the day. I am committed to ensuring that open political debate can flourish in a safe online environment, in which freedom of speech is valued but hate speech is not tolerated. I am a diligent worker with a fine attention to detail and I enjoy working both in teams and on solo projects. I am self-motivated and will bring tenacious energy to this role.

Christ. The way it slips out of me like mercury is disconcerting. Like I am made of bullshit, and my skin just contains it until I type.

Eventually I press submit on the application, and I close my laptop defiantly, as if I have achieved something.

I read a book in the lounge room to pass the hours until Dad gets home, when I will inevitably monologue at him about the intricacies of my mundane day. For most of my uni years I lived in share houses, in grotty rooms, so to live in a house with a stocked fridge and a parent who cares about my life is a treat, even if it does put me behind my friends in terms of life trajectory.

Dad gets home, goes upstairs to change out of his suit, then heads to the kitchen to prepare dinner. I hover around him like a well-meaning but unhelpful bee. Jude stares up at him cutely in a shameless attempt to procure a treat.

As he dons his apron, Dad asks how my day was, and I tell him I've applied for a fancy journalism job that will most likely solve conflict in the Middle East.

"That's my girl," he responds. "Private school education paying off. Could you fix my golf handicap next?"

"That depends," I say. "Can you get any better at golf?"

"I didn't raise you to be so cruel." He gives me a mock-hurt look and pulls a jar of pasta sauce from the pantry.

"And yet, here I am!" I do a kind of frenzied shrug-pirouette, arms up to down like a personified bottle-opener.

"And how was your day?" I ask.

"Well, I submitted my final designs for what may be the ugliest office atrium ever conceived, and not for the first time this year, I considered retraining to be a gardener."

"So just another day, then?"

"Indeed."

I tell him I'm going to shower and I'll be back down in a tic.

"As she wishes," he laments to Jude, and Jude stares back at me accusatorily; I have upset his favourite person, even if it is in jest.

When I return downstairs, Dad and I set the table for dinner, and we sit down to eat. He has made pasta; that is, he's made pasta sauce. That is: he's poured sauce out of a bottle into a pot and warmed it. He's boiled the pre-made pasta: we are not Italian.

He first started making this dish—if you can call warming a sauce and pouring it over packet ravioli a dish—when he and my mother divorced and, after a long fight in court, he got full custody of young teenage me. Dad grew up in a mining town in England where gender roles meant he'd never really mastered the whole "cooking" thing, but soon enough necessity meant he had to or we'd both starve. Occasionally when I was younger we'd have well-meaning aunts and ambiguously related older women come for dinner, and Dad would serve them variations on this meal, and they'd look at him, and they'd look at me, and you could see the pity in their eyes like, *Look at what this poor young girl is stuck with, look at how she lives with a single father who can't cook; look what life has already robbed her of.*

But what they didn't understand was that I loved this dish. I loved how plain it was; I loved how it screamed, "man was overwhelmed by the large supermarket." I loved my dad. I would trade a million fancy meals for frozen spinach ravioli and this man. I would trade a million mothers to hang out with this good dad; this good dad who wanted to be my father, even when the world didn't really want him to; this good man who went through hell to keep me.

So I sit at the table with my dad and eat this pasta like I have a thousand times before, and even though I am jobless and the world is absolutely ending and if I ever do have children they probably won't know what plants are and I'll have to try to find the language to describe a shade of green that used to exist and now doesn't, I'll have to try to conjure the sound of beaches for them—even though I know all of this, there is, incontrovertibly, a solace in this pasta ritual with Dad that makes me remember that there have been times I've felt safe and have had hope for the future, and that there are good people in the world who can be relied on, and that I might be hopeful again, it isn't so impossible a prospect.

I tell him more about the job—that it isn't journalism, actually, but comment moderation. That I'm not exactly thrilled about it but I feel I should do something, and this seems maybe more like what I should be doing than working in another shop.

Dad looks at me across the table with so much love, but I can see a little worry in his eyes too, a worry that he is getting worse at disguising as I am getting worse at disguising my sadness—or maybe I am just getting more sad. In exchanges such as this, over dinner, I jolly him and he jollies me, but there are pauses, there always are, when I lose energy for a second, forget to smile, go quiet for a bit, and then I have to jerk back into the present, express humour, express vibrancy.

His sadness at my sadness is the one thing I cannot stand; so much of my laughter is for him. So much of me waking up each day and continuing to live is for him, because I know that if I died he would die. And the fact that he exists in the world does give me the strength to keep doing the same. I think we are both scared of the inevitable future in which he won't be around, and anxious about how I will fare; if I will fare, more to the point. I mean, he would never admit to having that fear, he always says how strong I am, how I could take on anything. Sometimes I believe him, and sometimes I think it's just false bravado on his part. And of course I will survive; I'm being melodramatic. But am I? Is it melodramatic to say you fear not surviving? Survival is so unassured; for me it is a worry premised in realism. That we don't all admit to this is bizarre. The lies we tell ourselves and each other across the kitchen table.

We finish dinner, I wash up, Dad dries. I make him listen to pop music and he purports not to like it. We have a joke where he pretends he thinks every song I play him is Britney Spears, and I pretend to believe him. We are good at this joke, we have many years of practice. We started on tapes, then we had CDs, and now, here we are, making the same joke with Sonos.

My ex-girlfriend used to say that life was about "commitment to the bit," and if that is the case I am living life so much it's wild.

A week after I submit the application, there's a phone call from an unknown number. I have landed an interview for the comment moderator job. They are very impressed with my CV (three arts degrees?!).

I have never been good at interviews, and I think this relates to my not having had friends as a young child: it is just extremely clear in any interview situation that I desperately, desperately want to be liked. Unfortunately, the manic imperative I feel to win over each interviewer often results in bizarre slips of the tongue, in erratic hand gestures, in blurting out truly deranged shit that I don't even believe and have literally never contemplated before, let alone formed an opinion about.

I understand that desperation is an inescapable part of the interview dynamic, in that one person has the rock that the other person wants. But again, I have never "wanted" a job so much as I have wanted job offers. I would like to know that I could have the job, if I wanted it, and then I want to not take the job.

The nature of living, however, is that you have to pay for things, and during my undergraduate years I interviewed for innumerable terrible part-time jobs, most of which I did not get.

I think back to second year uni, to my fifteen-minute "chat" with Diane in HR at a company that facilitated business conferences. The position advertised was for a receptionist/office lackey, and no experience was required. The company headquarters took up one floor of a grey building in the city near the harbour. I had arrived late because I always arrive late. It was a hot, sticky day. My baby curls clung to my forehead like sweaty pubic hair, and my foundation dripped off my face and onto my collared crop-top. As soon as I got out of the lift and into the reception area, I realised that I would not be getting this job. It was not so much anything about the physicality of the office space per se, although that was unsurprisingly terrible, but more about the way that the dead eyes of the employees rolled over me with confusion. It was as if they could sense the mania that snap-crackled like electricity between the conductors of my unshaven leg hairs; they could feel that my presence was already messing with the equilibrium of their hushed sad space. I had never used Excel, it was so obvious.

Almost immediately after sitting down, I was summoned by Diane to stand up: appearing from behind a sliding door, she gestured for me to follow her into the beyond, which I did, with a gross speed that was off-putting to me, let alone to anyone else.

Diane did not introduce herself, I just surmised that she was Diane based on her appearance and also on the name attached to the rejection email I was to receive about half an hour later.

She led me into a brightly lit cave and asked me what I had studied at university. I told her art history, even though "journal article abstracts" would have been a more honest answer. Her face registered some affect at this; she told me that she had once hoped to study architecture.

I asked her whether this hope was as yet unfulfilled because she'd changed her mind, or because something had happened that had prevented her from fulfilling it. In hindsight this was a stupid question to ask in my position.

She told me that she hadn't got the marks to study architecture. She looked sad.

I now interjected manically, with false bravado and an evident inability to read the room. I exclaimed, "But look at you now, huh?!"

Diane looked at herself; I looked at her too. The view was unrewarding for both of us.

Diane did not like me and I was not going to get this job; nevertheless we continued on with the charade.

Diane asked me about my organisational skills, and I told her I was very organised. Now it was our turn to look at me: my unironed shirt belied my avowed time-management skills, as did my smudged mascara.

The next one was the kicker, the true evidential crux of my fundamental inability to tessellate within corporate environments. Diane looked me straight in the eyes, just knowing I was going to fuck this up. With the smugness of a maths genius asking a baby to explain the Riemann hypothesis, she said: "And if you were an animal, which animal would you be and why?"

I was panicking. The overhead light bright on my sweaty foundation skin, I stalled by commending the ingenuity of Diane's question. I knew what was expected of me: I knew that I was supposed to say that I would be a golden retriever because I am loyal and follow instructions well. Or a beaver because I am industrious and tenacious. Or I could have said I was a bird, thereby stressing my ability to always see the big picture, from overhead. But I did not say these things: I did not take these options.

"I'd be a meerkat," I said, "because I am both sneaky and vindictive."

I'd like to say that this response was entirely the result of conscious self-sabotage due to my lack of respect for capitalism, but unfortunately, I'd be lying. In that moment, the answer I gave seemed right to me. I wanted Diane to know that if I worked for her, I would get shit done, I would have no scruples, I'd be a corporate hack, I'd be her little bitch. I was thinking in for a penny in for a pound, I guess.

What I learned though, from Diane's dropped jaw, is that HR personnel don't actually want to be told the truth in job interviews. They want to relate to potential employees in the fabricated sickly-sweet language of neoliberal positivity. Diane wanted to hear about me wanting to be part of a team, her team, and I failed her. I'm sorry, Diane. I'm sorry for what I made you face that day. I'm sorry if it ruined your yoghurt snack break later. I'm sorry you didn't get into architecture—but, really, I'm not that sorry because you were a bitch in your rejection email to me, and I could see in the reflection of your glasses that you were typing it as my interview was still ongoing.

But that was then. This time, this time in the interview I will know what to say. I am older now than I once was, I've had more time to soak in the rhetoric, and I also do not care about the community moderator job other than the interior that it allows me access to, the vantage point it facilitates. This will make me canny; they will sense that I am canny but also totally unmotivated to become a journalist. I can imagine that most of the people they interview and hire for this position are obliquely intent on using this boring role to leapfrog into actual content production for the company, and that this would be annoying for the hiring managers, who simply want lackeys. I will therefore stress in my interview that I have no journalistic aspirations; that while I respect the work of the journalists I would be surrounded by, my own passion is for online community moderation.

I worry that I do not know how to dress for the interview, because I have no corporate clothes, and whenever I try them on they make me look like either a cosplaying child or a frumpy woman with no waist. I go with a voluminous pink dress, which is probably wrong, but no matter, I ace the interview.

This is in large part because the weekend before the interview I go to my friend Sarah's house to drink chardonnay and ostensibly "prepare" for the career grilling. I am determined not to repeat the meerkat fiasco. Sarah is my most competent friend. She has a jewellery stand for her earrings, so they never get all tangled together. At pub trivia she'll whip out some fact about transit policy in 1987 with such confidence that the rest of us just nod deferentially, like, of course Sarah knows that. Sarah works in comms and she has never once said the word "communications" to me—it's comms.

Soph was my best mate at school, whereas Sarah and I grew into our adult selves together at uni, where we both studied art history and bonded over our shared hatred of most other students. We particularly despised the mature-aged students, whose tutorial contributions almost always began with the disclaimer that they would like to "play devil's advocate." Sarah and I came out around the same time: she by sitting her close friends down in her lounge room like it was an intervention, explaining she was interested in women as well as men, but mostly women, and then opening up the floor for questions; me by bringing my girlfriend to a house party and proceeding to messily make out with her at all public events for the next few years.

Sarah knows that I am smart but she also knows that for all intents and purposes I am an idiot, and she is happy to guide me in the ways of the workplace, to translate the lingo into concepts that I understand.

"Hera," she says, as we are two fishbowl glasses of white wine in, sitting on the leather couch in her share house lounge room, "what you have to remember is that these people are bored and they just want to hire someone so they can get on with their day. You just have to come across as competent and not unhinged. And don't laugh when they say things about their corporate ethos, okay? Do not laugh.

"Google who started the company. Bring up that person's name within the first three minutes and say you admire them.

"When they ask you for examples of when you've made a workplace more organised, do not talk about how you used to steal belts during the one week you worked at David Jones and then gave the belts to Vinnies because there was a belt surplus in women's fashion and the belts kept getting tangled and that made it harder for the sales assistants to quickly select belts when customers asked for accessories to try on with their Ted Baker dresses."

"Well, then what do I say?"

"Tell them you like lists." Such authority Sarah has.

"Lists?"

"Lists. Tell them that though you have, of course, implemented many more complex time-saving strategies over your career, you find that the best organisation begins at the micro level, and for you, that means organising daily tasks and long-term projects in a series of lists, which you then mark as completed at each step." She looks at me meaningfully. "Trust me, people in offices love lists."

Bitch is not wrong. When I talk about my penchant for lists in the interview two days later, the HR women fucking froth.

"Ah! Mary-Alice loves lists too, don't you, Mary-Alice?"

Mary-Alice looks up from the other side of the conference table, where she's been doodling on my CV. "I do, I love them."

Snap!

I start the job two weeks later, after I've signed a bunch of tax forms and exchanged many pleasantry-filled emails with the company's HR woman. She recommends bringing a shawl to the office as the air conditioning is very cold. *We all have our office shawls! ;),* she writes to me, as if this is a fun situational bond rather than evidence of sexism in office design at the most basic level.

To kill time before I start online community moderating, I read a thick book about the wives of modernist writers and I become very angry about how Zelda Fitzgerald was treated. Scott basically stole her ideas and then had her locked up in a mental institution?! What was this world we were in?!

I've also been included in a company-wide group email chain in which everyone who works there, from lowly moderators to the editor-in-chief, has been forced to welcome me to the company in writing. I feel sorry for all of them, and for myself. How many of these do they have to do a year? Do I have to respond to each well-wisher individually?

Can't wait to have you on the team!

Like, yes you can? What are we DOING?

Zelda was GASLIT.

THE morning of the first day, a Monday that is to begin at 8:30 a.m. (insane), I wake agrog. I am not used to waking with an alarm, and I resent the noise. Nevertheless, I am determined to be peppy. If I am to slink into corporate life and judge everyone from my cubicle, I must ensure my demeanour is bright, chirpy, happy to be there. I have to look like I don't hate everyone and everything.

Sarah once told me that my resting face appears as though I am always thinking about a white man called Barry getting promoted, and as usual Sarah was correct in her assessment. My default expression is a kind of blank gaze, staring bleakly into the future knowing that it will look just like the past, interrupted intermittently by a little smirk if I happen to recall that "Oi Mister, You Me Dad?" Victorian doll meme.

Determined to rewrite the story my face tells before my inevitable office promenade, I practise a neutral smile in the mirror. I go to the bathroom and splash water on my face and say, "Get it, girl." I decide on a navy dress, I straighten my hair. I put foundation on my face and mascara on my eyelashes. I own only one pair of shoes—a pair of old Doc Martens—and the overall look is slightly undercut by this, yes, but last night, at Dad's behest, I polished the Docs and they are no longer covered in dirt and alcohol—another concession to the Man.

I google "News" and the news is bad.

I walk to the bus stop and look at the other commuters, wondering if they think I am one of them or if they can tell that I am a chaotic fleshbag in a navy dress. Two men in suits standing next to me are playing Candy Crush on their phones, separately, and another woman is on Tinder; they seem extraordinarily engrossed. Some schoolgirls are huddled around the bus stop bench bitching about their so-called "friend"—would you even call her a friend if she said she was going to get a matching group name with the core four on the back of her year twelve jersey and then when the jerseys arrived at school it turned out she just, like, hadn't done that? She'd gotten, like, "Maddison"?

"People are fucked," says one schoolgirl to the others knowingly. They assent; we all board the bus. People are fucked, she's so right.

I survey the territory. Everyone on the bus seems tired. One businessman sitting up front is listening to Ariana Grande, I can hear the chorus reverberating through his earphones, even as he strategically does not tap his loafers to the beat. Personally, I am listening to "Eye of the Tiger," as a private joke to myself, and I am not laughing.

We pass the shop signs I've known for my entire life. The furniture shop that was once a Birkenstock shop, and surely will be again, for all things have a way of moving in circles, and the widening gyre of Oxford Street Sydney is no exception. We pass the cinema I hung around in as a teen, hoping that someone would notice me. I fondly recall the first time I saw the film *Bobby* there. It was an ensemble piece about the assassination of the seventh Kennedy sibling with cameos from my then-idols Lindsay Lohan and Demi Moore. I remember how for weeks afterwards I would tell anyone who would listen that the film was "really affecting," as this was a phrase I'd heard used gravely by the floral-blazered matriarch of Australian film reviewing, Margaret. And the film really was very genuinely affecting. Did other people know about the Kennedys? Such bad luck, that family.

The bus makes a stop and the girls get off, merrily skipping into the school day that I would prefer to be having. You can't go home again, and you can't repeat high school forever, unless you become a teacher—and even then, I imagine, it's not quite the same. I muse on this, knowing that I will go home again, in nine or so hours, and then I will do so every day for the rest of my life.

Community moderation. Comments. Are dogs better than cats? Let's argue about it.

I am in my mid-twenties: I am allowed, even expected, to have an office job. But standing outside the tall building that houses the company for which I will now work, I feel almost comically out of place, like at any second someone will see me loitering at the doors and they'll laugh, like, *I'm so sorry but as if.* It's not that I have imposter syndrome in the corporate environment because of internalised misogyny, etc. Rather, it is that I simply cannot comprehend how anyone could think that me being here is natural. I fear my face will betray me; my eyes will surely roll upwards, contradicting my ingratiating grin.

Steeling myself before the grand entrance of corporate life (aka a normal door on a side street in the central business district), I enter the building and find the lift. I step in and smile brightly, as if there is a camera watching me.

The lift doors open and there I am, almost inside the very large, cold room where I will spend the rest of my life or so it seems to me on this morning. I take a seat in the reception, alongside a few others. We all ignore each other as we wait to be ushered inside the inner sanctum. The room is beige and reminds me of an abortion clinic waiting room, not just because of the corporate pamphlets and the linoleum, but because everyone seems sadly determined to gain entry to another room that will take something from them. They are just *gurning* to get inside and go sit at a computer or be interviewed by someone with a computer. When you get an abortion you can then leave the building, and you might be really devastated or you might feel really free—either way it's a decision you've made about your body and your life and you've had that choice. But everyone who works here will have to come back through the office reception area, day after day, having the hours of our own lives reduced, and by the time we leave at 6 p.m. each day not one of the decisions we've made in those past nine or ten hours will truly have been for ourselves.

I do see, by the way, that I am not bringing a positive, growth-mindset energy to my first day on the job.

Finally the HR lady appears, and she ushers me into another room. I am allocated a locker for my "personal effects" and already I am trying not to laugh, thinking of the contents inside the Lurpak butter promotional canvas bag I carry: my wallet, three pairs of underpants, headphones, nine tampons, a travel vibrator, two novels, a notebook, two beer caps, a bottle of sake, and a fountain pen. I am also told that I am to return my work-issued laptop and headphones to this locker each day at the end of my shift.

Then I am taken to my desk, which is also the desk of six other people. It isn't a hot-desking scenario; it's just that it is a large desk, with four people at computers on one side, and three people at computers on the other. I am to be on the four-person side, with my fellow community moderators. On the other side, the spacious three-person side, are chairs that will soon be filled by people I am immediately made to understand are in every way superior to me, as they are journalists. Like, *journalists*. If italics could be understood to constitute a certain deferential vocal tone, then the HR lady uses them here. She doesn't say it but she may as well, for the message is clear: do not disturb the *journalists*.

Externally I smile the smile of someone who is grateful to be here (*get it, girl*), and in my head I smile the smile of someone who is satisfied because her predictions about everything being awful are correct. I smile the smile of any woman who, at the behest of her partnered-up girlfriends, goes on a Tinder date with a guy who looks like a wanker on his profile, and on the date the first thing he talks about is his love for Elon Musk, and she just sits there, ecstatic, holding back a tear of self-congratulation, thinking, *Yes, exactly. Exactly as I imagined.* She holds on to this satisfaction in her own perceptiveness for dear life for the rest of the date. She holds on to it as he orders for her; she holds on to it as he talks about his car; she holds on to it as he tells her he "doesn't usually go for dark chicks"; she holds on to it as she for some reason hears herself agreeing to a second date and, one day, to marriage. When she dies she is smiling, thinking about how she predicted all of it.

I've been told to arrive at 8:30 a.m., it seems, so that I can be sorted out before the madding crowd arrives at 9 a.m. At this stage it is just myself and Ms. HR, and I have the privilege of surveying the abandoned desks from the night before—of noting line after line of desk cluster, of hypothesising about desk-sitters' relative journalistic ranks based on the quality of fast-food wrapper next to each keyboard. My desk is at the very forefront of the room, meaning that if I ever venture beyond my desk hub, it will be obvious that I have no professional reason for doing so, that I figure myself to be a kind of exceptional-Ariel type—that I want to be where the people aka *journalists* are.

The HR lady leaves me there with a handbook detailing the corporate ethos, saying I should read it over the day and not feel too bad if it takes me a while to get through as it is thick. I could read this but I could also one day still be an astronaut; "could" is an interesting word.

Around 8:45 a.m. a cloaked figure arrives at my cluster. The cloaked figure wears many layers of loose black clothing— scarves, cardigan, jumper, amorphous pants/skirt?—and atop her head is a visor, like you'd get for free at a sponsored sporting event, and atop the visor there is a shawl just kind of nonchalantly sitting there, entangled with a scarf. After sitting down at her chair and arranging her screen just so, and after pulling from her handbag all the items that she might need for the day, not making eye contact with me throughout this entire process, she announces herself; she says, "I am Alison."

And she is; she is Alison.

Alison is a cagey bird, who seems not to mind that she is in a cage but only that she is now being forced to share her cage with me. I think she likely has her priorities in the wrong order, but

I am also aware that not one thing I do will change this. Such immediate antipathy from someone tends to indicate that the problem is not you, but them. Then again, perhaps I say this to myself because I am frequently disliked on sight. No matter: we must all do as we can to live, I guess.

Alison doesn't want me to live, and why should she? She looks about fifty-five, with the posture of someone much older. I'm sure in her position I would immediately hate me too—this relatively fresh-faced girl with an obviously disingenuous smile.

I look at my phone. Only four minutes have passed since Alison arrived, swathed in fabric and disdain. The other two moderators will arrive in eleven minutes, if they are on time. I hope that they will at least be closer to my age, if nothing else. I allow myself, for a second, to dream that I might like them, but then I kick myself. *Hera, do not get your hopes up; you will only be disappointed.*

Journalists have begun to filter into the office. I assume they are all journalists, that is. Soon I will learn that some are IT people, some are web designers, some are editorial assistants, some are fact-checkers, some are subeditors. I sit there, pen in hand, ready to write down information if any is given to me. I produce shy smiles for those who glance over me as they waltz further into the space, laptop bags swinging with importance.

Eventually a very small brunette woman arrives at my side of the desk, acknowledges Alison with a nod, and proceeds to turn on her monitor. She looks to be in her mid-twenties, and she shivers as if she is freezing.

She does not introduce herself to me, but I instinctively understand that this is out of shyness, not rudeness. Something about the tunnel vision with which her eyes focus on her keyboard makes me think of an unpopular kid I knew in primary school, who once came up to me in the playground at lunchtime and said, "My mum told me that people who are bullied in primary school actually do way better in the real world than the bullies," and then looked away kind of wistfully, as if willing herself there, into that future. I feel fond of the small brunette—protective, even.

"Hi! I'm Hera," I bellow at my mysterious moderator peer, sticking my head around Alison's chair, which sits between us. "It's my first day here—any tips from a fellow trencher?"

She looks at me and giggles. "Oh, I'm not sure . . . Bring a shawl, I suppose? It gets so chilly in here. And say hi to Steve when you can."

I don't know who Steve is and I refuse to bring a shawl, this refusal growing stronger each time shawls are mentioned.

The mysterious stranger hasn't told me her name, so I ask. It is Mei Ling. She offers no more info than this, and that is the extent of our interaction for the day.

Now the energy of the room shifts as a tall blond woman wearing wide-legged black trousers and a fuck-off aura enters the space. Clocking me, her face goes slack for a second and then recomposes, like she is bracing herself to visit her grandma or do something else that she feels bound to do but isn't particularly enthusiastic about.

"You must be Hera. We are so happy to have you here! The community moderation team is the backbone of this newspaper and we couldn't function without you, our unsung heroes!"

I laugh, hastily turning a guffaw into an obsequious giggle—I hope suavely, but I know not.

"I'm Sally, the editor-in-chief, and I sit just over there." She points to the furthest corner of the room, and I am amused by what her definition of "just" must be. "Alison here is a veteran, and she'll show you everything you need." She is looking at her phone as she says this. This turns out to be the first and only time Sally ever speaks to me.

After studiously ignoring me for a while, Alison says it is time

to introduce me to the rest of the office. She and her many layers
of fabric stand, and we begin our slow march. Alison leads with
the embodied exhaustion of a Holocaust museum tour guide,
and I clock the effect her approach has on many of the desk-
sitters, who avert their eyes and attempt to look busy so as to
discourage communication.

Those unlucky enough not to have acted fast enough are
treated to an introduction to someone who will have absolutely
no bearing on their lives or work. We all pretend this is not the
case—I ask them about their role, and they ask one or two questions about me, until we each feel enough corporate pretence has
been performed and we can all go back to our separate realms:
they to their Twitter feeds, and myself and Alison back to our
desk.

The fourth chair on our side of the desk is still empty, so I
ask Alison who sits there. She looks into the past, reaching for
a name.

"That was Tim's desk. Tim resigned last week."

"So, it's just the three of us moderators then?"

"That is correct."

Myself, Alison, and Mei Ling. The three best friends anyone
could have.

I want to die but, devastatingly, this does not occur. I am very
much alive, and I am sitting on a rolling chair.

Alison decides that the best way to teach me my role is to
have me observe her as she does her own job. This involves me
spending the next seven hours of my life straining my neck and
watching her scroll, watching her laugh quietly to herself, watching her toggle between windows exasperatedly. On occasion I
pipe up and ask Alison if she might indulge me by explaining
what it is that she is doing. At this she sighs, seemingly expressing her hope that osmosis might already have set in by now and
that I will just know what to do without further instruction.

"Community moderation," she tells me, "is about people."

I mean, true.

"Our readers deserve a say in the conversation, and so we open comments below articles in order to facilitate this. However, sometimes things get heated, or we are bombarded by trolls trying to derail the conversation. Do you know what trolls are? Yes, well, it's our job to moderate those comments and make sure conversation is constructive and respectful."

"So we delete racist comments, basically?"

"Ha!" Alison scoffs as though I am a child underestimating the sting of a bluebottle.

She looks me in the eye, clearly readying herself to give me a teachable moment, her diction slowing down to a condescending crawl.

"No, we don't just 'delete comments,' Hera." She uses air quotes to highlight how foolish my assumption is. "This is not China; there are laws here. There is free speech. This is not Tiananmen Square. We are not comment *deleters*, we are comment *moderators*."

I discreetly lean back in my chair to see if Mei Ling's expression changes at all during this impassioned speech but she's cleverly obscured her profile with a curtain of hair. I make a note to myself to grow my hair.

Eyes back on Alison, I decide to ignore the Tiananmen Square analogy. "Of course. My mistake. I guess my question is, then . . . how do we moderate comments if we don't delete them?" I am genuinely confused.

The expression Alison makes now is the facial equivalent of cracking one's knuckles in readiness for a large task.

She launches into a diatribe that involves a lot of colour-coding and many acronyms. Basically, to comment on the site, users have to create an account. If we see that they have made a comment that is blatantly racist, homophobic, or otherwise fucked, we are to furnish them with an email warning. They then become "orange" in our system. If they do it again, "blue." If they do it again, "yellow." If they do it again, "red." After this: account suspension.

If they don't make a hateful comment for the following seven days, they go back to being uncoloured, and the process begins again.

"Okay, and what if they just make another account and go on to pull the exact same malarkey?" I am hoping "malarkey" will bridge the generational divide between us.

At this question, Alison's eyes spark, but not because of my canny vernacular. She is ready to drop some truth bombs.

"Do you know what an IP address is, Hera?"

I have existed on the internet in Australia and have wanted to stream shows from the US before they've been made available down under, so obviously I know what an IP address is, but I don't think this information will be received well here, so I say, "No, please tell me, Alison."

"An IP address is the individual number attached to a person's internet connection"—wrong—"and so we can see when a commenter's account is made using the same IP address as a previously banned account. There are a lot of old hats doing this, Hera, a lot of people trying to beat the system, swapping between accounts. But I find them. I always find them."

I decide not to ask Alison if she knows that it is extremely easy to generate multiple IP addresses.

From what I can gather, my job will involve this: reading each individual comment on each individual news article, deciding whether each comment is constructive to community dialogue or not, and, if it isn't, changing the colour attached to the commenter's account.

Another large chunk of my day will involve doing this but with a slightly different focus: copyright. If anyone inserts a hyperlink into their comment, it is my job to click on that hyperlink and see if the site it takes me to is an official site, or whether it is a site that is breaching copyright in some way—i.e., if the link takes me to Lady Gaga's official YouTube channel and blesses me with an official music video for "Bad Romance," all is well. But if that link takes me to a non-official Gaga account, to a—dare I even say it—pirated Gaga rendition, then fuck, guns are out. I am deleting that comment faster than you can say "Gaga oh-la-la."

This is a real job, and it is mine.

I take facetious notes as Alison monologues to me.

TERF means trans-exclusionary radical feminist, this is a slur against second-wave feminists. A. says be vigilant about account users who use this term, they tend to stir the pot unnecessarily.

And then next to this note I draw a little cartoon of a pot, like I am a twelve-year-old, because this is how I feel: like a bored humanities kid who plays up in maths class, much to the chagrin of the teacher who knows that this kid will probably not fail the exam, despite putting in no effort.

On and on, pages full of nonsense biro. I am digging my nails into my legs just to keep my eyes open.

By the time the workday ends I am exhausted. Part of me had hoped, perhaps foolishly, that there might be after-work drinks, where I'd get access to office gossip, or at least extend my circle a little beyond Alison and Mei Ling, but this does not transpire. My shift finishes at 5:30 p.m. and by this time half the staff have already begun to filter out.

When Alison begins to pack up her things, I look to her for confirmation that I too may leave.

"Of course you can, your shift is over."

Of course I can, my shift is over. Silly Hera!

I carry my laptop and headset to my locker, and I make my way to the lift. The lift goes down. I walk through the lobby and exit onto the street, where real life is happening. People are striding determinedly in many directions, bent on getting home, and I am one of these people. It's only been one day but I understand the grim expressions I see with far more clarity than I did this morning. I see the sad reality of the commute. I feel sorry for every single person.

I get on the bus, and on the journey home I do not consider the inner lives of my bus comrades; I'm too tired.

My arrival at the house coincides with Dad's.

"Hera, you look like you've been hit by a truck."

"Good to see you too, bud—Jesus."

This evening I feel no manic imperative to share my day with Dad, a state of mind he intuits once I respond to one too many of his questions with "Mmhmm." What would I tell him? That the world is brutal and on multiple occasions I considered standing up from my desk, going downstairs, and throwing myself in front of a bus? Dads do not want to, and shouldn't have to, hear this. He's been working his entire life; so has everyone else. I must suck it up.

The next day is a Tuesday; the day after that a Wednesday. I know this because I have to be aware of days now.

A routine has been established, in that I sit, Alison sits, Mei Ling sits; we all sit. We have our counterpart community moderators in the UK and in the US, and each morning before we get started on the day's work we have a videoconference in which they communicate the night's happenings so we're all caught up on which particular opinion piece about Palestine has been blowing up in the comments. It is amazing how desensitised everyone is. A guy called Mark, skyping us from his cubicle in London, yawns visibly as he tells us about state-sanctioned genocide and how readers are "not being very chill" about it, and we yawn visibly back. Alison sits with her shoulders down, indicating that the weight of the world has never not been on her.

There are all kinds of acronyms to learn; so many different ways to categorise groups of people in internet slang. I'm not a total luddite, I do know some of the acronyms just from life (LOL, am I right, fellow kids). But on my third day I miss the meaning of a whole comment exchange on an article about working from home. One commenter is calling everyone who works from home a "Wuslim." I'm aware from a previous Google search that Wuslim means "white Muslim," but I really can't understand what that has to do with people who work from home. I ask Alison if she can relieve me of my ignorance.

"Ah," she says. "You don't know Wuslim?"

"Yeah, no, I do, I think. I just don't understand why calling someone a Caucasian Muslim would be a) an insult or b) contextually relevant."

She looks at me like I have so much to learn (and I guess I do), then wordlessly turns back to her monitors.

Mei Ling studiously ignores this exchange. I'm starting to think Mei Ling might be a genius.

I get back to scrolling. I scroll, I scroll, I colour-code, I scroll. I contemplate Zelda. WWZD?

She would not be here is what.

I receive a notification on my browser—ping! Mei Ling has added me as a contact on the internal IM. I am *buzzing*. What does this mean?

The dot next to her name is green; I watch the ellipses dance: she is typing. I know I should do work and then just return to this window when I get a notification that she's actually sent the message; this would be the logical thing to do. But there is something about the typing ellipses that pulls me to stare directly at the screen until the text comes through. They tell you not to look directly at the sun, but you do it anyway, don't you? *Don't you?*

Ping!

Mei Ling Chen: *You get used to her, I promise.*

I look over at Mei Ling's shoulders. She has not looked up, she has not changed her posture at all to intimate IM complicity. Her hair is not completely obscuring her profile at this moment, and I can see that she is not smirking, as I do whenever I receive an amusing text in silence. I am thoroughly impressed by her subterfuge.

I consider typing back: *Like you can get used to the smell of shit if you sit in it long enough??* But no, I will bide my time. Mei Ling and I are not there yet. Slowly, slowly, Hera. I need to say something that invites further banter, but that could also be interpreted as earnest work chat if I misread the situation and Mei Ling is actually just being a supportive girl boss in a corporate environment.

Hera Stephen: *How long will it take until that happens, do you think?*

A pause.

Dots pop up, dots disappear.

Ping!

Mei Ling Chen: *You just have to wait until you give up on all of your dreams, and then everything becomes a lot easier. The moment will come, have faith.*

Oh my god.

Oh my god, Mei Ling is funny. Mei Ling is funny *and* depressed. My two favourite things in a potential friend. I am *beaming.* I am *floating.* Mei Ling, you saucy devil, you sly dog, you also hate this!

I stifle a guffaw. Mei Ling looks up. I catch her eye—I have to! I have to catch it! She smiles knowingly at me, and I back at her.

I now have an ally on my side of the desk. This must be how Brutus felt when he first realised Cassius also had a boner for killing Caesar. Don't google that, I don't know if that's how it went. Let me have this.

The day becomes much more psychologically manageable now, as Mei Ling and I get into the rhythm of messaging each other screenshots of particularly chaotic comments from the articles we canvass for hatred and copyright noncompliance.

That thing I said before about cats and dogs? That was not just a hypothetical. That Wednesday afternoon I spend four hours of my life moderating a comments section on an opinion piece by a well-known Australian journalist who has had the temerity— nay, the fucking *gall*—to write that cats are better than dogs, and to put this in her article's headline. It's like she actively wants to incite another world war. Have we not suffered enough?

The comments start off reasonably amicable. @petmum agrees with the journalist's position. @petmum also has a cat, and she loves her cat. She is pro cats.

Brilliant, so far so good.

Next up @dantesinferNO agrees that *some* cats can be nice,

but he doesn't like the attitude of most cats, who act all haughty. @dantesinferNO only thinks that cats are better than dogs if you are comparing a really good cat to a really bad dog.

Not quite the point, but fine, yes, whatever. Pass.

@drunkinlove now contributes the inevitable cat gif to the conversation. They choose the one where Salem the talking cat from *Sabrina the Teenage Witch* does some weird stilted puppet *mwahaha* laughter and you can almost see the hand inside the stuffed animal moving it around.

I am fine with this, I appreciate a well-timed gif. Do I wonder who @drunkinlove is, and what they are doing in their life that means they have the time and inclination to contribute a gif of a cat to an opinion piece about pets? Yes, I do wonder this. But again, this is all kosher, all above board. No need to get my digital highlighter out just yet.

Now @truthbot enters the conversation, and here's where it begins to turn. My spidey senses are tingling; I feel chaos in the air.

@truthbot: *dogs r obviously better than cats, author sounds like a pussy bitch.*

@truthbot: *hope she gets splayed & stops wining*

I assume @truthbot means "whining," but how are we ever to know? Some things on this earth will always remain mysteries, and I think that's beautiful.

@petmum returns to the fray: *Honestly, @truthbot, I think you'd do better not to spread such meanness around. The author likes her cat. Some people prefer cats.*

Then the inevitable:

@gleesimp: *you missed out on birds. Birds are the best pets. My mum died of cancer and my bird was the only thing that got me through.*

@debby: *What about goldfish? Did the author of this piece ever even consider that? Feels like she should have, if she was going to* rank pets. *This article is DRIPPING in privilege. Author doesn't even consider that most people can't afford dogs or cats, or even any pets at all?? Obvious to me that she's from family money.*

Imagine if this exchange had occurred this morning, when I didn't have Mei Ling to send screenshots to.

The fourth day of the week is Thursday: I am learning. But my mood is turning again, just as fast as it changed yesterday. After the high of the Mei Ling revelation, the low of another morning in this office brings me right back down. I sit and scroll as journalists trundle past me, talking amongst themselves about the state of the world. Not one of them makes eye contact with me. Today's article topics include climate crisis, geriatric alcoholism, and football. My eyes are dry, my back hurts. How can this be my life.

On Friday, more of the same.

The one differentiating factor today is that I notice another journalist working on the other side of the monitors. His British accent differentiates his mutterings from the other concealed voices that constitute the soundtrack of my days here. His colleagues are welcoming him back from a holiday, I think; it's hard to hear. At one point, I am angled in such a way at my laptop that I can see through a crack between two monitors, and I observe a sliver of his face.

It's a nice face.

Alison, perhaps sensing that I am distracted, reclaims my attention; she announces that I am to watch her read a comment section on an article about disappearing coral on the Great Barrier Reef. I will myself to keep my eyes open as I watch her scroll.

The rhythms of the office are already familiar to me: what is new and strange becomes mundane so quickly. When "news" happens there's a charge in the air, all the journalists puffing up like inflating jumping castles, as they put in harried calls to sources. My side of the desk, of course, is unaffected by these bursts of energy: we plod away, always playing catch-up, speed-reading ever-unfurling scrolls of digital garbage, signalling to a user in Perth that it's not okay to call another commenter a towelhead, moving on to the next line.

After the coral exercise, I skim-read articles about Gaza, a woman who had cancer and bought a dog, metalworkers in the US, a British TV personality who's killed herself, a nurse who's won the lottery, youth unemployment in regional Australia. I am not being paid to fully read the articles, but to grasp enough of them to be able to contextualise each comment at their ends and then decide whether it is probbo or not. Is that racist or is that just the other side of the argument? I have three arts degrees, so I tend to err on the side of it's racist.

As I sit and stare at my laptop, I hear the journalists on the other side of the desk nattering about national politics, speaking with vehemence as if their ideas might ramify somehow. Suddenly, I am on the verge of tears, which I know is dramatic, but it is not something I can control. I have never felt so mentally and physically paralysed. I didn't predict just how much this would bother me, this exclusion from news-making. My eyes begin to burn; my body is slightly humming, shaking, trying to contain the sadness. I need to leave this office immediately, like when you know you're going to vomit and nothing else matters but getting to a toilet *now*.

So far this week I've been eating lunch at my desk, unsure if I have the right to leave the office, too afraid to enquire, but today I must risk it. I must get out. I hurriedly ask Alison if I can take my break now, and she looks at me like "duh." "You should have taken your break earlier, Hera," she mutters exasperatedly. "Think about how what you do effects the workflow." I am so close to crying at this. Instead, I tell Alison I will do so and I beeline for the lift, head down.

Exiting the building, I am shocked by the brightness of the

sun. It hits me savagely, like one of those slap-bracelets we used to whack on each other's wrists in primary school. It has been this bright outside the whole time I have been inside, I realise. The whole time I have been watching Alison read comments, messaging Mei Ling, yawning about genocide, scrolling; the sky has been a perfect blue.

I don't know where to go to buy food. The task feels impossible. People in suits walk around with takeaway bags, but from where? I walk a few blocks, and eventually I find a sushi shop next to a phone case store. I buy two chicken katsu rolls and walk another few blocks until I spy a bench to sit on. When I open the sushi bag I see that I have not been given soy sauce, ginger, or wasabi. This is the straw that breaks the bisexual's back. I heave out a cry.

There are moments in life that stay with you, not because they are special in a good way, but because they are moments of complete flatness before something else inevitably happens. I always forget this, but it is true: something always happens.

Eating this dry sushi, I am utterly dejected.

My workday contains no achievable goals, no satisfaction: just comment, after comment, after comment.

I can already feel myself slipping into despair. I've just started, I can't quit. I can't quit.

I recall the boarder incident, I recall the years since school in which I have been training myself to react less viscerally to disappointment in situations and in other people. I recall my ex-girlfriend telling me that I was "a lot." I recall that it is this job, or no job. What I most want in the world is access to people, to understanding how they cope. This job has to do: I have to do it.

But en masse the whole thing is so pathetic—the men in suits buying takeaway coffees, rushing across the street to get in to the office before nine; the forced smiles between colleagues who both happen to be reaching for the last bagel; the fact that we all read Marx in first year uni, or if not, at least a paragraph or so of Walter Benjamin was relayed to us by a stoned high school paramour, and we lay on the lawns outside our schools or between tutorials, and we never thought that after this hiatus we too would end up cogs in the machine, and grateful to be so, and grateful to get home to Netflix.

Or perhaps, I am beginning to suspect, as I chew this sad sushi, maybe everyone else but me foresaw this even then, and thought it best not to mention it; like not telling your wife you've lost your job until after your anniversary dinner because you don't want to ruin it. Like not telling your best friend that you've slept with her boyfriend, even though you've already slept with her boyfriend, and like, you can't un-sleep with her boyfriend . . . she's going to find out and then it's going to be worse. Just fucking tell her! I've been re-watching *Fleabag* but haven't we all. All that time spent acting in bad student plays and debating the merits of polyamory, drinking cheap beer and laughing in the sun—had everyone been plotting, all along, secretly applying for graduate programs and perfecting the art of existential complacency so that when the time came they were ready to switch gears? Had everyone else been playing along with a fantasy that only I was too thick to realise could not last forever? I guess I thought if we all really didn't want it, then we all really wouldn't do it. Like the schoolgirls on the bus, like the promises we all made to get matching group names on our school jerseys: it turns out everyone got their actual names printed, and only I had committed to "Beef Cheeks" embroidered above "Class of 2012" in Cambria forever.

People are fucked, the girls are right, but I am also a fool. I should have known, but I didn't want to. There are so many things I don't want to know, but the universe keeps telling me stuff like an incorrigible gossip, like a school friend on pingers for the first time, not making sense and not stopping for breath.

I stand up. I must make my way back to my self-imposed prison.

Nearing the office building, I spy the British journalist from the other side of the desk. He is also about to enter the lobby. I can see him more clearly from this vantage point. He looks about forty, handsome, but stressed, distracted, lined. He is wearing a checked shirt tucked into his business pants, his torso is long and his legs are not, and the contrasting fabrics highlight this. I also have to enter the office via the lobby, there is no other way to get inside, and I have to get inside, for reasons having to do with capitalism.

I am so tired, I rose so early. I know that I have it in me to be vivacious. I've been vivacious so many times before, when the situation has demanded it. I've been taught to be vivacious my entire life; it feels like every film I've ever seen has involved a sparkly smart white woman who makes ordinary situations dazzle, who surprises everyone with her nuanced take on Simone Weil while downing a shot of tequila in a sports bar.

But this kind of nuanced and approachable vivacity requires so much energy, and my sushi has not made me full; I am still hungry. I have so many hours to go of the workday, so many more opinion pieces to read, so many more hours of chipping away at an unending block of text, so many asides from Alison.

Inside the lobby now, I enter the lift, I smile at the journalist. Will I be vivacious? Will I make a comment that proves I follow the news? Will I be polite and ask about his lunch? As he was not present on Monday, I've not been introduced to him, and I figure that unless I talk to him now, he will remain anonymous to me maybe forever. Nothing about this man indicates he'll be any more receptive to my attention than the other journalists in the office. Nothing about this man would ordinarily spark my interest. But I am so, so bored.

Fuck it, I decide. I make eye contact and cannonball into

conversation. "Hi, I'm Hera. I'm the new community moderator. I think my desk is near yours. Who do you hate most in the
office?"

He looks at me for a second like, *Did she actually just ask
me that?* And then he bursts out laughing. It is the first genuine
laugh I've heard all week; he is laughing like he's been snapped
out of a fugue state.

He has a vein in his forehead that becomes more prominent
when his eyes widen.

"Well, Hera, new community moderator, I don't know that
I'm at liberty to divulge that information."

The lift doors open, and he gestures for me to exit first. I can
sense the mood shifting, I can see his smile receding as he trans-
forms into office mode before my eyes, so I decide to invite our
newfound camaraderie into the sacrosanct corporate space. As I
exit the lift, I look him directly in the eyes, which are very close
to my eyes at this moment, and mouth, "Well, who?"

He responds with a very small smile, one that could mean
"wouldn't you like to know?" or "you've crossed the line but you'll
learn office manners in time" or "I'm actually thinking about my
father's dementia" or truly anything else, I do not know this man
or what his smiles mean. And then he walks around to his desk,
on the other side of mine, where his face and presence are hidden
by the giant monitors that divide our table like a changing room
curtain made out of Dells, and we are in different worlds again.

He starts talking to his fellow journalists about a café owner
in Sydney who is being evicted because of thinly veiled anti-
China sentiment. The three of them are engrossed, trading stories about the good work they've each done, covering the unjust
racial profiling of small businesses in Sydney's western suburbs.
He doesn't talk as much as the others do, and I am not sure of the
dynamic—if they are all journos, if one of them is more senior,

which beat or beats they cover. I return to my tabs, I resume clicking and scrolling.

Well, that's that, I force myself to think. I punted, I lost. Back to the grind, back to Alison and Mei Ling, back to death. I can't stand it.

After about an hour of this torture, I excuse myself to go to the bathroom. I'm in familiar territory: I'm on a comedown. In that lift, I felt something, I felt like this place might have more to offer me. But now the future is closing in on itself in my mind, endless loops of beige. I enter a cubicle and I sit down on the toilet. The fluorescent light overhead turns my legs a marbled white, and I observe how my flesh splays, how my thighs touch. I let myself cry again, just a little—silently, of course.

I don't know how I am going to do it—the rest of today, and then next week and all the weeks that will follow. Two people enter the bathroom, talking about some story they're working on. It's a piece about negative gearing, and they're brainstorming which MPs might give them the most incendiary quotes. All I can think is: these women are so in their own lives. They seem to be really in them. And I don't mean this in a cynical, judgey way. I am jealous of them; incredulous, even. I don't know how to be in my own body, my own mind. I want to care about a story, any story.

I wait till they've left, and then I leave my cubicle, wash my hands, wipe the wetness from under my eyes, and return to my desk. Before I put on my headset, Alison tells me that in future I should try to build my bathroom break into my lunch break, and I thank her for her advice.

Around 5:15 p.m., a ping from my screen. I assume it's a message from Mei Ling, giving me the tea on what's transpired in my absence.

I press on the IM notification and the chat pop-up box emerges.

The message is not from Mei Ling: it's from Arthur Jones. Who is Arthur Jones?

Whoever he is, he's just typed: *Doug.*

Who sent me this? Who is Doug?

I look up from my screen and around the office like a character on the phone to their stalker, who's just revealed that they are *inside* the house.

And then I see him, the British journalist from the lift, with the laugh. He is standing up from his desk, the top of his head visible over the monitors. He moves in a way that suggests he is swinging his laptop bag over his shoulder. He rounds the desk corner and, making eye contact with me, smiles another small smile, a shrug of a smile. "Good evening, Alison, always a pleasure," he says to her, and she blushes. And then, to me, when Alison has turned back to her screen, he mouths, "I hate Doug." And with this he steps out into the corridor that will take him to reception that will take him to the lift that will take him to wherever he sleeps at night.

I am alight once more, new energy surging through me; the thrill of a challenge.

It's on, then. It is that simple.

I have found the source of sustenance I will need to survive the office. For two minutes today I have been reminded that I am a person.

I am going to hold on to it, of course I am.

That night I am meeting Soph for dinner after work. This is an exciting prospect for me because Soph, like all of my friends, has by this stage had a nine-to-five job for some years. Until now, I have had to sit silently at such dinners as my friends and their partners take it in turns to lament their boredom or anxiety, to complain about the manager they hate or the promotion they have not received. When we are done with the first round of career commiserations, I might be able to slip in a comment about something I've read that day. But university study is not real work, that is the unspoken consensus, and I cannot possibly understand the stress my friends are under. Whenever I have attempted to equate my own stresses with theirs I am swiftly rebuked, and so I have learned to keep quiet until at least a few bottles of wine have been consumed, and the grievances aired become broader, more existential. I don't have an office enemy who keeps taking credit for my slideshows, but we *are* all going to die.

Now I am *one of them*, though, and I too can complain about my day.

Soph and I have arranged to meet at 6:30 p.m. at an Italian restaurant, the pricing system of which has not changed for as long as I've been alive. The downstairs area is a café where my friends and I used to come after school to drink coffee and pretend to be adults with our counterparts from the neighbouring boys' school. The upstairs is a restaurant, with the same gingham tablecloths I imagine they used in *The Sopranos*, having never watched *The Sopranos*. I arrive at the restaurant early, so I linger on the stairs for a few minutes, observing the scene below. I can feel myself momentarily buzzing into a better mood than I've been in all week, because of the British journalist, and because this, now, this is what I live for: being in the world, observing the action, all the small insanities that constitute our days.

The table in the corner next to the street is taken by an elderly gentleman with a newspaper, an address book, and a glass of orange juice on ice. He keeps looking around furtively and then quickly pouring slugs of liquor into his glass, which I love: I love his commitment to the performance of concealment in each pour, as if he hasn't been drinking booze brought from home at this table every evening for the past fifteen years. I love that the waitress never calls him on it, I love that she studiously looks away each time, so the charade can continue.

I see some kids in school uniforms doing what my friends and I used to do, sitting in a huge clump of energy and unmet potential, two empty coffee cups between seven of them, legs splayed across each other at random, like pick-up sticks. The waitress is looking at them from behind the counter like she would enjoy slitting their throats, but occasionally she smirks when one of them says something undeniably amusing.

"Did you guys notice how Mr. Bradshaw gave an early mark to everyone but me?"

"That's because you're a shitcunt, Marcus."

That's because you're a shitcunt, Marcus. Fuck it, I love these teens, I love the waitress, I love Marcus.

I continue up the stairs, remembering when Soph and I used to be those teens; when we did not know what our lives would entail and moments were spent in the present.

Soph now works in international diplomacy, and she is forever hinting at things she couldn't possibly tell me ("NDAs, you know?"), and then drinking wine and telling me anyway. It's not that big a risk for her, since I have little interest in foreign policy and forget everything she tells me anyway. Even if I did want to try subterfuge, I don't know anyone who would be interested in buying secret facts about Malta.

Even though Soph and I now live rather different lives, we began adulthood in the same swirl of vague artistic ambition. At school we were both going to be bohemians; we decided this one day when our art teacher showed us a photograph of Francis Bacon's messy studio, and solemnly told us that Bacon's male lover killed himself while on the toilet. We thought this was brilliant. I'd be a painter and Soph would be a novelist. I'd never painted but she'd certainly written, and it made sense to diversify our talents and, thereby, our bohemian social circles. In hindsight, aspiring to the lifestyle of an alcoholic Irish painter with a face like a globe and a penchant for misogyny was perhaps not the best plan, but we had little material to work with at that point, and it seemed to us that it was this or a life of business deals, there was no in between. We planned to move to Europe after school, and by Europe we meant "somewhere with lots of garrets." We'd seen *Moulin Rouge*, we knew how Europe worked.

As it happens, later never came—or, it did come, but it was different from what we'd pictured. When we got our Higher School Certificate results, Soph did well and so did I. It seemed a shame to waste the marks, or so everyone around us said. I found myself being slowly realigned to this perspective, like a lobster being boiled to death in a gradually heating pot. We could always start uni and then defer; better to enter the system and then have the choice, that was the agreed logic.

Soph enrolled in law/media and communications, and I enrolled in a Bachelor of Arts—a gesture to bohemian Paris. We'd both be at the University of Sydney, as it had been conveyed to us since birth that choosing any other university would be akin to not going to university at all.

Talk of moving to Europe was temporarily postponed, until swiftly enough what was temporary became perpetuity—a transition I've learned happens quite frequently. They say that habit is the great deadener but they don't also tell you that habit is all there is.

Soph quickly embraced her law studies. As the mark to get into law was a minimum of 99.75, you were saved the trouble of telling people individually that you were really smart. Soph fitted right in with these people who strode around campus with their torts textbooks highly visible underarm. These students seemed not to own bags or backpacks, as I noted one day when we were sitting on the grass by the library.

"Poor things," I said sympathetically, "always wrestling with their piles of heavy law books, not knowing that a contraption exists that would make transporting them so much easier."

Soph laughed at comments like this for the first two weeks or so of university, after which the idiosyncratic habits of the law cohort were off limits. I didn't mind; if I'd made her decision, I would have committed too. What would be the point in studying law if you couldn't also embrace your inner dickhead and expect that no one would call you out on it? I quite liked this for her—I liked the world that she granted me access to, and I liked the fact that I was not part of it.

Upstairs, I sit at our usual table on the balcony and wait for Soph to arrive. I think about which work anecdotes I'll narrate to her and consider contriving the existence of a water cooler in the office, to add some bureaucratic texture.

Soph descends on the table in a blur of movement, jacket flung over chair, backpack hurled beneath seat. "You will not believe what Jacinta did in the team meeting this morning."

I suspect that I will believe it; I have heard tell of Jacinta's antics before.

Bread arrives. I eat the bread and wait for my turn to talk.

Jacinta hijacked a meeting she was not leading, taking credit for Soph's work on a recent project. I agree that Jacinta is a cunt who deserves only bad things, and this appeases Soph a little, but not much. She will destroy Jacinta, she claims. I do not doubt this: Soph is smart and mostly motivated by vendettas—although this lies under a deceptively sweet surface—and she recently broke up with her boyfriend, so she has the time.

The workplace dynamics of Soph's office are interesting compared to those of most of our friends. A lot of the people she works with are on postings from foreign countries, so they're all socially footloose and fancy free in a city that is not their own, and they are sleeping with everyone in their orbit. Most have partners back home but there seems to be a what-happens-on-tour-stays-on-tour mentality.

By the time our pasta arrives Soph is on a roll, going on about some trade campaign and how the marketing team are trash at liaising with graphic design, making life tough for anyone who actually works on *policy*. To be fair, they do sound like they are trash. I mean, I am technologically illiterate, but even I know how to add events to iCal. Most of the time my iCal events are just reminders from myself to stretch, but the principle remains.

Eventually, when she's unwound enough, Soph asks how I'm doing.

I find myself narrating the events of my week like my life is an amusing sitcom in which I am the hapless protagonist who keeps turning to the camera to shrug as a laugh track plays. I tell her about Alison's visor, about how she told me she wears it indoors to detract from "the glare." I tell her about Mei Ling, about how she is an ally but still inscrutable. I tell her about the work that is crushing my soul. Soph listens, she nods, she expresses dismay at the right moments. She is still the same Soph from school, in this respect, silently watching me make a mess.

As I go on, however, it occurs to me that Soph is merely going through the motions. She is holding back, I think, because she can't quite believe that I am actually doing this, that this is actually my life. She is responding like it is all a joke. This is because I am framing it like it is all a joke.

I have myself in a double bind. I either maintain the sardonic surface, keeping the vibe light, or I switch the tenor entirely and admit that this job is already making me feel like I am receding into greyness, and I just don't know how I'll do it, I don't know how I'll last, and I'm scared that I will feel this way for the rest of my life, economic conditions being what they are, and food and shelter not being free. I have always been the arty friend, the one who floats on by. Me doing this job was supposed to be a "bit"— Hera's working in an office, how mad! And I am now finding that it might be impossible to maintain that conceptual divide, if the "bit" I am doing is actually just my entire life. I have been working in an office for one week, and already this is where my head is at.

After a while Soph does seem to catch on that, though I am doing my best to make despair funny, I did not actually have a brilliant week.

"Babe, be real: was there not one moment in the past week where you felt, like, interested? Surely there was, like, *one*?"

I think back on bad sushi, racism, IP addresses. Doug. I hate Doug!

"Oh well, Doug, I guess," I say.

"Doug?"

"Doug."

I remember Arthur's eyes on mine, how his focus sharpened when he realised how few fucks I gave, how I wasn't being deferential to him because of his rank, like most in my position would, how I didn't do office-speak. I let myself luxuriate in the memory of making someone laugh in a place that does not have laughter.

"Well, there's this guy in the office."

Soph's face animates; this has piqued her interest. She loves NDAs, and she loves workplace fucking, and she loves hearing about people in other workplaces fucking, and she's been encouraging me to try sex with a man ever since my ex-girlfriend and I broke up.

"He's pretty old, he looks, like, forty or something, and he's, like, absolutely senior to me—not on my team, but, like, he actually matters in the office. I don't actually know what his beat is, but the vibe is like . . . Okay, so your dad would probably read his column over breakfast and be like, 'Hmm, an interesting point he's making here about militia in Hong Kong,' and then maybe at dinner that night your dad would tell his boomer friends that he read 'an interesting take on the Hong Kong situation' that morning."

Soph nods; she understands what I mean.

"But the thing is, this guy—his name is Arthur—I think maybe he's flirting with me, and I think I'm flirting with him too, and I actually think he's kind of gorgeous? But he's my work senior and also my age senior and maybe he's just being friendly, and also I am very bored at work so it could just be that I'm blowing this way out of proportion in my head . . ."

As I am talking, I am also wondering whether what I am saying is true. Am I dramatising feelings for the sake of conversation, or do feelings grow when you voice them? I am mostly sure that my monologue is an accurate representation of my emotional state—but I also know that I live for drama. I go on. I'll speak it now and work out if it's honest later.

"But I do just have this kind of resolute feeling in my stomach that something is going to happen with him, and that he might like . . . matter?? It's crazy, I know that's a crazy thing to feel or say. But yeah, he messaged me today on the internal IM and I felt, like, genuine elation, which . . . maybe it's just a silly work crush, but there it is, and now I just want to talk to him again."

I'm pleased with having a reason to use "internal IM" in a sentence, and with the effect that this rant has had on Soph's interest in the conversation.

Soph is *on board* with whatever is happening here.

"Hera, listen to me, and I don't say this lightly: you need to fuck this man."

Who knows if he's even single, who knows if I'm even interested? But I've got nothing else going on. I may as well follow the thread and see what happens. This is how people get through working their entire lives, right, by dreaming about fucking or actually fucking their colleagues? I've seen *Grey's Anatomy*, this is not my first rodeo. If I'm really going to embrace corporate culture, it's basically imperative that I fuck the old guy, right? Who am I to defy tradition?

It is clear that Soph has little to zero interest in Arthur apart from the, and I quote, "big-boy banging" he will give me. I suppose it would be cooler if this were my main concern too; if I belonged to a school of liberated young women who saw sex as a tool for intergenerational dominance; if I was the type of person who could actually perform this manoeuvre while remaining unscathed. Unfortunately, I do not have the emotional dexterity to compartmentalise in this way. My feelings are a sludge of inter-twirling glob; my feelings are a child's finger-painting, where everything's been so thoroughly mushed that the whole page has just turned a murky brown and is devoid of any semblance of tonal integrity.

Soph's suggestions that I wear a naughty little skirt into the office à la Bridget Jones seem to conveniently ignore the fact that Daniel Cleaver is a dickhead and Bridget deserves better. I tell Soph not to Daniel-Cleaver Arthur; Arthur does not warrant that wrathful characterisation, at least not yet, when all he's done is mouth, "I hate Doug." When all he's done is be attractive to me because he looked at me like he presumed I had thoughts in my head. Maybe he is Mark Darcy.

And not only that, I tell Soph, but I won't wear flirty little skirts into the office because, first, I don't own any flirty little skirts, and second, it's fucking freezing in the office, the cool temperature is the office's dominant contextual signifier. Has she not been listening, has she not been reading?

The waitress clears our plates and glances over her shoulder to wordlessly convey that we are by now the last customers in the place, and that she'd really like us to fuck off so she can clear up and go to bed.

Outside, Soph orders an Uber, and after a big hug and a reciprocated "Get it, girl," I wander up the road to the bus stop. I have not reached the stage in my life where I can justify the ordering of an Uber while sober; Ubers are luxuries strictly reserved for nights of blackout drunkenness in which public transport is no longer an option.

On the bus I ponder the mental states of my fellow travellers. It's 11:30 on a Friday night, but we're not in a particularly bar-filled area, so there aren't many of them. There's the bus driver, who looks like she wants to die, if only she had the energy to do so. There's a homeless guy on the back seat whose elaborate set-up is admirable; he's got blankets, he's got a range of bottles, he's got a book perched on his lap while he reclines and takes in the city from his state-chauffeured joy ride. There's a woman in a tailored dress whose extreme forward focus indicates to me that she is trying very hard not to be sick. Occasionally she sways jerkily as the bus turns a corner. My guess is after-work drinks turned large. I feel for her. She is my corporate sister, my gal in the dugout.

When the driver pulls up to my stop, I salute my bus family. The homeless guy salutes back; the woman gives a small, embarrassed smile; the driver indicates no change in emotion, but this is okay, she's tired, and she's at work. She is my affectless queen.

As I climb into bed I think about all that has transpired this week; so much and also absolutely nothing has happened. Some moments I have particularly narrativised, have footnoted in my head as potentially significant, I do see that. I see the contours of what will become a story that I will tell myself about myself. When I dream, I dream of Alison.

The second week of the office job rolls in, and then the third, like the sea rolls in—because it has to. And there I am, still bobbing in the wake.

You know that scene in *To the Lighthouse* where it's like "time passes" and then Woolf just skips ahead, and everyone is like wow that is so radical, that crazy Modernist, she really just went and did that? I'd like to use this opportunity to say that Woolf clearly never worked in an office as a comment moderator (don't @ me, I know there weren't like, work rights for women then). Because I feel every second of time passing. I feel every five-minute interval. There is not one moment where I conveniently zone out and then I am in the future. My present is the screen in front of me, and my present is my scrolling mouse, and my present is aching for my lunch break each day, aching for sweet release.

Days pass and I do not have a chance encounter with Arthur again. Despite his sitting about one metre away from me, on the other side of a monitor, we have very few opportunities for interaction.

In situational workplace comedies on television there is usually some sense of communal camaraderie—there is a false idea perpetuated in these shows that every person in the office is socially linked because of their specific shared geo-temporal existence. Maybe this is so in some offices, maybe some people just walk in the light. But for me, no. The office is clearly delineated into clusters of staff who think each other brilliant and equally important, worth talking to, and then there is everyone else. Everyone else is marooned, alone at their desks, unconnected to the fray. There are the IT guys. They come in all types, incoherently scattered about the floor like random guests at a wedding who don't fit in to any established social group, and so find themselves seated with the children, or with the bride's cousins, or with the groom's work friends from two jobs ago. There are the stats people, a subset of the IT people with a little more clout, as they get to tell the journalists when they are going viral, and therefore reap some goodwill by egotistical association. There are the basic hardware people, my favourites, because their situation seems most similar to mine in its mundanity and monotony and lack of overall goal. The main job for these hardware people is every day to turn on and off the laptop of a boomer journalist named John whose "bloody thing wasn't bloody working again." There is the HR woman and the receptionist. These two seem to exist in their own little sphere, clearly figuring themselves to be the backbone of the organisation, unaware that the journalists do not consider them to be people. There is the security guard at the door, Janeel. I like him, as he now jokes with me each morning about it being "another day in paradise." This joke does not get old, and indeed, only accretes hilarity with each re-use.

Mei Ling and I continue to develop a comfortable and necessary rapport, but it rarely extends outside the world of the office. I think we both recognise that considering we each constitute each other's primary reason for not offing ourselves each day at work, it might be a bit much of an ask to feature in each other's social lives as well. We never take lunch breaks together, as lunch breaks are strictly one after the other, so the comments desk is manned. Further, we don't hang out after work, because the primary concern when the workday ends is to get the fuck out of that over-air-conditioned beige abyss, and to think about it as little as possible in the remaining hours until we have to return. As such, though I soon feel as if I see and talk to Mei Ling more than anyone else in my life, I know very little about her.

Alison sits between us, inhibiting the possibility of talk, and so our exchanges remain digital.

The only other person with whom I have regular exchanges is Ken, one of the journalists on Arthur's side of the desk, who has taken to wheeling his rolling office chair around to where I sit at the end of my side when he needs an inconsequential banter argument settled, or when he is looking for someone to tell him what to buy his wife so she'll be less hostile. Ken does not know one fact about me, other than that my name is Hera and that I work in a spot that is physically proximate to him.

There is also one IT guy, Ian, who clearly wants to become my friend. He keeps dropping by my desk to ask if I want to go to the pub across the road after work. The first time he did this I was tempted to say yes, and then persuade Mei Ling to come too. I like the pub, I like drinking, I reasoned; what is not to like about this prospect? This is what colleagues do. I am a colleague. But then another day he reveals that he and his friends will be playing Dungeons and Dragons, and I don't know how that game works but I do know it is not something I want to know about, let alone do. I picture myself downing schooner after schooner as three slim men in their thirties move pieces around a board (I guess? Like I said, I have never played this game). I don't enjoy the picture my mind makes.

I tell him, "Thanks so much for the offer, Ian, it's just that I have plans tonight. Another night, though, yeah?"

So now he stops by my desk every day at 4 p.m. to ask me again. Spoiler alert: today will never be the day.

I feel bad, but not bad enough to play Dungeons and Dragons in a pub near work with three male strangers. Mei Ling pings me an *Arrested Development* gif when Ian returns to his desk. It's the one where Lucille (in a fabulous pink Chanel skirt suit, like the one Marge wears when she gets into the country club) responds to Michael flatly: "If that's a veiled criticism about me, I won't hear it and I won't respond to it."

That gif could mean so many things in this context. I respond to Mei Ling in text rather than gif. I type: *I won't hear it, and I won't respond to it.*

We have a job to do, after all, which is to colour-code profiles on a screen until we die.

One Monday morning, into the fourth week of my tenure, Alison is being particularly tetchy. A comment moderator in the US has failed to flag to our "team" that a big piece is coming out today which has the potential to be very divisive. With pieces that are obviously going to stir some shit, I've now learned, we usually "pre-moderate" the comments. This simply means that instead of deleting them or categorising them post-fact, as the conversation unfolds before our eyes, all the comments go into a kind of digital waiting room until we've assessed whether they are crazy or not. Our US counterpart's unintentional omission is not particularly difficult to resolve. Indeed, all we need to do is click a button on the back end of the website that will change the comments section to "pre-mod." But due process is everything to Alison, and she resents this international oversight, the extra burden it places on her, the disruption to her "workflow."

Alison requests that the editor-in-chief come over to our desk, so she can be fully briefed on the "situation." Sally dutifully arrives, pulls up an office chair next to Alison, and sits there, resigned to listening to Alison's tirade for a full five minutes. After the five minutes, Sally clearly feels that she has done her bit as democratic overlord, she has demonstrated her care for a lowly member of her staff. Sally can sleep well tonight, knowing that no one can accuse her of office elitism. She cuts Alison off mid-sentence with a raised hand.

"That's extremely valuable information, Alison. I really appreciate you feeding that back to me. I will have words with the Washington team, and we'll get this sorted. I've got to run— keep up the good work."

And with that, she is gone. Alison is mollified for about a minute, until it seems to dawn on her that Sally hasn't asked who to email in the US, which she would need to know if she were actually going to do what she has just promised.

For me, one benefit of Alison's morning of ranting is this: it brings attention to my little side of the table—not in any systemic or prolonged way, no, but in one very specific sense. On my screen, a message pops up from Arthur, under "Doug," which is the single word that has constituted our chat thus far.

Arthur Jones: *How does Alison spend her Sundays, do you think?*

I am freaking out but trying to remain calm. I will in no way suggest that I have been gagging for Arthur to message me again for the past two weeks.

Hera Stephen: *lol. How long have you worked on the same desk bank as her?*

Arthur Jones: *When I started here four years ago, she was already here. I think she's been here forever.*

Hera Stephen: *Right?? I honestly think she was born and will likely die in this room. I think she sleeps here. I think she makes a nest under the monitors each night.*

I hear a stifled laugh on the other side of my monitor. This gives me a rush akin to a nang high.

Our chat continues in this vein for the rest of the week, and response times become shorter each day. By Thursday it's a near-constant exchange. My job is easy to multi-task with, but I do wonder how he's getting any work done. I spend my morning commutes thinking about what I'll say to him that day, googling what films were popular in the UK in the early 2000s, scrolling through Twitter for niche jokes I'll appropriate.

Hera Stephen: *Thoughts on Sally's leather skirt today? Getting very Lucy Liu vibes.*

Arthur Jones: *Exactly what I was thinking. Perhaps she'll*

educate the IT staff on their pivotal role in the means of production? Viva la revolution.

Hera Stephen: *Ahhh, I see—another Charlie's Angels fan in the room. Also, maybe, a fellow socialist?? Fuck I was obsessed with her as a kid.*

Arthur Jones: *I remember seeing that film in the cinema when I was at uni. Did more to persuade me that Marx and Engels were relevant to my life than any of the readings I was set.*

Hera Stephen: *Oh my god you so did every reading, didn't you? Like, you absolutely highlighted parts and wrote notes and earnestly engaged in tutorial chat. Am I right?*

Arthur Jones: *Hera, you are so right.*

The Friday of this first week of this new chat routine, I have plans to see friends after work. Sarah has moved into a new share house and is using her comms salary to rent the biggest room. She's having myself and Soph and a few other people we know from uni and school over for cocktails on her balcony. These kinds of evenings usually end in me drunkenly forcing everyone to play "Never have I ever," a game that people are resisting more and more the older we get and the more everyone's life experiences become grounded in office work, missionary sex with a long-term partner, and hiking on weekends.

I am vaguely looking forward to the evening, because hanging out with these people feels like hanging out with family, I have known them for so long. Many of them have known me since the years in which I wore my hair in a high pony every day; intimacies like this cannot easily be replicated with friends you make as adults. But I'm also not looking forward to it, because it is quickly becoming apparent to me that my whining about work is not being particularly well received. This is disappointing, as access to shared self-pity is one of my main aims in doing this job. It appears, however, that I will have to endure several more years of corporate life before my friends will accept me as one of them. The sentiment seems to be: "Call us once you've worked there for four years, Hera, then you can begin to understand how depressed we all are."

For this reason, among others (including: lust, lust, lust, boredom, lust), I am quick to ditch my plans, giving my friends almost no notice, when Arthur IMs me at about four thirty to ask if I want to join him and some other journos from his team at the bar across the street after work.

Would I like to join? *What a silly question*, I think. Obviously I would like to join, Arthur. This is what I have been waiting for the past three weeks: you, in a bar, with me. I say Mei Ling will join too, if that's all right. He assents, sure. I IM Mei Ling and tell her sorry but she has to come. After I send her *buzz buzz bitch it's me again you have to come* three times in a row, she acquiesces.

Mei Ling Chen: *Urgh, fine.*

Because it's Friday, people start to clear out of the office earlier than usual. Mei Ling, Alison, and I are bound to our stations until five thirty, however, as that is how shift work works.

Arthur and his team begin to filter out around five fifteen, a swarm of "beers beers beers" and self-congratulation.

He stops at our side of the desk on his way out, looks at me and says, "See you there shortly?"

I nod. "You know it."

Alison looks aghast. It is all I can do not to laugh. I won't satisfy her curiosity with an explanation, even though she so clearly, desperately wants to know what is going on, why I have come to figure in the life of a journalist, someone from *the other side of the desk*.

Looking back now, I see that an outsider reading this scene might perceive that a powerplay was being established: I the eager young ingenue; Arthur the creased older man. On some levels that observation would not be so far from the truth. I certainly wanted him more because he was a figure totally outside my normal realm of interaction. I did want him more because of the presumption that I could not have him, this presumption based on my professional worthlessness compared to his salary, superannuation, and vaguely recognisable byline.

But it would not be fair to characterise this dynamic as totally predatory on his part: I saw myself as a predator too. Perhaps a warped sense of agency on my end, but I felt it nonetheless. I was Hera and I wanted Arthur, and I saw no reason why I shouldn't have him.

In truth, though, also, okay, I cannot deny that I was quietly eager to be granted access to the other side of the veil. I wanted to be privy to the discussions these higher-salaried men and women had with each other, the dynamics that formed and shuffled over Friday drinks. I wanted to know how they spoke out of office, and if the air of self-congratulation was puncturable or not. I wanted to see them get drunk. I wanted someone to say something homophobic and then struggle to talk their way out of it, seven beers deep. I wanted to see if they genuinely liked it, this life they were living. I wanted to see what Arthur made of it all. Because something told me he was watching too.

Maybe I gave him too much credit from the beginning. But what is lust if not generosity persevering? I wanted him to be what I needed, and so that is what he became.

THE bar is Mexican-themed, staffed by white uni students, obviously. It is dark and sticky and until now I've only ever ended up here very late at night; it is weird to see it with this much clarity. Mei Ling and I cross the threshold into a long, thin space, with booths multiplying away into the distance like dominoes in a hall of mirrors. I spot Arthur's table towards the back, and we make our way over. I am very aware of being watched. I doubt Arthur has alerted his co-workers to the fact that we will be joining them, and they are probably going to be alarmed by interlopers approaching their sacred booth. A few faces turn when Arthur waves us over, and I can see some small double-takes, like, *Where do I know her from?* I see Ken see me and arrange his face to conceal disbelief that I can exist here, in this space, and not just as an addendum to the desk he sits at.

I assess the situation and judge that there is only one viable way to deal with this scenario. I could let myself slip into the booth like an uncomfortable ghost. I could allow Arthur to introduce me and Mei Ling to the group, and let him dictate the terms of our acceptance, meaning we will be introduced as comment moderators and then swiftly ignored in conversation. (Mei Ling probably wouldn't mind this, as she does not actually want to be here.) Or, on the other hand, I can bellow. I can make it clear that I will not be dealing in office hierarchies here. I believe that a bar is a beautiful egalitarian space in which all are equal, as long as everyone can pay their round.

I stand at the end of the booth, Mei Ling next to me, looking at her phone. As always, I am impressed by her talent for dissociating when it is tactical to do so.

I look around the group and exclaim, "Hello, everyone! I'm Hera, this is Mei Ling. Thanks, Arthur, for extending the invite. Lovely to see you all outside of the freezer. Next round's on me— what are we drinking? You have to say beer because I am paid like shit."

"Beer!" a man in a short-sleeved shirt exclaims from the back of the booth.

"The good man said beer, so beer it is. I'll be back in a sec with jugs."

I catch Arthur's eye; he is smiling incredulously. I wink and walk away, back to the bar, telling Mei Ling over my shoulder to take a seat and rest her weary legs.

She rolls her eyes at me. She's never seen me in a social

situation, let alone one like this, in which I am so clearly playing a larger version of myself to get what I want.

Hera! you might say. *Hera, this is your first opportunity to bond with Mei Ling outside of work! Surely you should use this opportunity to tighten the bonds of female friendship and plebeian solidarity? Surely you should ask her about her life, and she you, and you can each become more than side characters in each other's lives, more than bit parts with no past, family, or life outside of your own narrative?*

To you I say: *Now is not the time, shut up. I'm walking back to the booth and these drinks are heavy.*

When I return to the table, my offering of jugs is received with adulation and fanfare. I slip into the booth opposite Mei Ling, both of us on the outer, having arrived last. She is shaking her head at me, smiling. I shrug my shoulders, like, *What of it?* She laughs. I decide she is a middle child, between two sisters. I make a mental note to ask her sometime whether my guess is right. I turn to Ken and ask him what he wanted to be when he was seven.

"Palaeontologist," he says, after thinking for a moment. "Definitely a palaeontologist."

"And do you feel that reporting on financial markets for a media outlet scratches that itch? I imagine it's all the digging without the dirt, no?"

He falters for a second then understands the joke. "Yeah, I'm a regular Indiana Jones."

"Raider of the cost sharks, am I right?"

This gets a good laugh, and he clearly likes how it represents him, so he repeats it loudly to the rest of the table.

"Raider of the cost sharks! Arthur, where did you find this woman?"

"Port Douglas," responds Arthur.

Finally, someone who can keep up. Everyone else obviously

has no context for this, and they display signs of confusion accordingly. Arthur clarifies.

"No, I jest. As you know, Ken, Hera works just next to us, with Mei Ling. I figured they could do with a drink, considering their manager is Alison."

"Ah, Alison," says a woman in a pantsuit across from me. "She's insane, isn't she? She once reported me to HR for using one of her teabags. I thought they were communal!"

Everyone pipes up with an Alison story. It seems she is something of an office legend, and not in a cool way.

The jugs get drunk and more are purchased. The evening wears on, the eyes get glassier, anecdotes are swapped and exaggerated, facts are disputed, people eventually begin to leave in ones and twos, Mei Ling among them, off to their nights, off to their weekends.

The group dwindles until there is just me, Ken, Arthur, and pantsuit lady, whose name, it seems, is Killara. At first I think I've misheard her, and that she thinks I've asked her where she lives, as Killara is also the name of a Sydney suburb. When I question her, though, my ignorance is exposed, as it transpires that Killara is a Dharug name meaning "always there." Embarrassed, I decide that I must find an opportunity and then quite literally die for Killara; it is the only way I can redeem myself.

Ken decides that a good thing to do now is to rib me about my mistake. "I thought your generation was supposed to be 'woke,' Hera." He makes inverted commas with his fingers when he says this.

"Come on, Ken, chill out. It's a common mistake—people make it all the time . . . if they're *racist!*" And Killara turns to me, eyes bulging accusatorily. Then she bursts out laughing.

It's a joke. Thank god. She is joking.

Arthur observes my red face and cheeks, my stuttered apologies, my efforts to joke along. He does not join in the teasing. He can see that my veneer has been momentarily shattered, and that I do in fact care what people think of me. He can see my white guilt shining through, like a fluorescent light bulb covered by a decorative and flammable shawl in a university student's bedroom.

It is also possible that he sees none of this. It is possible, even likely, that I am so extremely aware of my face and my flush and the tenor of my voice in this conversation that I am projecting my awareness onto him, a relative stranger who may well be thinking about sport at this very moment.

But don't you think it's true that sometimes you just know? Sometimes you meet someone and know that they understand you and you understand them. You might not ever see them again, but for a moment in time, you're both aware that you are looking at the situation you find yourselves in through the same window, whereas everyone else around you is looking at it from somewhere else entirely, maybe from the ground floor, maybe through an open doorway. It's not necessarily sexual, either, although it often is charged with this. It's like joining a group of strangers and friends standing in a circle in the backyard of a house party, and swiftly noticing that that man there, next to your housemate's brother, is going to be your party partner this night. Others make jokes but you and he do not laugh, you've ascended to a different plane, in which the only thing that is funny is the comically timed eye contact you keep making. You split off from the circle, you don't need those losers, you might not even know each other's names, you might not swap names for the whole evening, you are closer than names. Names are for chumps.

Others try to join your splinter group, seeing as you look like you're having such a good time. They quickly leave; they don't speak the language you two are composing.

The rest of the party find the two of you insufferable, and if you weren't one of this pair, so would you. But you are, so you don't. You are laughing too hard.

At the end of the night a mate drives you home, and the next day you vaguely remember loving this man from the night before, but you don't ask around about him, you don't fish for his last name, you don't try to get in contact. In sparks of laughter cutting through the smog of your mind, you know that what you had was perfect and, what is more, you'll always have it. And besides, in this life you'll find each other again, of that you have no doubt. Whether you'll remember that you've met before when this reunion occurs is another question, but it won't matter, you'll do it all again; in thirty years' time you'll be at a restaurant and you'll wait next to the man in a queue for the unisex bathroom and you'll get to talking and you'll recognise it then too. You won't necessarily recall that he's the same man from that party all those years ago, but you'll have that familiar sense that this person knows you, and you know him. You'll have each other cackling about the restaurant's name, how all you can think is: I love how unapologetically this place is a drug front. And then one of you will go to the bathroom and then another stall will open up and the other will enter it and the timing will work so that you won't run into each other again at the sinks. Again, you won't search for him in the restaurant: you'll return to your table smiling, and no one at your table will know why you look so pleased; they'll just assume you had a good piss, and you'll let them think this.

What I am saying is that this is the kind of foreknowledge I had the more I talked to Arthur: I felt that we already knew each other, and that neither of us could control this; it just was. Something about the set of his eyebrows, their furrow, something about how I could feel him looking right in and seeing right through me. He might tell you that he didn't do this, that

I was always a mystery to him, that this enchanted him. But I think he knew from the beginning exactly who I was, and how desperately I wanted to be truly seen by someone whose gaze I valued. Maybe he didn't know that he knew—but he knew. From that night in the bar when I made my gaffe, he could see that for all my bravado, I was not unbreakable. I wanted to be loved, just like everybody else does. In this regard I'm not so different from every other person who has ever lived.

IN the Mexican bar, we are all quite drunk. At some point, the service stops. It is time to leave. I want to keep looking at Arthur.

We all stand up. Ken and Killara say they're walking to the train station, are we coming?

I tell them that I get the bus, so I'll walk the other way. Arthur looks torn, and then says it makes sense for him to walk that way too. I think we both know that we do not want to get the bus, and that if he really intended to go home he would order an Uber. But perhaps I am misreading everything. Perhaps he thinks I am clingy and desperate, and he is not at all interested, only polite.

It's just us now, standing outside the restaurant. He is shy. I'm certain that if I motion to leave, he will acquiesce to this version of the night. But I'm also almost sure that if I stay, he will stay. I decide to have the guts for both of us. I say, "I'm fucking starving, are you?"

And he almost sighs in relief and he says, "Oh my god, Hera, I am so hungry. Do you know anywhere around here open this late?"

I don't, but the assumption he is making is that because I am young I will also be cool, and that I will know all the late-night eateries because of my debaucherous lifestyle. I say, "I'll think of somewhere," and surreptitiously check Google as he puts on his coat. There's a Chinese restaurant nearby, one I know from when I was a kid, and it's not cool but it's open, and so this is where I lead him.

He is drunk, drunker than I am, and it amuses me very much, the dopey smile that has now taken over his face. He very much wants to be led, this is clear to me.

At the restaurant we are seated by a window. The space is almost totally devoid of patrons. No music plays; it is aesthetically sterile.

Arthur seems nervous, perhaps aware for the first time how drunk he is. Hesitating over the menu, he chooses a few things, all brilliantly terrible choices, things that will absolutely not turn out well in this establishment, and I couldn't care less what we get, but to put him at ease I choose a few things too. We order the food and two glasses of wine; he is extremely polite to the waiter. Like deferentially polite; more polite than I am even, and I am very polite.

Before the waiter comes back with the food, we have fifteen minutes in which to sit, and he seems to feel the weight of this, the expectation to fill the silence, and he seems tired suddenly. It's okay, I'm used to cajoling energy in others. I ask him about his work, his life, his biggest fears. He responds to each question thoughtfully but succinctly, pausing after each answer to look at me directly and say, with a question mark tied around his shoulders like a sweater on a hot day, "If that makes sense?"

I ask him if he lives with housemates or has his own place, and then kick myself because he is a proper adult with a job, and proper adults with jobs don't live with housemates, they are beyond that. The question highlights our age difference, something I have been trying not to do in any material way—or, rather, something I have been trying to highlight only when it reflects attractively on me. Not when to do so is to magnify my own relative poverty, inexperience, and out-of-depthness. My youth can only be flashed around in jest, as a joke we both enjoy because it is clear I am the older one, really, in the dynamic. I know more, or at least we both act as though I do.

He answers my housemate question without suggesting that he finds it amusing. He says, "No. No housemates. I have my own place. I rent it."

His place is quite close to my place—which is my father's place—as it turns out. I make fun of him for having financial stability. "Your own place!" I exclaim. "Oh-la-la! I didn't realise I was having dinner with the King of England. Christ, I would have brought my signet ring."

He laughs shyly into his chest, like he is embarrassed about how he has money and I do not. At least, this is what I presume he is uncomfortable about. Hindsight is a dish best served earlier, but it never is. It is inevitably served after the bill has been paid, when you are fucked and full and powerless and bloated and stumbling.

The food appears. It is bad—who would order honey soy chicken?—but after a mouthful I am full anyway. He demolishes it, forking chicken into his mouth behind a curved palm and a napkin, like a girl in a rom-com trying to eat a burger gracefully on a date. This strikes me as gorgeous. He has long, slim fingers, I notice. I ask him if he plays the piano. He says that no, he doesn't, but he is clearly flattered by the question, that I could imagine him playing piano.

At one point in the conversation he pauses and he looks at me imploringly, like he is asking me what to do, how best to live his life. I decide not to tell him; we girls must have our secrets, am I right, ladies.

From time to time his feet graze mine, and each time he apologises.

I ask him why he moved to Australia. He takes a moment to respond to this, like he is considering which answer to give.

He sets his fork down, looks at me, and explains that he came here on a holiday after finishing university, and he fell in love with an Australian girl, so he stayed.

"So romantic!" I exclaim. "Like a movie!"

"I suppose," he answers. "I suppose it's like a movie."

"All right then, favourite movie: go."

He picks up his fork again, has another mouthful. "Hmmm . . . there are so many, but probably . . . *Before Sunrise*?"

"Oh my god, Arthur, fuck off. It is so not."

When we finish our meal, and our wine, it turns out he has already paid, which he must have done when he went to the bathroom. I admonish him awkwardly, because I don't want to presume anything, I don't want to enforce a tone he does not want to set. If this is a work dinner, between colleagues, we should pay half each. But no, he has already paid. He set the tone. It was he who set the tone. I have to remind myself of this in my retelling. I tend to overestimate my own power when I think back on this night, almost like I am trying to absolve him of guilt for what happened after.

It is late as we board a bus and take it to the depot closest to both our places, but neither of us suggests an Uber. We sit next to each other mostly in silence, on the back seat, our legs touching very slightly when the bus jolts.

The bus arrives at its terminus. Either a line is crossed now, or it is not.

I am not going to kiss him first. I make a decision in this moment. If anything is ever to happen between us, it has to be him who makes the first move. Not because of gender roles, not because I don't think women can propose, but because he is so timid, so unsure, and I want him to know, when he kisses me, that it is because he very much wants to. And he will kiss me, I know this. It is just a matter of when.

At the depot we stand very close to each other, not touching, and he looks at me, and I look at him.

I move in; I hug him. I give him a wide smile. I say, "I'm going to walk from here, Arthur."

He takes a second to calibrate this new information, about me walking, and then he smiles too. "Yes, well. Are you sure? This was nice, Hera."

"Yeah, it was. It was nice."

"We'll have to do it again some time . . ." He tapers off as he says this last bit, perhaps regretting it.

I say, "You got it, bud." And I stride off into the night, toward my father's house, alone, as if this sort of thing happens for me all the time. As if my heart is not beating out of my chest.

At work on Monday, I fear that the weekend may have washed away what happened on Friday. I have no way of knowing if the ratio between my level of anticipation and his is totally off. I sit in my office chair, I plug my laptop into my monitor—or, rather, I plug a laptop into a monitor. Nothing here is mine, and I would be wise to remember that.

Come lunchtime, no message has appeared from him. He is sitting an arm's length from me, at a desk on the other side of my monitor. Every time my IM pings, I jolt with adrenaline, and every time I am disappointed that it is Mei Ling, I feel guilty. I engage in tepid banter with her. It's someone's birthday in the office and we take turns speculating about what the birthday man wants for his birthday, knowing nothing about him other than the fact that Sally has deemed him worthy of a cake from Coles.

Mei Ling Chen: *he wants a head massager*

Hera Stephen: *he wants head*

Mei Ling Chen: *he wants to forget the past six years of his life*

Hera Stephen: *he wants to forget*

Mei Ling Chen: *okay yeah so you had a fun weekend it seems? Chirpy*

Hera Stephen: *Okay fine, yes. He wants to pull a rotisserie chicken out of his backpack for lunch and for no one to say anything about it, to just, like, act like that's normal.*

Then I receive a message from Arthur. Ping! I immediately sideline my chat with Mei Ling.

Arthur Jones: *Did you have good weekend?*

Hera Stephen: *Yeah, I had a surprisingly fun Friday night actually. You?*

Arthur Jones: *I was thinking the same thing.*

EVERY two minutes or so for the rest of the time I work in this office, barring a few specific days, I will receive a ping from Arthur. Every minute that he does not reply to my reply, I will die. Again, the fact that I can carry on this near-constant exchange while still fulfilling the duties of my job is yet further proof that my role is entirely pointless, but alerting Alison to this reality will not be particularly helpful to me, so I keep this little truth nugget to myself.

I read a lot of novels and he reads a lot of news. We are the gender binary, except neither of us likes cars. He tells me things about the things happening in the world that he is turning into content; I tell him which March sister I think he is. (He thinks he is Meg but I think he is secretly Amy, fearing that he might actually just be mediocre, not brilliant, and if given the opportunity he would throw his sister's manuscript on the fire and then immediately feel really bad about doing so.) I tell him he is Meg with Amy rising, and then I have to explain all of astrology to him, because he does not understand the rhetoric, it is a foreign language to him, the way I speak, the words that my friends and I use, the slippage of levels between irony and sincerity and earnestness and melancholic capitalist apologism at play in the CoStar discourse that modulates our sentences and thoughts.

He really takes to the star signs thing, though, I think because it is fun and silly and these are things that he does not usually allow himself to be, and also because astrology is essentially self-construction in metaphors, and what better way to tell someone that you are becoming obsessed with them than by innocuously mentioning that your chart is telling you big changes are stirring in your life at the moment? You're not being earnest, you're just sharing the science. It's so infantile it's mature, maybe? Don't answer that. Regardless, it is endlessly fun to receive and pore over the links he sends me, to astrology.com, to dodgy regional newspaper horoscopes telling me to buy a horse that day. Inevitably his chart will tell him to loosen the fuck up, as this is a hallmark of his sign, and it is never not satisfying to send this to him accompanied by a little *btw fyi xx*.

He is addicted to smoothies; I am addicted to tobacco. He likes running; I like sitting. He loves Australian rock; I love pop bangers.

I send him songs to listen to, and he listens to them. He quotes lines from them back to me when we're talking about other things. He tells me he has emotional motion sickness when reading the federal budget. A few weeks into our frantic messaging, I ask him if he wants to join me on my lunch break in thirty minutes (a huge gamble that pays off). He says he has just taken a DNA test and it turns out that he is in fact one hundred per cent that bitch. It is hard to explain why him saying these things is so funny to me, why it makes me smile so widely to receive an out-of-context refrain from a trap song I enjoyed in my teens in response to a question about house style. But then again, reading what I just wrote, I see that it is not so hard to explain, actually. An older white man on the other side of my monitor coming to know and love the bizarre assemblage of pop references I have accumulated since my youth, using them to entertain me when he should actually be concentrating on war crimes in Bosnia— that's entertainment. How could I not love that? How could I not be falling in love with him?

He also sends me songs to listen to but I generally don't listen to them because he has terrible taste. He came of age as a white man in Australia in the early 2000s, need I say more.

Three weeks into our non-stop IM conversation, he sends me

a song I actually know, and I don't listen to it properly until I'm on the bus home that evening. It is by a young woman and it is very sad, about how all of her friends are having babies and she feels ambivalent about this but then ambivalence turns to jealousy but then the chords don't shift and we get the feeling that she is just floating in this middle place of indecision, and that this place is actually where she has consciously chosen to be. I wonder why he sent me this song. I hazard a guess that this is his masculine way of telling me that he wonders whether he has missed the fatherhood boat and that he has mixed feelings about this. Of course, he never talks to me about why he likes the song, and I don't ask, because I fear the answer, or the conversation that an answer might spur into existence. As the weeks pass I am increasingly aware that there is more to his emotional furtiveness than shyness; I am aware of a spectre residing in all our conversations. But I choose not to push it.

The woman in the song, the one who is thinking about her friends having children, she is older than me in real life, but only by half a decade or so. My friends have not started having children yet, but I'm sure they soon will, and then I'll be singing this song. I am in no financial position to have children, but I doubt that I ever will be: I've known for some time that if I ever decide to have a baby, it will be based on feeling, not circumstance per se. My friends are waiting for mortgages before they procreate, but I will never have a mortgage unless I win the lottery, and look, if I won the lottery, I'd buy the house outright, right?

So if I don't have the mortgage to tell me to spawn, then what will tell me to? Feelings of inadequacy as a woman? Boredom when all my friends are busy going to play dates and I'm alone on a Saturday afternoon? And what would I be able to give to a child, anyway? I don't even mean that in an eco-conscious way, though people my age who are morally superior to me are deciding to be childless for this reason. The planet is dying, I don't not know this. And I have thought about it, I'm not immune to the discourse, it's just that I really don't think that my one child (or maybe two) is going to hasten the end of the earth in any discernible way when billionaires are still flying to space to fill their existential voids. Rather, if I raise them right, they might even get to see some of the good bits of this place before it all ends, and maybe if they're better at times tables than I am they can even help fix it?

But putting aside the planet for a minute, there is the question of me as a mother.

When I was a child, I had a little book of secrets—not figuratively but literally. In it I wrote my deepest, darkest gems of knowledge, information that I'd gleaned when I was not supposed to be listening. In my childish scrawl, backward b's and slanting lines, I recorded the dirty truths I'd become caretaker to. I was gullible so long as the person who told me lies was at least two grades above me in school.

I recorded that a girl in year six said she had travelled back in time. I listed the instances I went out-of-bounds in the playground. And a secret disclosed by my mother: *Mum says Dad meets men in parks.*

Another entry, between the bombshell revelation that my grandmother was not a Catholic and my own confession that I had made my friend Natalie let our Barbies grind up against each other. This one written with visible anger, pen incising the page like a scalpel: *Mum says I would be a mad mum.*

I don't remember the context for this comment, but I know it stung. I'd always had a feeling that I was a different, comparatively weird kid, but what kid doesn't dream of growing up and no longer being weird, and having un-weird kids and being an un-weird parent? From childhood my mother had ingrained in me a belief that my life would be harder than other people's lives, because of who I was as a person: because of my personality.

As I grew older and distanced myself from my mother, I tried to think less about her indictment of my maternal potential; she was not a good mother, so why should I care what she thought? But we latch on to criticisms of our personhood when we fear they might be accurate. I always had the feeling I was at least partially mad, and so it was hard to completely disbelieve my mother.

LISTENING to this song Arthur has sent me, I am taken back to feeling like I will never be able to access the joys that other people experience because that is my pre-determined lot in life.

Arthur is perhaps feeling bad that he is not a father at age forty or whatever he is, because of circumstance. But here I am, at age twenty-four, thinking I will never be a mother, not because of circumstance, but because I do not deserve children.

I cannot and do not tell Arthur this.

Thinking about him wanting kids, however, makes me feel a sensation I've not felt before: a kernel of wanting. It's premature, of course—I haven't even kissed the man—but I let myself imagine. I want to be the one who can give him the experience of fatherhood; I want to trick the universe into letting me have my own family to love, that will love me back. I imagine how happy Arthur would be, seeing me with our child. I picture how natural I'd look cradling it. I imagine what joy I might rediscover through the infant's eyes, and how I would never tell it that it is mad. I also know that this feeling I am having is bad, for feminism and so on: I shouldn't want to achieve happiness by providing a man with happiness. But I do also truly feel that this is how I will achieve it. I've tried making myself happy with no external forces and it absolutely has not worked. I can always find fault with myself, I can come up with a million different ways not to receive the joy I scrounge for. But if I do it for someone else, if

I make *them* happy, well, that is incontrovertible, that has value. That would make me matter.

The song ends and the bus lurches forward, and taking in my surrounds I realise that I've missed my stop. In a panic, I press the button and at the next stop I jump off and begin the march back to my father's house, attempting to walk with a swagger that suggests this is what I meant to do: getting off at this stop is not a mistake but a choice.

Dad and I "make" tacos, and we eat while watching the news. For the first time in my life I know more about the news than Dad, which he enjoys. I school him on public responses to policy, and he is performatively humbled. As we wash the dishes, Jude helps by licking the dirty plates in the dishwasher.

When I get into bed I think about Arthur, and I wonder where he is lying, and I wonder if he is thinking about me. It occurs to me that I can think about him when I touch myself.

A part of me is scared that if he could somehow sense that I was touching myself while thinking about him, he'd be grossed out rather than turned on. Isn't that the worst thought? Not just that the person you like might not like you in that way, but that you wanting them might actually be repulsive to them? Like, if you made a move on them they might feel violated; you might become the kind of person you hate, even if you didn't mean to.

Another part of me thinks no, he is too sacred to be shelved with the things I usually think about to get off fast. I debate whether it would honour or degrade him to use his image to come. I decide I don't know him well enough yet. It's strange; I've never thought ethically about anyone I've masturbated to before. Is this love? In porn captions and erotic stories on the internet they always spell "coming" as "cumming" and I don't know if that is the masculine version or the American version or just the correct version of the word when it's sexualised. But I feel in my bones that if I were ever to orgasm with Arthur, I would not cum; I would come.

I fall asleep without masturbating, so perhaps I am an ethical person.

Life goes on, Alison keeps hating me, Mei Ling and I keep up a pleasing co-dependence for the hours that we are in the office. Arthur and I keep messaging; the pings of his missives structure my days. My friends keep living, keep working, keep brunching. A malaise has settled over Sydney, over all of us, in different ways. One Saturday, six weeks into my corporate existence, two weeks after my dinner with Arthur, I go to a farmer's market with Soph and we are both hungover, having had separately manic nights the evening prior, she with her work friends and me with my spiritual friend Daisy and her new boyfriend Johan, whose main charm seems to be his reliable access to ketamine. Between gulping organic bubbly fruit beverages like they are IV drips of plenty and deciding between hydrangeas and peonies, Soph stops and declares, "I feel like I am in *Eternal Sunshine of the Spotless Mind.*"

"You feel like you've wiped your memory of a lost love and now you want it back?"

"Nah, that's not it you bloody loser I feel like . . ."

"You feel like you want to dye your hair a vibrant colour that doesn't suit you?"

"Hera!"

"You feel like you want to see everything backwards? You feel like you're Effy from *Skins*? You feel like you want to fuck Jim Carrey?"

I'm not particularly helpful when I'm hungover, clearly.

"Fuck off, Hera!"

At this point she pauses again. People are having to swerve

around us as she philosophises, but I'm too deceased to feel bad about the bottleneck we are creating.

She explains, "I feel like I am the person at the desk in the memory-wiping clinic and every day I just like, I do the same shit and see people make bad choices. Like, my job is to smooth things out with false promises about how things will be better. And like, Kate and Jim shouldn't have deleted each other, and like, I essentially facilitated them doing that? And then I just do it to the next pair and collect my money, and then I use that money to buy this eleven-dollar juice because I get blackout every Friday night? I don't know—it all just seems a bit, like, do you remember when we said we were going to move to Paris?"

"*Bien sûr*, Soph." I remember it well.

"Yeah, well, I just keep having flashbacks to when the prospect of moving somewhere like that was so exciting, like I genuinely felt like another world was possible if I just went there. And now if someone was like, 'I will pay for you to move to Paris,' I'd be like, 'Eh, but how different would it be to here, really?' Do you know what I mean?"

"*Absolument*, Soph. *Absolu*-fucking-*ment*." I say, "I think I'm falling for that guy I told you about, at work, and I don't know if it's because my feelings are real or because it's something to do."

"Amen," she replies, and does not enquire further.

I rest my head on her shoulder and we walk around the market this way, stumbling awkwardly like a pair of school dads in a three-legged race for charity. We select a bunch of peonies from the flower stall and we head back to her place, where we lie on the couch watching *Buffy* until Sarah rocks up with wine and tells us to behave like human beings and drink.

After a few glasses it becomes easier, after a few bottles the hangovers are forgotten. I begin to tell Sarah about my work man, expanding on what I have already said to Soph. I say that I am finding it harder and harder to tell which bits of my life I am actually feeling. I say that I feel like I am in a daze all the time. I say that I feel things when I am with Arthur, and when I am messaging him, so this must mean something, right?

Sarah looks at me seriously, like she is considering my proposition with the gravity it deserves, and then she says, "Hera. Hera, do you remember Max?"

I do. I do remember Max.

I arrange my face to express confusion, as if I don't already know exactly the point she is trying to make. My raised eyebrows suggest that yes, yes I might remember Max, who's to say?

Max was a boy I met when I was seventeen. Max was a boy I met and tried to convince myself I was in love with. Max was my crash course in becoming someone else's fantasy. To Max I was an enigmatic nymph. I was the first girl Max had met who understood his cinematic references. Max was the first boy I'd met who seemed genuinely interested in what I had to say.

Max is how I first learned that someone loving you is not the same as someone knowing you.

Max didn't know that inside my skinny body was a fat person waiting to break free.

Max is the only male person I've ever slept with.

When Max told me he loved me, I told him I was gay, which is what I have believed up until very recently.

Sarah is trying to suggest that my infatuation with Arthur is an echo of what I once felt with Max, and that it will pass. I resent the comparison.

All I ever wanted with Max was to feel more, and I didn't. But now I do feel more. It's definitely different! I tell Sarah to fuck off and pour me some more wine.

We're all sprawled around the couch; Sarah and I are sitting on it, and Soph is for some reason adjacent to it, on the floor, doing unenergised, sloppy push-ups. Adrienne would say her form lacks integrity, and she would be right. I ask Sarah if she remembers Nick Tyrell, from first year uni, to overhead pass the conversation away from my own romantic patterns back to hers. Here if you need!

Sarah says, "Hera, you know perfectly well I remember Nick Tyrell. He was the only man who has ever mattered to me."

I reprove, "Sarah, you say that about every man you've ever given a wristy to."

She looks at me sagely, seriously, reverently. "And I mean it—every time."

We all burst out laughing, and Soph collapses from the plank she has been perfunctorily attending to.

Soph announces, from her fetal bevel, that we need to go out; it is time to leave our pity party and embrace the world, the world being the bars within walking distance of Soph's house, and the streets in between.

I am approaching a level of drunk where I feel that I could do most things extremely competently: the world is open to me, I might be able to speak French, who knows? I could steal a plant; I could grow a plant. I could tell any bouncer that I've had two wines with dinner and I would believe it and so would he, maybe.

I wonder what Arthur is doing at this very moment; probably sitting on a couch somewhere, also getting drunk with his friends, but with more money, and with less laughter. I imagine they are all talking about *The Wire*, or a mutual friend's recent pregnancy announcement. They're probably swilling grenache around in Riedel glasses; they've probably eaten a meal on plates, with cutlery. They're all probably about to retire to bed, to their homes. Maybe the wives are putting their pashminas on. Maybe the men are using the term "the missus." Maybe one of the mis-suses is giving one of the men a playful punch on the arm for this, but really she likes it, because it means she is safe: she has made it to missus; she is someone else's problem now.

Maybe with all this going on around him, just maybe, Arthur is in a silent reverie on the couch, thinking of me. Perhaps his friends pirouette around him in their goodbye routines, and he is silent and still, imagining me.

The audacity of my mind!

I glance up and Soph is painting liquid eyeliner on her eyelids—with remarkable acuity, considering she is fucked.

"Where are we going, Soph?" I ask.

"To the world, Hera, to the world."

"If we were to be more specific, though?"

"Mr. Moore's, I reckon."

I see the evening flash before my eyes; the beers we will drink, the conversations we will have, the hangover I will wake up with tomorrow.

"Brilliant."

I smear lipstick on my pout, Sarah does up her shoes, and we exit one building to enter another, where the drinks are expensive and everyone is a graphic designer aka either unemployed or designing the logo for a tech company.

I make myself believe that I am enjoying this, through sheer force of will.

We are not the prettiest people in the bar, but we are the loudest, and this counts for something. Soon enough we have captured the attention of some long-haired men, and Soph is entertaining them with a story of international diplomacy, full of winks to things no one knows anything about, but the camaraderie is being established.

One of the men focuses on me, as if he has just adjudged in his mind that I am in fact here, sitting at the table, next to him, a subject he can engage. It always feels so icky, when men do this; when something in their posture changes and it's evident that they've decided they want to try to fuck you. I have not had sex with a man in seven years and I thought I never would again, because I detest the feeling of being an object for male evaluation. But as well as this, shamefully, I also detest the competitive edge that arises in me whenever this occurs: I hate that I want to be wanted by people I do not respect. Have I not slept with men because I find them structurally repugnant, or because I fear rejection?

Tonight, however, in the loud bar with the dark booths and a growing obsession with a person of the male variety not in this room, I think: Let's give it a go, hey? How bad can it be?

The long-haired man says he likes my jacket—and he is right to say so, it's a great jacket. I tell him thanks, and I compliment his short fringe. I'm pretty sure he's had his eye on Soph, or maybe Sarah (good luck with that, mate), but my seeming indifference to him has intrigued him, I can tell. He starts bigging himself up, like this is a fight he now wants to win, because it's hard.

It's not that hard, I think in my head. If I drink enough I'll probably sleep with him, he's fine. I don't know if I'll be any good at it, mind you. It's like the opposite of first-time gay nerves. I know how to eat out a woman but do I know how to ride a man? Seems unnatural.

He asks me what I'm thinking about, because I've been silent for a beat or two.

I consider all the things I could say in this blank space, all the scenarios I could bring into being with the opening and closing of my lips, the gymnastics of my tongue.

I contemplate telling him a version of the truth, which is that being in this bar makes me remember a time in first-year university when a group of new friends and I had traversed the streets of Newtown at night, drunk on life but mostly alcohol, and we'd all been so thrilled that we had found each other, and that the city was now accessible to us in a way that was not possible previously, when we had been annexed to our various schools and weighed down with heavy backpacks each day on the morning commute and the return home to our childhood bedrooms. How a girl whose name I cannot now recall had started leaping in a zigzag down a laneway and we all followed her, and somehow we were all singing a song that we were making up as we went along, and the song made sense to us, it was joyous and loud. And how now, if I found myself in a group of people in this exact same situation, I would not feel those feelings anymore, that elation—and I wonder if life is just trying to encounter new situations that will bring you back to old joy, or if there is new joy to be found and, if so, where is it, does he know?

I tell him I'm thinking about climate change.

He tells me he thinks about climate change all the time too, and then describes his home-composting process in detail. His hand has moved onto my leg, and neither of us acknowledges that this is so. It is inevitable; it is all inevitable.

When I sleep with him later that night I imagine Arthur. It's over so quickly, it's disconcerting. In lesbian sex I have been trained in reciprocity as the bare minimum: I know to touch her, to lick her, I want to make her feel good. Even if it's just a one-night stand, I'd like to think (and I do) that there is respect between us.

With this man (what is his name? I can't ask him again; I've asked him so many times) I feel like this is a transaction, but also like every insecurity I've ever had about my body and my personality is probably true and glaringly obvious, and he's likely just doing this to get off, and I should be grateful that I'm allowed to be involved. Where do these thoughts come from? Why is my immediate instinct to hate myself even when none of the evidence suggests I am undesirable?

No matter, I put the thoughts aside. I am here on an anthropological mission: I am here to have sex with a man.

His share house is a terrace, his bedroom is the room at the front on the ground floor. His bed is a mattress on pallets, because of course it is. I can't see much else as we do not turn the lights on, we get straight to it. Or, rather, he does. I am a vessel, I am a receiver, I am everything I imagined a woman would be made to feel like in straight sex. And I don't know if I am making myself feel like this or if I am being made to feel like this. I try to assert agency: I scratch, I pull. But it is all so fast, and he cums almost immediately, and I realise: at least in this regard, physically, there is nothing to be worried about. Having sex with a man is the easiest thing in the world.

When I leave his house in the morning, I do not wake him up.

It's been three months since I started my new corporate life, and at work I am now an accepted part of the machine—not a particularly valued element, no, but a cog that inescapably exists, for some reason. I can be relied on to make a joke when something stressful happens that all the journalists are anxiously buzzing about, and then they can tell me how lucky I am to have a job that is no way near as demanding as theirs. Inevitably I'm aware that something is happening in the news cycle before most of the journalists, because it is my job to monitor audience reactions, and people who spend their lives commenting on news articles are pretty quick to broadcast their opinions. In the time that it takes for a topic to trend on Twitter I can guarantee you that Darren from the Central Coast has already commented twenty-five times directly into the comments section attached to the primary news article on the media outlet's website.

When the news cycle directly affects Ken's work—that is, whenever it has to do with financial things, which, like, everything does, as there is nothing Ken does not see as directly related to the stock market—he whistles and singsongs to his desk colleagues, "I'm hustling for that dough today, fellas!" repeating it like an out-of-tune advertising jingle. And sometimes, if he feels the need to incorporate a visual gag into his routine, he stands up and asks me loudly, over the monitors, "How's the nail-painting going over there, Hera?" and chuckles to himself. Alison ignores these exchanges, as if she were deaf and blind. Usually I do the same, but sometimes I'll respond, simply to give Arthur a laugh—simply to hear Arthur's laugh.

I'll say, "Mate, it's all quiet on the Western Front, and since you ask, only my middle finger is painted, want to see?" or something equally infantile. It's the only level Ken exists on, discursively, and you have to meet him there or else he does not understand.

Then Arthur will message me: *Did you have a crush on Lew Ayres, be honest.*

And I'll respond: *No, I wanted to fuck the front itself.*

And he'll say: *That's my girl: direct action.*

And then I won't respond because he's just typed the words "that's my girl" and I know it's a flippant turn of phrase, but come on, that's flirting, right? We are flirting. If we are not flirting, then I have seriously misunderstood what flirting is my whole life.

It doesn't matter. It does not matter. We've been messaging for two months. Nothing has happened between us except a Chinese dinner; nothing may ever happen between us. Except obviously it will.

ANOTHER Friday rolls in, and around 2 p.m. on this auspicious day, Ken creates a WhatsApp group called "News Bros" and I am included in the group, while Mei Ling is not, which I feel bad about, but I am not secure enough in the group to start making requests about additional members. For starters, I am the only non-journalist in the chat. Though it is unspoken, it is clear that I am a special exception, and that this would usually not occur. There you go: you just have to be young, smart-mouthed, female, reasonably big-titted, with no avowed journalistic aspirations of your own, and then you too can be invited into the drinks inner circle.

The plan tonight, for a change, is the Mexican bar next to the office. Ken informs us that we will be "getting loose" as his missus is out of town for the weekend. I wish I had been there when Ken first learned the phrase "get loose." I can imagine the unadulterated glee that must have appeared on his face when he realised he'd happened upon a phrase that was so imbued with one hundred per cent pure Kennish energy that it would inevitably become his lifelong catchphrase.

I tell Soph that I might meet her at a party later in the evening, but I know perfectly well that if Arthur does not leave drinks early, neither will I.

ARTHUR does not leave early and neither do I.

Throughout the feigned casualness of the evening that extends on and on, as both of us go through the motions of talking to other people, we always end up next to each other. Someone will get up to go to the bathroom and then, bam, it's Arthur's leg against mine in the tightly stuffed booth. Or I'll be putting all my effort into concentrating on Killara's story about when she and her friends rigged the election for school captain in year twelve, and despite Killara's story being pretty funny, and despite my determination to be more in this space than to be someone who craves someone else, every time my eyes leave Killara they meet Arthur's, because Arthur is always looking at me and trying to seem like he isn't. Even when he's talking to someone else, I can see that he is attempting to simultaneously follow the conversation I am having from across the table. I can see him do his very small grin when I make a joke, while he's also conversing with some colleagues about the state of funding for investigative journalism in this country (it's bad, is the consensus).

It's become apparent to me this evening that Arthur is in fact Ken's boss. That he is also the boss of most of the journalists at the bar right now. Because Arthur is quiet and has never mentioned his specific role to me (unless he did when I first met him, and I forgot), I've made it a point to not ask him much about his work, because I don't want to seem sycophantic, I don't want to give the impression that I am interested in his world because

I want a leg-up or a tip. It has occurred to me that he might be the boss, but I discarded that thought: I have never seen him yelling, and his general air of deference does not a boss make, or so I presumed. But, no. Killara makes an offhand reference to a deadline he's set for filing, and then it dawns on me, of course he is the boss: I manifest hindrances to happiness. Of course he is the boss: I always have to do the hard thing.

The drinks, much like the years, start coming and they don't stop coming. We do shots, we do beers, I buy a round of margaritas because I am drunk enough not to care about the pillaging of my bank account this entails.

Someone—I assume Ken—suggests karaoke, and suddenly we're all out on the street, stumbling towards the city like a bunch of unwieldy schoolchildren on an excursion.

When we arrive at karaoke, after making our way up a concrete flight of stairs in a dingy building between a theatre and a Chinese restaurant, the staff are expecting us: Killara has called ahead, it seems. God, she's good. She orders drinks for everyone, she corrals us into our booth-room. Two roving mics sit expectantly on the low table that we sit around, and now picking songs is the only task left. It is not lost on me that Killara has organised this, and not one of the men. I barely know the woman but I want to hug her, I want to say, "Fucking etch, am I right? You rock." I do not think a man in an office has ever organised karaoke, even though every man in an office has hogged the mic at it.

I do not deign to make song suggestions of my own; I will happily add to the chorus of whichever forgotten banger comes on next. I'd prefer to look too nonchalant to go through the large, sticky, laminated booklet and enter my song preference with the finnicky remote. Admittedly, I am silently rooting for one of Ken's obnoxious, nameless (to me) colleagues to pick a Springsteen song, as I have essentially been rehearsing his entire oeuvre every evening of my life, while washing up after dinner with Dad.

But, no. It's Bon Jovi, then Journey, then Macklemore, then Psy.

I've been distracted, but have nonetheless kept a silent eye on Arthur, who is seated across from me, in a corner of the booth, looking at his phone, looking tired. Perhaps he does not like karaoke, or perhaps he fears his authority as the boss would be undermined if he picked a song and did it badly.

I join in on the singing from time to time, but I do not dare attempt to procure one of the microphones, which are being monopolised by the Ken-adjacent men.

A brief pause as one song ends and another begins. I look up and see Arthur watching me, doing his half-smile. I am gratified and I give him a small smile back.

And then I hear them, those melodious opening bars, that harmonica. I look around to see a few people cottoning on and groaning.

Ken goes, "Who the fuck picked this and not 'Born in the USA'?"

A voice begins to sing the opening line, softly, but loud enough to be heard over the backing track. It's a low voice, and it is not brilliant, but it is one that means what it is singing: "I come from down in the valley, where, mister, when you're young . . ."

Someone yells "woo" and then the room is pretty much silent, apart from the voice singing the song. It occurs to me that there is only one person this could be, because no one else would have the power to command silence for a ballad in a room full of drunk people.

It's Arthur; of course it's Arthur. I look to him again in the corner and he's holding a mic. He catches my eye and gestures to the other mic, which is on the table in front of me. I have no idea how he has managed to orchestrate this, or why no one else is picking up the second mic, when with all the other songs the mic has been fought over like the flag in a Nippers game.

"C'mon, Hera, the mic is screaming your name!" Killara yells with glee, and the rest begin to chant: "Hera! Hera! Hera!"

I'm certain that most of the people are only chanting because this is the first time they've been able to ascertain my name.

Right, well, that's that then. I have to do it. To refuse would be to look like a bad sport.

But they don't know how vulnerable this is going to make me. How, if I were to picture my perfect evening, it would be singing "The River" with Arthur in this very room, with him having picked the song.

What about me screams "saddest Bruce Springsteen song"? He knew.

I join in on "then I got Mary pregnant" to screams—mostly because people are drunk but also because, as it happens, I can sing. And I can sing this song with my eyes closed, hands behind my back.

When everything went down with my parents, my dad and I used to sing this in the car. We had the album on a tape. Dad would always drum on the steering wheel between the verses. He said that one day I'd understand what this song meant even more than I already did, and what he foretold was correct.

Arthur's beaming now; he's looking at me like I hold every answer. And I'm trying not to look at him too much as we continue to sing together, because I know that my face is like the surface of a lake, rippling and responding to every breeze, every skimmed pebble, and I really would prefer that the entire office not see the yearning that is pulsating from my very being.

By the time we get to the final verse, the silence around us is a reverie; it's like everyone is remembering a time in which they were happier than they are now. I don't have to worry so much about not looking at Arthur because I am certain that everyone is looking inwards.

So I sneak a glance, and he's still singing at me; and now I am smiling back broadly, I can't control it. I lean in to the melodrama with the final "ooh-oohs." I am harmonising two octaves up, I don't even care that I'm showing off, I want to show off in front of him. I want him to see and hear what I can do; I want him to know the way that I feel things.

When the song ends and the music fades out, everyone applauds and then they quickly move on—"Hips Don't Lie" is up next and the Kens have reappropriated the microphones. Our song becomes just another moment that happened in the night.

But not for me, of course. For me, something has shifted.

AT midnight we get kicked out of the karaoke place, and everyone starts heading to the train station or organising Ubers. I sense a presence beside me and it is Arthur, hands in pockets.

"Want to share an Uber?" he says. "From what I recall we live pretty close to each other."

I glance around to see if anyone is taking in this interaction; thankfully they are not.

"Sure, okay. Why not."

We sit in the back of the Uber, the middle seat empty between us, and talk in muted tones about the evening, about which were the worst songs to endure.

After a pause he says, "Your voice is something else. I knew you would be able to sing."

"And I somehow knew you'd pick the saddest song on the list," I counter.

We are driving down a familiar highway and I know that in a matter of minutes we will reach my house, and then I'll get out of the car and this moment will be over. I cannot endure the prospect of allowing that future to happen, and I feel that neither can he. But I was the one to extend the evening last time, I will not do it again. We sit, we wait. Finally, he breaks.

"Listen," he says. "Want to get one last drink?"

"All the bars will be closed now, Arthur."

"Yes, I suppose you're right. It's just . . . I don't want to go home yet."

!!!

I consider my options. I decide.

"I know it's maybe weird, because I live with my dad, but he'll be asleep, so, well, do you want to come in to mine for a drink? We've got plenty of wine—or whisky, if that's more your style, Mr. Boss Man."

"I'd like that very much."

"Okay," I say, looking down.

And so we sit in silence for the rest of the trip, except for Arthur telling the driver that we'll just be making the one stop, as it turns out.

It is very, very weird opening the front gate and having Arthur follow me down the path to my house. This is not work, this is not the bar near work; this is my place, and I am guiding him.

I tell him to sit on the couch in the front room while I go and get the drinks. I am careful to do this quietly so I don't wake Dad—not that he'd come downstairs if he heard me, but just because, well, he'd work out what was going on.

There is an ease in my body, in my speech, in this room, in this house. And here Arthur is: the man who looked incredulously at me that first day in the lift, not the man beyond my reach behind the monitors. That being said, when I return to the lounge room with wine and two glasses, he is clearly nervous. As I set the glasses down on the coffee table, he rearranges his hands, he thanks me politely for getting the wine. When I sit down, his body is not close to mine on the couch; he is performing respect for my bodily autonomy and I really wish he wouldn't.

I've also brought my laptop in from the kitchen, and I press play on a mellow playlist. The sad girl pop of Maggie Rogers slips through the laptop speakers and into the air around us.

Arthur's feet are on the ground, while I lift mine up and cross my legs on the couch, facing him.

We start talking about everything; he is drunk, he is funny, he is thoughtful. We even get to climate change, and children. He starts talking about cows and methane gas emissions and how really child-bearing is the least of our problems when it comes to the planet dying; and he knows lots of statistics that I don't know and I cannot help but be impressed by him, by the fluency with which he outlines arguments that I myself would not venture for fear of seeming ignorant or callous. He is not being those things, though: it seems like he has really thought about it, and this is something I like.

I say, because the wine has loosened my tongue, "I'm also just fearful that I wouldn't be very good at it—being some kid's mum, that is. I think maybe the climate change argument is just a way for me not to say that I'm just terrified I wouldn't actually have much to give a child in this world. Do you know what I mean?"

And he looks at me very seriously and he says deliberately, slowly: "Hera, any child that has you for a mother will be the luckiest child in the world."

Somehow we are sitting close together now. I don't remember that happening, but here we are.

I am so touched by what he has just said.

I scoot myself forward, knowing that if he rejects me I will die. I wordlessly trace two fingers around his jaw.

Making a decision, he reaches for me; he has me. His hands are around my face, and then they trace my shoulders, my back, my waist. He kisses my collarbones, my cheeks, my lips. My lips. I feel my body release. It gives in. Of course. This is what I want. I know now what I want in life.

You laugh, but I'm serious.

I stop him. I say, "Either you leave now, or we go upstairs. The choice is yours."

I want him to be sure. Oh, how I want him to be sure.

"Let's go upstairs."

So we do.

Standing in my childhood bedroom, next to my bed, Arthur lifts my dress above my shoulders and places it on the ground. I try to reciprocate. I clumsily undo his shirt buttons, I throw his shirt to the floor; but when I get to his belt, I fumble. I am drunk, yes, but I am also not used to male clothing. Sensing my panic, my shaking hands, he smiles at me, pushes me away softly. He unclasps his own belt, he wriggles out of his own trousers, and I watch him. Arthur is standing before me in his jockeys, and I see that he is hard. I want to make a show of myself for him. I unclasp my own bra, and I remove my own underpants. Wordlessly, I step toward him, and I drag his underwear down his legs, leaving him to step out of them. I step back, stand up straight. I want him to look at me looking at him. He groans. He steps toward me and kisses me. He takes me by the shoulders and pushes me onto the bed. I can feel all of him pressed against me, and we are wet and hot and slippery. It is a blur, the way we move together, we kiss and grasp and lick. But when I feel him enter me, I experience a moment of clarity. This feeling is something I will fight for.

PART · TWO

I'd like to tell you how we woke up in my bed the next morning, tired and hungover but content. How maybe he was absentmindedly stroking my back when I came to consciousness from sleep. Maybe how I'd had to sneak him out of the house to avoid Dad seeing him. Or how I'd thought, screw it, I was going to dig in, and I'd just escorted him downstairs and introduced him to Dad.

I did not do these things, though, because after we made love, only a few minutes after, in fact, his phone started ringing. And in my blissful state, I told him to answer it, that it might be important. And he, drunk and groggy, did answer it, and someone was speaking to him and they were annoyed; I couldn't hear the words but I could recognise the tone. And I could tell that it was a woman. And he said, "Yes, yep, I'll be home soon. A bigger night than expected. Okay. See you soon."

And I looked at him with understanding dawning, and he looked at me knowing that I knew, and then he said, "I'm so sorry, Hera." And then he left. I lay naked in bed, staring at him as he pulled on his pants and his shirt, as he did up his belt, and then he opened my bedroom door and closed it behind him, and a few seconds later I heard the front door closing and I was alone in my bed, totally alone. That is how it happened, and I wish I could tell you otherwise.

His smell was on my body, on my sheets. The slight hollow his shape left in my mattress remained. My body was still raw, wet, open. And even though what I felt was a terrible, terrible emptiness, a part of me had known that something like this was going to happen.

Somehow, I fell asleep. And when I woke up the next morning, only a few hours later, he was still not there, and I was still alone, with nothing but my memory to assure me that what happened actually happened. And what *had* happened? It was unnerving to realise that while I thought one thing was happening, it had actually been something else entirely. Or had it? Did what I feel somehow not count now? Was it to be retrospectively erased?

I couldn't. I couldn't erase it, even if I had wanted to, which, unfortunately, I didn't.

I had felt happiness.

And even though I was queasy, even though he had lied to me and the path ahead, should I choose to take it, would be filled with landmines and problems and likely wouldn't take me where I wanted to go—even though all that, I knew that if he didn't stop, neither would I.

My decision to continue is a difficult thing to come to terms with, maybe. Perhaps you'll suggest that I should have halted at this point, as it would have been the ethical thing to do and it would have protected my feelings.

But what I really wanted was feelings to protect. And here they were. So I would go on.

The hangover that greets me the morning after I first have sex with Arthur is clingy but not murderous. In a daze, I spend some time pottering around downstairs, clearing up the wineglasses and bottle Arthur and I left by the couch in the living room, thinking how when we drank from them everything was charged with promise, and now there are just errant red stains on my father's carpet. The metaphorical potential is too vast; I am overwhelmed.

This afternoon I am having a picnic with Soph, Sarah, our uni mate Daisy, and another mate, Ben, who did law with Soph but is forgiven because he's not practising. Dad's in the kitchen, reading the newspaper, when I go to tell him I'm leaving. He has a date tonight which he refuses to admit is a date.

"Grown men don't 'date,' Hera. We are simply two people who find each other interesting, having dinner."

I roll my eyes and say, "Sure, Dad, have fun on your date."

As I exit the kitchen he is smiling to himself.

Arriving at the park where I am to meet my friends, my phone lights up with an Instagram Messenger notification. That pink, that purple, that beauty! He's added me, he's sent a message. His profile picture is an abstract shape, and it reminds me pleasingly of old people on Facebook who have the generic face outline as their display picture either because they can't work out how to upload a photo, or because they have loudly voiced concerns about online privacy despite having social media accounts.

The first line revealed on my home screen makes my heart flutter and fall all in an instant, so I click it and delve in, knowing that he will see that I've seen it; I am taking this gamble with my pride.

It reads: *Hi. Thank you for last night. I can't stop thinking about it. About you. I hate asking this, but I have to: would you mind please not telling anyone about it?*

I feel the breathy relief that comes with the first text after sex: this is an affirmation that it happened, that there will not simply be immediately reciprocal ghosting, a relegation of the night into the past. But with this, there is also the simultaneous understanding that I am already consigned to his secret shame. I wonder how I can retain dignity in this situation, or if I can.

I take a breath and type back. I am attempting to keep the momentum going, keep him staring at his phone, but I also hope to establish the upper hand (not that I have it, why am I even trying).

Hey. Um, you're welcome? Unfortunately I can't stop thinking about it either. Like, all the time. And so sorry, but I've already emailed HR, that ship has sailed.

And then, two seconds later, I type:

Of course I'm not going to tell anyone, Arthur. I'm not a psychopath.

Him: *I still smell like you.*

Me: *Bottle it and you'll make a fortune.*

My friends arrive and of course I tell them everything. Well, not everything. I focus on the months of sexual tension culminating in earth-shatteringly good sex, and then the betrayal. I don't tell them that since last night I've engaged in further text conversation with him. I decide not to highlight that I've already taken the unethical position and allowed the flirtation to keep going, after I know the truth.

It's a sunny day and the grass is green and I want to frolic in the goodness of it, because that purity has already been snatched away from me. Let us drink cider and eat strawberries and laugh in the light about my conquest. Let them see my happiness, let me have it, just for this day.

They want to see photos, so I show them. The options are limited, as I've not taken any photos of him directly, but even on his google-able work profile, he is lovely. They exclaim that he has such beautiful blue eyes (like I don't already know). "Hera the heartbreaker!" they exclaim. "You will ruin this old man!" They don't know how close to the truth they are, but also how far from it too.

It is Sarah who makes the inevitable point—that someone who cheats on their partner might not be the best person in the world.

Luckily for me the others are unconcerned, for now at least, by how this reflects on his character. The betrayal element is neatly passed over as Ben declares, "God, all men are dogs, hey. Who gives a fuck. Anyway, how was his dick game?"

Even though Soph and Sarah know from our previous conversations that I actually happen to give a lot of fucks about Arthur, and that him having a partner who isn't me is less than ideal, we all act otherwise for my benefit, for the benefit of the bit. We delight in the drama, and in the shared pretence that I am emotionally unaffected—I got in and got out, and with a story too. In their eyes, if I do it again, it will be with the power. I certainly don't tell them how I had to try not to cry when he got the call.

The next day, Sunday, I sleep with a guy called Rav so I can continue to tell myself I have agency, that I am not just submitting to the part of mistress.

Men! It seems I sleep with men now. It's no big deal, sexuality is fluid and I hate myself, so many things can be true at once.

Arthur is one of many, I repeat in my head and to my friends. I can't just be waiting around for him, and I will not.

So I log in to Bumble and there I find Rav, someone who has agreed to sleep with me by swiping right on a still image of my face, and I him. Going on these apps is like going to a party in high school as a size fourteen: you are aware that while you are likely not any guy's first option, by the end of the night you will probably be one guy's last. It's about deciding to accept this reality, or not. In high school I was thin, but because this thinness was achieved through starvation, I never felt that it was truly mine; it was just something I was caretaker to, for a bit. Now I have a body that eats, so it is me and I should be more inside of it. But I can't help feeling that it is temporary, and that any version of my flesh that I present to a man will be false. None of them is the real me, just a passing stage for this mass I inhabit. In two years' time I will be different from how I am today, I know it. I offer no promise of stability. I don't feel this way with women. Why is this?

Rav is nothing; Rav is adequate at sex. When I feel him inside me for the first time, I feel physically penetrated, and that's about it. He is playing Tash Sultana from a Mini Bose the whole encounter. I keep having flashbacks to Arthur, how when we moved from the couch to my room, Julia Jacklin was playing softly from my laptop, and when I looked at my laptop yesterday morning, the battery was flat. When I charged it again, the song playing was "Someday."

I am told that there are two kinds of people in the world: those who listen to the lyrics of songs and immediately apply them to their own lives, and those who let the beat or melody take them, barely registering the words. As you might have guessed, I fall into the former camp. Someday, someday, someday.

The following morning at work, having raced from Rav's bed, where I foolishly fell asleep, I am on edge.

Alison starts the week by telling Mei Ling and me that we have to be extra vigilant over the coming days, as elections are popping off in a country that has significance to Australia and the US, and there is bound to be a lot of vitriol spurting through keyboards and onto our screens. (I should add that in the entire time I worked in that job, not one commenter's account was ever suspended. Vigilance meant blue to orange to red; vigilance meant seeing something and then doing nothing, except making it evident that we had seen it.)

Mei Ling IMs me, asking how my weekend was after News Bros drinks. I tell her it was uneventful. Hers was nice, except for when her Deliveroo guy forgot to pick up the sauce that was supposed to go with her kebab; that was pretty bleak. I confirm that "pretty bleak" is the correct assessment, and we move on into our days. A lot of people are posting links to an unofficial film clip for "Beds Are Burning" on an article about the Australian government's updated policy on fossil fuel emissions, so much of my time is taken up removing these links, only for users to repost them, incensed about the nanny state.

Around lunchtime, my computer pings again. This time it is Arthur, asking for my phone number. It has clearly not occurred to him to access my number from the News Bros WhatsApp chat, which I find endearing. I message him the digits, exhaling as I press enter. He doesn't call immediately, which makes sense as we are at work, but of course my stomach is at zero gravity as I consider all the things he might want to say. Though rage over his relationship status should be my guiding emotion, instead, my biggest fear is that he will tell me Friday night was a mistake, that he's sorry, that we should keep it professional from now on. I don't know how I will be able to continue this job if that is the case. Then there are the permutations of the other option— permutations that involve not stopping. These are good, I like these permutations, even though they also terrify me.

When I am on my break, walking around the alleyways near work, pacing, pacing, I receive a call from an unsaved number. I take a breath and accept it.

I huddle against a wall like a fugitive as I hold my phone to my ear. Misty rain filters through the sky and onto my top, which is a burnt orange cotton and easily marked.

There is silence, and I will not speak first. I stare at the wall opposite me, the graffitied ground floor beginnings of a tall tower block, and I wait for him to begin.

"Hi," he says, as a greeting.

"Hi," I answer, as a question.

Always this reticence, always this nervousness! The intimacy that can be erased in such a short time. The task of building it up again, line by line, brick by brick. Don't you remember how it felt? Can't we just talk like we're still there?

"Look, I'm sorry for my message on Saturday; I was kind of spiralling."

"That's okay, I understand." I mean, I do and I don't, but I want him to keep talking, and this is the response that will facilitate that.

"It's just, well, things are complicated, my marriage is complicated, and I'm sorry you had to find out that way—but, well, I've never done anything like this before, and I suppose I wanted to say, I understand if you don't want to have anything to do with me now."

Oh, so not just a partner, but a wife! Excellent. And I wonder what he means to imply by telling me he's not done something like this before. Does he assume that I have? And is he trying to tell me that he's not like other guys, he's a good philanderer? And why do I feel myself already falling for this?

I exhale slowly, letting my silence fill the space as I consider what I can say that is true.

"Arthur, I . . . It's not like this is normal for me either. And I know that I should not want anything to do with you now, but, like . . . well, I do. I really do? And so I don't really know what that makes me here; it's less than ideal. So . . . I guess, what do you think about that?"

I can almost hear the relief from his side of the phone. After a few beats he returns the serve; a meek kind of lob concentrated on landing within the singles court and nothing else. Speed sacrificed for precision.

"Well, if that's the case, Hera, you should know that over the past two days I have thought about little other than seeing you again."

The lob is in. I can't contain my smile; it takes over my face.

And I know that this is wrong. I know that by accepting these words I am becoming complicit, more complicit than I already am. But my feelings started before I knew this was cheating. They started out pure, and does this not count for something? I have never wanted to be a mistress, adultery has not been on my twenties bingo card. But I do want love—who doesn't? I want to fall in love with someone who loves me back, and here I am, falling.

So I decide. Standing in this dank alleyway I decide I'll settle for a sliver of the love that I want, in the hope that one day soon, there will be space for it to become more. Perhaps you think this makes me weak—pitiable even. But experience has taught me that I rarely care enough about anyone, romantically, and here is this man, whom I do care about, very much, and he's offering me some of himself. Why would I choose the potentiality of nothing if there is a chance that I can have something now? I am so sick of not caring about anything. I am so sick of moderating comments. I am so sick of not having someone I want to hold.

He construes my silence as a return shot, and so he continues the rally, this time with a middling groundstroke into the centre of the court, placed courteously, inviting my response: "Tell me if this is too much, but, well, do you want to meet up again? Outside of work, I mean."

I laugh. "Well, yes, Arthur, obviously I would like to 'meet up' again. And though I cherish our sporadic interactions in the office, I think somewhere that isn't the office might be more appropriate."

I steady myself here, readying myself to say what I want, cringe be damned.

"And if by 'meet up' you mean do I very much want to kiss you again, then that's a yes too. What did you have in mind?"

Even though we've now had sex and are seemingly embarking on an affair, just mentioning that I want to kiss him seems daring to me, like I am throwing out an insane, unrehearsed line of dialogue during a show. I wonder at myself, at the roles that I can play—and at the roles that any one of us can play, at any time, if we just decide to. They really are all open, all the time.

It's his turn to laugh with nervous excitement.

I feel like he's planned this conversation in his head but is terrified now that he is actually having it. He manages to spit out, "Well . . . how about a hotel?"

I stifle a laugh. How am I in this situation? But laughing would ruin the tone.

I say, "All right. Let's go to a hotel. Do you have a usual one you do this kind of thing at?"

He says, "Hera, I think you know perfectly well that I don't."

And so it happens that I find the place, I book it, I use my anaemic debit card to do so.

Four and a half long days of comment moderation later, on Saturday afternoon, I walk from home to a small hotel a suburb away. I consider putting on make-up, wearing something sexy, being alluring. But I decide that this is not how I want it to be between us. I don't want to engage in a performance of erotic confidence; I don't want to be a noir queen. My face is fresh from a shower, my outfit is a loose pair of pants and a green jumper I like. My skin, by the time I reach the hotel, is a little slick with sweat: it is a sunny day in Sydney.

As I approach the building, I see a locked gate, and I realise I don't know how to get in. Is there a code that has been sent to me in an email? I have no idea. Once I made the booking and sent Arthur the address and the time at which we were to meet, I considered logistics taken care of.

Loitering outside, I scroll my phone and cannot find the answer. All I can find is evidence of the galling truth that I booked the room on a website called dayuse.com, a URL so glaringly directed at people having affairs that I both resent and respect it.

I feel both grown up and like a child in this moment. I am an adult woman. I am embarking on an affair. And yet I live with my dad, I get nervous at parties, and I've never bought groceries more than a day in advance of when I plan to eat them. I don't know what to do with my hands when I'm uncomfortable. Mistresses are supposed to be confident—I am a fraud.

A few minutes later, while I'm still standing at a loss on the footpath, a car pulls up, and out he steps. He too looks unsure of himself. Taking charge with false bravado, like I did that first time at the Mexican bar, I say, "Glad you could make it," and I plant a kiss on his lips. He, being taller than I, has to lean down to receive my kiss, and I notice that he is a little reticent to engage, probably because we are in a public space where anyone could observe the adultering he is doing. He also appears surprised by the kiss, by the swiftness with which I make a move, which is amusing to me, considering what lies before us. I am not here to fuck spiders: I am here to fuck him.

He has his laptop bag (I assume he's told his wife he has to go in to work) but we have no travel bags, there is no ruse of an overnight stay for the benefit of the concierge. I tell him I don't know how to enter the building, and he offers no constructive suggestions. I google the hotel and call the number that materialises on the search results page. After inarticulately expressing to the woman on the phone that we are outside and asking if we can please come in, the gate beeps green and I push it open.

The reception is quaint, tidy, functional. I approach the desk and tell the woman I have a reservation. I determine that she absolutely knows what is going on, and I wonder if she finds our awkward and excited demeanours humorous, or if it happens so often that it is now mundane. She asks if we are visiting the city and I say, "in a way," which I am quietly pleased to note results in no affect crossing her face. She is my kind of woman: inscrutable. She gives me the keys, tells us where the room is, and informs us that check-out is 10 p.m. We make faces and sounds to suggest that this is not out of the ordinary.

I begin to walk up the stairs to our room, not glancing back to see if Arthur is following. I have the keys, after all. The reservation is in my name. It is my room; he can join me if he wishes. Our silent march continues till we reach our destination, and my body feels laughable to me, all the ways that it is screaming out for what it wants. I feel my hips swaying as I walk, like some dance of seduction, which is ridiculous, so I try to control them.

We reach the door, finally: I can feel his hand on my lower

back, gently pressing where my waist succumbs to my hips. It seems he does want to join, yes. I can't wait any longer. I turn to face him and this time he moves forward, and he kisses me. It is not a hurried kiss, and it does not feel wanton.

We pull apart for a second.

"Hi," he says.

"Hi," I respond.

He looks at me so seriously. He says, "I've been wanting to do that ever since I left your house, and before that . . . every day before that."

I don't know how to respond to this, I feel like anything I say will sound overwrought, melodramatic, false. So I don't say anything. I smile instead. I am pleased but disconcerted. This is not the snappy text exchange we've perfected, it's earnest and for this reason it is jarring for me. If this is a game I'm not sure how to play it.

"Well, come on then," I direct. I unlock the door and we cross the threshold into our air-conditioned paradise. It's a small room but it is full of light. There are shadows on the walls from the trees swaying outside.

What would someone who felt comfortable do now? I kick off my shoes, jump onto the bed, and sit on it cross-legged, in the centre, bedspread blooming forth from around my posterior in all directions, like a petal. I look at Arthur, who stands to the side of the bed, watching me, smiling.

I should say something sexy, I know this is the moment. But I can't do it. Instead, I purr, "Arthur?"

"Yes, Hera?"

"Your laptop bag is really hot."

He laughs. "I bloody knew you wouldn't be able to resist a quip about that! It's hot, is it?"

"Oh yeah," I respond gravely. "Really sexy. Girls famously

can't get enough of men who wear satchels for their technology. Reminds us of James Bond."

"Well, in that case," he raises his eyebrows, "do you want me shaken . . . or stirred?"

I cannot deal with this, especially with his accent. I burst out laughing, rolling my eyes as I do so.

"Come here, you big idiot." I pat the bed.

He jumps onto the mattress next to me and we lie there for half a minute, fully clothed. I think we are both taking a moment to acclimatise to the extreme strangeness of the situation, and getting familiar too, with the sensation of being alone together sober. It seems neither of us has read the manual for how to have an affair.

"Arthur?" I question.

"Hera," he replies.

"Did you bring condoms?"

He laughs. "Christ! She's direct."

I hold his gaze like a dare: "I told you I like direct action."

He gestures to his pants. "More like erect action."

Again I stifle laughter. "I cannot believe you just said that."

He does an American accent: "Best believe it, baby."

"Wow, okay." I begin to undo his shirt buttons. "I'm going to need you to stop talking now."

"I can do that. But just so you know, the condoms are in my laptop bag." He winks, which should make me want to leave this room and never come back, but it doesn't. I see humour in every stupid thing he does.

I go to his bag and I remove a condom, still in its packet. I place it on the bed.

Slowly, slowly, I remove his shirt. Together we undo his belt, we slide his pants off. He is hard and the feeling of that is still strange to me, despite my recent heterosexual escapades. I don't really know how to approach his penis, I'm tentative with it. I do not remove his underwear yet.

Instead, I get up and stand in front of him at the foot of the bed—I liked the performance of undressing in front of him in my room, and now I want to do it properly, theatrically. I remove my jumper and my pants and—surprise!—I'm not wearing anything else underneath. I chose not to wear undergarments just to see his reaction, and it is worth it. He lies partially upright, gobsmacked in front of me. This is how I have dreamed of him looking at me. I am emboldened.

"Arthur," I direct, "take off your underpants, and then touch me."

He hurriedly acquiesces, flinging his briefs to the floor. "Yes, ma'am."

I pounce back onto the bed, and our bodies meet. We hold each other, we grab. He reaches down to feel me and I am dripping. He traces his finger gently, he is being sensitive, he is being slow.

I cannot be slow now. I reach for the condom and I try to open the packet but I can't work out how.

"Arthur, help me, please." I hand him the plastic square. He rips it open and I watch him as he slides it over himself. I am trying to remember what to do for next time.

Business taken care of, I push him down, I straddle. I lower myself onto him, and I take him in me. Whimpering, eyes on each other, we begin to make love.

People write about desire all the time, and I read the poems, I see the films. I've had sex a fair bit, I'll not pretend I haven't. But nothing can prepare you for that moment during sex with that one person with whom it all makes sense, like, *Oh. Oh, I see now. I understand.*

Today we don't say it, but I think we both understand: I know, he knows, that whatever this is, it is different. The circumstances may be sordid but what is happening here, between us, it's not normal. It feels gigantic. It feels like we have brought an immense force into being, and we are now caretakers to it. I've never felt like this before, like I am guarding magic.

Later, in the heat and sweat of crumpled bedsheets, he produces a bottle of wine from his laptop bag, and we find two water glasses in the ensuite, and we drink from them, talking slowly and laughing.

After a while of contented silence, I decide to say what I am thinking, in case it isn't clear. I say, "I think you know this, but I'll say it anyway. This . . . this isn't a game for me, Arthur. I'm not in this just for kicks."

"Well, that's a relief."

"I'm being serious, Arthur."

He is chastened. "I know, I know, I'm sorry." He pauses. "I . . . don't know what to say around you. I lose my words."

"Okay, well, then just say what you're thinking. Try that."

"I'm thinking . . . I'm thinking that this is something else. And I'm thinking that I don't know how to do this."

"Do you think that I do?"

"No, no, I didn't mean that."

"Arthur, what are we going to do about this?"

We've slept together twice. I'm not going to give him an ultimatum. I will not be that woman. But I want him to say something, anything, to indicate that he feels the enormity of this like I do.

He exhales. I can hear his mind whirring. "I . . . I don't have all the answers now. I was not prepared for . . . this. But I want you to know, I'm not taking any of this lightly."

He's not taking the hint, is what.

"Okay . . . okay, but Arthur, I guess what I'm trying to get at is . . . like, is being with me something you want?"

I can't believe I just asked that. I feel like a teenager.

He lets out a chuckle. "Hera, I thought that was obvious."

It was??

"Oh right, okay then . . . So we're in a bit of a pickle, hey?"

"So it would seem."

With this, he hugs me tightly, and I nuzzle into his shoulder, thinking, *Fuck.*

I don't really know what it is that he's just affirmed—he's said he wants to be with me, but he also hasn't said he wants to be with *just* me. I can't ask anymore now, it's too desperate. I decide to wait and see.

Eventually, we have to leave the hotel. We do not stay till check-out. I have a dinner I planned on purpose, so I wouldn't be alone and dejected after this, and he has to return to his wife. He doesn't put it in these words, of course. In fact, in the time we are together, her existence is rarely, if ever, mentioned between us.

We return the keys to the concierge. I have no doubt she's heard our spirited fucking, and I try to apologise to her with my eyes.

"I'll see you at work, Arthur," I say when we are standing outside on the footpath once more, and I walk away without giving him a chance to say any more. I am ziplocking the afternoon. No more dialogue; just a feeling that I hold on to as I stride away, Sydney seeming more alive to me than it has in a very long time.

AT dinner, I don't talk about anything out of the ordinary I've done today. We are at a Lebanese restaurant we all know very well; a place we've been shushed at by patrons from the nearby theatre many times before; a place we feel comfortable enough in to ask for more flatbread without guilt. My friends and their partners report on how they have filled the hours since breakfast. Not one of them has fallen in love in the daylight we have seen today. I pity them, while knowing that if they knew my situation, they would likely pity me.

Throughout dinner, I check my phone. I find the fact that he is still messaging me on Instagram, which is so clearly not his digital home but mine, charming, even though it is also a symbol of the subterfuge he is engaged in. It's unlikely that he uses the app for anything else. He has, like, four photos on his account, one of them of her and him, clearly taken years ago, which I try and fail not to obsess over.

A green dot tells me he is online.

Dot dot dot, he asks me how dinner is.

I reply: *Spirited*.

I remember spirited dinners, he types back.

I smile to myself, at the little secret hoard of emotion I now keep in my pocket. I want to take him to my dinners. I want him sitting next to me, rubbing my leg when Sarah is being ridiculous, laughing at my stupid jokes when no one else will. I want to give him back the world that he has absent-mindedly lost, somehow, in amongst the years that separate our ages. I want to be the one to show him that there is still joy, and, in showing him, see it for myself.

At dinner, the discussion turns to sex work—would you do it, is it ethical, is it feminist? I find this conversation rather tired in general (yes, it can be feminist; yes, it can be ethical; no, I likely wouldn't do it, not because of ethics but because of my inability to emotionally compartmentalise sex from other areas of my life), but I am happy enough to engage in the talk with this crew, as it seems some of the boyfriends are considering the issue for the first time. It is always important to encourage the boyfriends when they have thoughts about things that are not directly related to their own lives or to bitcoin, as there is no guarantee it will ever happen again.

John (boyfriend of Angela) has recently read a think piece in *The Atlantic* by a woman who says sex work is the ultimate feminist fuck you to capitalism, because it allows her to own and sell her body for direct profit, whereas usually her body is capital in someone else's deal. He does not say it in these words. What he actually says is, "This chick was saying that being a prostitute is just like the most honest bargain you can do, as a sheila, and I thought, 'Power to you.'"

Angela rewards John for his progressive thinking by giving him a pat on the arm, as if to say she approves. The other men take from this that John's is the right opinion to have among the womenfolk, and so start exchanging truisms about sex work being the oldest profession, and how sex is a service like any other.

At this, some of the women demur; the men may have gotten overexcited in their argumentation, it is felt.

I have no partner to rally with or to teach, so I eat more hummus and let the conversation flow to its inevitable destination, i.e., Soph saying that it's about the right to choose. No one can disagree with this; everyone loves choice.

Sex work: good or bad? I type to Arthur.

Sex good: work bad, he responds.

I chuckle and then I sigh. I look up to my dinner companions, who are still talking animatedly as if the world at this table is all there is. But I have discovered another world. And I am going to colonise it.

We spend the next few weeks like this: work on the weekdays, hotels in the evenings and on the weekends. It is possible that we are single-handedly propping up the Australian hospitality industry. Work is still deathly boring, but most of my time in the office is spent messaging Arthur, occasionally making out in the stairwell. He tries to be surreptitious, whereas I am secretly begging to be caught. Mei Ling does not comment on my surely perceivable distractedness. Killara has taken to bringing me back takeaway coffees when she returns to the office from what it is that her job allows her to do—leave the office, interview people, be in the world. Occasionally, she even tells me about the stories she is working on, although she draws the line at asking for my takes.

The IM chat between Arthur and me oscillates between banter and feelings. I push the feelings when I can, using innocuous celebrity gossip to segue into more emotional territory. From time to time I consider the very real likelihood that this chat could at any moment be read by our employers, but rather than being scared by this prospect, I find it calming. I find it calming because surely Arthur knows that this is a risk, and the fact that he's willing to take it suggests that he is more invested in talking to me than he is in keeping his own job. This is what I tell myself.

Hera Stephen: *Okay re college admissions scandal, do you not feel like Glenn Close should play an older Felicity Huffman in the inevitable movie?*

Arthur Jones: *And Teri Hatcher to play Lori Laughlin, to rekindle the Desperate Housewives tension?*

I am obsessed with this response, obviously.

Hera Stephen: *hahaha you are such a gronk. Okay: Desperate Housewives: which one are you?*

Arthur Jones: *I can be anyone just please don't say I'm Mike, I couldn't stand that guy.*

Hera Stephen: *You're not Mike, Arthur.*

Arthur Jones: *All right then, who are you?*

I consider my options.

Hera Stephen: *Look, I want to say I'm not Edie, but something about her rings true for me.*

Arthur Jones: *There's a lot to love about Edie!! Just please don't get electrocuted and die.*

He would care if I died! It's a low bar but I'll take it.

One morning I am sitting at my desk, as usual, and I am scrolling through the comments on yet another op-ed, finding it difficult to concentrate because of the fact that Arthur has just sent me an IM that references making me come. He and I are getting more comfortable writing about the things we want to do to each other—these conversations start during the day at work and then seamlessly switch to Instagram messaging once we leave the office, which I think is a cute nod to the separation between work and play. Like yes, we're using office time to message about fucking, but we are respecting the workplace because we're using the internal IM to do so.

Dirty talk at work does have its challenges, though. Take right now, for example: it is 11 a.m. and Alison is sitting next to me and I am unbearably horny as I try to keep track of a comment thread about cuts to federal arts funding. A user who calls himself @donaldbadman is pleased that less funds will be going to "theatre wankers," @changeagent agrees that theatre is classist, @curiousgeorge is concerned that cuts will detrimentally affect the cast of *Home and Away*, and all I want to do is masturbate.

I type this last bit to Arthur and I see his dots emerge and then disappear. Finally, his response comes through: *Well, then lean in, Sheryl Sandberg. Suffragettes died so you could touch yourself at work.*

And for this reason, for feminism, I find myself orgasming on an office toilet seat not ten minutes later. When I return to my desk, Arthur messages me: *Tell me you made Emmeline Pankhurst proud.*

Babe, I respond, *she is crying tears in her grave.*

IT'S not all sex, though. That's one thing I'm learning about affairs. In films and television there is so much emphasis on fucking, and don't get me wrong, a lot of it is this—but even more of it is waiting. Arthur and I technically spend weekdays together at the office, only metres apart, but mostly all we can do is message each other. When we are not at work, there are hours and sometimes evenings we get to spend in each other's company— but even more so there are hours of typing *I miss you*, and *I wish I was with you*, and *What are you doing now?*

Usually in relationships, after a few dates or so, if the thing isn't already fizzling out, you begin to introduce your paramour into your circle; you test out how they'll tessellate in your larger life, how they'll get along with your friends. The judgement of your friends and family influences how you see your potential partner, no matter how much you tell yourself it won't. And the quality of the time, too, is different—it'll be spent with others, at barbecues, at drinks, at parties, on the morning commute.

Whereas when your relationship is secret, this necessarily limits the number of parties involved in the development of your intimacy. There is you. And there is them them them. Abstracted, removed from the rhythms of shared daily life, the two of you will tell each other everything. You teach each other your lives, because description is the only access each of you has to the other's other existence.

It's like when Hallie and Annie plan to swap lives after summer camp, so they spend all their time in their little cabin memorising the floorplan of the other's house, learning what nicknames their family members go by.

Instead of meeting my friends, he hears about them, in much detail. He knows that Sarah is the most reliable, the one I'd trust to be there in a crisis. He knows that Soph is what I think I could have been, if I'd chosen another path, and that though she makes me feel alive in a way that is idiosyncratic, there is a part of me that will never quite trust her, because in Soph I see the part of me that takes, and in Sarah I see the part of me that gives. In every story I tell him, he forms a tapestry of understanding; he sees my world as I see it, and I have never given this to anyone else before, because they've seen my world with their own eyes, and I wouldn't dare to presume that my own view of my life is more reliable than their view of it.

Arthur has such a good memory for details, so much better than my own. After a while he begins to tell me when I've already told him a story, and I love this; I imagine that when there is not a single story I have not told him before, then that is the day I will be truly happy, because he'll have the complete image of me, and he knows me, and he hasn't left.

I can tell that he does not have many people to tell his own stories to, even though that is technically what he does for a living. But the stories he tells at work, they are not his. He does not have many friends, and I understand from the way he talks about her, which he only does rarely, that his wife has for a long time been his best friend, and that now she is the person he lives with, and that he is immensely deflated by this. I can tell that he feels guiltier about this than he does about the sex; because the thing is he laughs with me now and he does not laugh with her, and he promised her that it would always be the two of them laughing, and he thought he'd keep that promise.

ONE Sunday afternoon about a month into our new routine, we are lying in a hotel bed in the city. We have made love, and now we are idly chatting about work. It turns out Arthur also hates Ken, which is hardly surprising news but vindicating nonetheless. I ask him about the first time he saw me, whether he felt that there was something there, like I did, or whether it took longer for it to build.

"Aren't you a little fisherwoman?" he responds.

I whine, "Oh, come on, babe, spill. Be real: were you immediately obsessed with me?"

He gathers me into his side, strokes my back, and tells me that no, he was not immediately obsessed with me. He was immediately intrigued, though, and he immediately knew that he wanted to know more.

"Oh my god, Arthur, you know that's the same fucking thing, don't pretend. You *immediately* knew that you wanted to make love to me in the Castlereagh Boutique Hotel, didn't you?"

He sighs. "Sometimes I think you can read my mind."

And with this we're kissing again, and he's going down, down, down, me having explained to him that in lesbian sex eating out is a must every time, and that I have standards.

After I come, he slithers up the bed and we are squished together again, like purring cats.

His phone vibrates with a text, and he goes to read it over the side of the bed. I can tell from the stiffness in his body it's from her.

When he returns to me he snuggles in, and I do not ask him what the text was about. But she is on my mind. What is she doing right now, and where does she think he is? Is she out with friends, shopping for groceries for their dinner tonight? What hold does she have over him?

"Arthur?"

"Yes, my sweet?" (He really does say things like this, and for some reason, instead of finding it repulsive, I bask in it.)

"How long have you been with your wife?"

He looks at me seriously. I know he is going to answer me. I seldom ask him things like this, and honesty is part of his schtick—his image of himself as an honest man is what keeps him ticking, I am learning. So he will not evade if and when I enquire. It's just that most of the time, I prefer not to ask. I prefer not to know, and I prefer not to remind him that I am the other woman by asking. Right now, however, I am entangled in bed with a man I am coming to love, and I need to understand what I am dealing with. How much ruin I will cause, if I get what I want.

"We met when I came to Sydney on holiday after uni, which I think I told you? And then . . . we stayed together."

"Okay," I say, processing. "So you're telling me you've been with your wife for, like . . . almost twenty years?"

"That's what I'm telling you. Yes." He swallows, as if deciding whether to tell me more, or readying himself for it. "Before you, I've, well, I've only ever been with her."

I almost choke on my own saliva. This information is not what I expected. I am shocked by it, and yet for some reason I am also comforted by it. This is all so new to me, this being with an adult man. But here he is telling me that I am only the second person he's ever slept with. So perhaps our situations aren't quite so different.

"Holy shit."

He laughs nervously. "Holy shit indeed."

When I don't speak, he continues, "When we first met, she was . . . she was so smart and fun and—"

He pauses, I assume because talking about her like this might feel like a new betrayal of her.

I try to temper it, I try to keep it light-hearted, to avoid revealing how extremely invested I am in this conversation, how I am hankering for any little crumb of information about her he might offer me: "So she's no longer smart and fun? Seems harsh, babe."

His smile is pained. "No, she is. She's still all those things. It's just . . ." He trails off.

"Okay, so why are you here with me?"

"Because I can't not be, Hera."

It's not an answer, but I'll let it go for now.

And it's not as if I am unmoved by this revelation, the twenty years I am apparently blowing up. And yes, I might not have started school when they met, and in some ways this makes me feel small, silly, compared to what they have. But I have loved, I have lived some life. I feel myself feeling for her, and for him. But I also feel for myself. And I have parents who no longer love each other, if they ever did, and I truly wish they'd both had affairs earlier. For my sake, if not their own, I wish one of them had left. Sometimes a promise you make is not a promise you should keep, I learned that young. I know that sometimes the best audience for your jokes is yourself.

I move on, into safer territory. I ask him about his childhood and he tells me about growing up—like me he is an only child—and being good at sport but not good enough. He describes his mum, her dependency on him, about the rage against the world that courses through her and that he has always had to live with but has never really understood himself. I tell him that I think his mum and I might understand each other, and he hesitates at this but then agrees. He tells me about his schoolfriends, some of whom are living in other parts of the world now, some of whom are still in the town he grew up in. He manages to catch up with most of them once every couple of years, when he goes back home to England to visit, or when they come to visit in Sydney, but he never sees them all together.

He says he envies the ease and bounty of my friendships, is impressed by my social life and my full calendar of people to see; he wishes he could be more like that.

"But, Arthur," I say, "it's not ease. It takes effort. I'm always trying."

He smirks as if to say that he does not believe this. I smirk like neither do I, because this is the game we play; we pretend that I am a socially together person. I am young and financially insecure. If I don't have the appearance of social ease, then what else do I have?

I say, "Sure, yes, Arthur, I have a million friends, and I am living the time of my life."

I love being alone with Arthur. But I love being seen with him too. When we are outside of the office and not in a suburb close to his house, we hold hands as we walk, and I feel proud to be the partner by his side. I enjoy the role I get to play. I must look like a normal woman out for the evening with her boyfriend. This thought gives me pleasure. And maybe it's internalised homophobia, maybe I enjoy being presumed to be straight. But it's something else too. I suppose it's just . . . I've never been seen as this woman before. I've never been perceived as a carefree ingenue out on the town with her man. It's satisfying, to play to the tropes you know so well.

And I don't know how to articulate to you the joy I feel one evening when, in the week following his relationship-timeline revelation, Arthur tells his wife he has a late-night call at the office so that he can spend the evening with me, and on our way to a bar from dinner we run into Colin, my old manager from a job I had in my late teens.

I am on a high with Arthur anyway, and then to see Colin, it's too much! I'm so thrilled to see him, this person from my past, and I am so, so happy that Arthur gets to watch me interact with him. Arthur never gets to see how I interact with people in my life outside of work, and I never get to introduce him to anyone I know. This feels like the perfect level of remove—Colin is not so close that him meeting Arthur will complicate anything, but he is close enough that there is familiarity there, and mutual care. Introducing Arthur to Colin is another step in expanding Arthur's and my private universe out into the real world.

"Colin!" I yell, and I bound up to him on the sidewalk, Arthur trailing shyly behind.

We hug dramatically, like teenage girls when they haven't seen each other for a day.

"Hera! How are you, you gorgeous thing? It's been years! You look fabulous!"

Arthur is still standing a few feet away, letting me have my moment, and Colin and I chat excitedly. I soon ascertain that Colin is a Buddhist now, and he goes by a different name. I am trying to hold in my disbelief, as when I worked with Colin he would come into work still pinging, delighting us with tales from the evening prior—the poppers, the twinks, the dancefloors, *the twinks!* But good for him, I think to myself, he's clearly happy, even if being a hot drug-taking homo sounds much more enjoyable to me than being a Buddhist.

As I squeal in delight I turn to Arthur, ready now to introduce him. He is smiling silently, looking a bit hesitant. I immediately understand that he is weighing up the probability that Colin might know someone he also knows, thereby revealing his adultery to the world. But the odds are so low. I decide to plough ahead.

I introduce Arthur as my partner and for a moment Buddhist-Colin shifts into more of the Colin I knew. He puts his hands on his hips and says, "Hera, you sneaky thing! When I knew you, you were a baby dyke, and now look at you, you have a boyfriend!" Turning to Arthur, he asides, "They grow up so fast, don't they?" and then he winks.

Arthur does not know what to say to this and it is extremely fun to watch him struggle to come up with a response. Eventually he goes with, "That they do."

Soon enough, Colin says he must depart, he must get home and meditate. I hug him goodbye, Arthur says it was nice to meet him, and we walk on into the night.

I am energised, gigglish. I exclaim to Arthur happily, "Arghh! Colin. I'm so glad you got to meet Colin! He let me play the *Les Mis* soundtrack on repeat through the shop speakers! What a bloody sweetheart!"

Arthur laughs and stops me walking and, putting his hands on my waist, he lifts me up and spins me around. Setting me down on the footpath again, he gives me a kiss and says, "You really loved that, didn't you? You honestly really loved seeing that guy." He looks both proud and bemused, like I'm a crazy pet he adores.

Arthur loves that I love love, and because this is so, I can happily embrace this part of myself when I am with him—the part that has so much joy inside of me, the part that delights in the world. If I said this to Sarah and Soph, they'd probably tell me to find the joy myself. They'd tell me a man won't solve my depression, but what do they know? I'm trying alternative medicine. I'm a fucking pioneer.

For the first two months of our relationship, we never spend a whole night together. When we are tired and full after dinner and sex, we do not get to fall asleep wrapped around each other. I do not know if he snores. He doesn't know that I thrash around when I'm dreaming. We do not get to wake up next to each other. I don't know if he showers or has coffee first in the morning.

But one weekend, he decides to tell his wife that he's staying at a friend's holiday house. I do wonder what kind of relationship they have, if he is confident that such blatant duplicity will not be caught out. If I lied to Sarah about going away for the weekend, I foresee that this ruse would last all of about two hours before she somehow figured out that this was not the case. Do they not talk to each other, do they not talk to each other's friends? I let it go: not my problem! I get a night with Arthur—who cares how this is possible?

It's an Airbnb this time, and he's booked it, which I am delighted by. So far it's been me booking the hotels. It's in Surry Hills, in a quiet, tree-lined, terraced street, and it's clearly someone's actual house. There are family photos on the walls, and there are spices in the pantry, and there is no concierge we must play-act for. It feels like a place that a regular couple would stay in. It feels like a home we could have.

We open the wine we have brought, and we pour it into actual wineglasses, not water glasses appropriated from a hotel ensuite. We sit on the couch (the couch!) in the living room (the living room!), and I snuggle up to him and tell him about my week, about how on Wednesday morning the barista at the café near work, where I now go most days and order a flat white, looked at me and gestured, "The usual?" And then, when she passed me my coffee, she had made me a skim mocha. A skim mocha! This is who she thinks I am as a person. She thinks I am the worst person in the world.

"She should be shot," Arthur decrees.

Exactly! She *should* be shot. He gets it.

We start googling restaurants in the nearby area, reading out customer reviews to one another.

Arthur suggests a pizza place about a block away, because Drew from Melbourne says, *The crust reminds me of Brunswick.*

I counter with a Spanish place a seven-minute walk away, as Antoinette (mum of four) promises, *Wide chairs, clean bathroom.*

We settle on Japanese, not because of a review but because Arthur has never tried gyoza before? I really do have to show him the world.

As we walk to the restaurant, he takes my hand, and I once again observe other straight-passing couples smiling at us approvingly, with no hidden meaning in their eyes. I do feel guilty that this thrills me so much. Whenever I walked hand in hand with my ex-girlfriend, the expressions on the faces of straight passers-by were either stony or overly encouraging—like they wanted to convey to us that they were allies; they approved of our lifestyle; they'd definitely voted for gay marriage. Every day we were in public was a fight we were in with the world, and it was a fight I was glad to be having, but it does get tiring, fighting all the time.

At the restaurant the goodwill continues: our waiter tells us we are a gorgeous couple. Arthur and I laugh, maybe for different reasons. I am cosplaying as a normie girlfriend and I am getting away with it! We drink more wine and stuff ourselves, and our laughter monopolises the space but no one seems to care. They seem happy for us.

When we get back to the Airbnb we are drunk. Arthur is

attempting to do a Scottish accent and he is failing badly. He collapses onto the couch as I go into the kitchen to make us some tea, and from there I can see him now and in the future. I can see him on a couch that we own.

As is our custom, we retreat to the bedroom, and we christen the house by having sex in it.

I have felt flat for a lot of my life. My natural vibrancy was lost somewhere around Year Eight, I think, if I had to timestamp it. Generally, I feel like I am walking in a straight line through fog and I just have to keep going—not because I have any expectation that there's something good on the horizon but because if I stop I'll die. But occasionally—very, very rarely—the atmosphere in the air around me will change. It will become crisp, clear, for a second, and I'll have a feeling in my head that is like the clouds parting and for a moment I'll sense this promise of *promise*. For a flash, I'll just know, that there is more to come. That I won't always feel like I do now; I might feel good again. It goes away as quickly as it comes, this premonition, and it is never more specific than that.

What I am saying is that having sex with Arthur feels like a shortcut to accessing this sense of promise whenever I want.

When Arthur is inside me and my eyes are on him and our bodies move in tandem; I remember that I was not always sad, and that one day I might not be again.

Perhaps this seems to you like a low bar for love. But trust me, and if you know you know—it really, really isn't.

It's been building for some time now. I've wanted to let the thoughts settle, but they've only been intensifying. And in the afterglow of sex, I feel it rumbling, this thing I need to say, this thing that has been jumping around inside me. I am terrified, of course. I am terrified of his response. But I also know, at least I think I know, that if he allows himself to tell the truth in return, all will be well.

"Hey, Arthur?"

"Yes, sweetheart?"

We are lying on the bed and he is running his index finger up and down my spine.

I'm glad I'm not facing him; if I was, I don't know that I'd have the courage to speak.

"God, okay. I feel like such a dork for wanting to say this."

His breathing quickens; he knows, I'm sure of it.

"You can say it, Hera. Please say it."

As usual, I will be brave enough for both of us.

"Arthur, I love you."

He turns me around to face him. He is beaming. He grabs my shoulders and draws me in fast. He kisses me like he is thanking me.

He pulls away just enough that he can look me in the eye, and when he speaks it is like he's been holding it in too.

"Hera, I am ridiculously, hopelessly in love with you."

I laugh a little. "Well, that's good," I whisper.

"Yes," agrees Arthur. "I think it's very, very good."

And despite all the bad, it *is* good. It is very, very good to feel this way.

It is always easier to justify the dubious decisions we make to ourselves than to our friends. This is why we sometimes omit details when telling a story at brunch—we say that we slept with the guy, but we don't mention he had a Southern Cross tattoo, for example. I have not been telling my friends about my relationship with Arthur because I fear their judgement, and because I know I won't listen to their advice if it is advice I do not want to take. I don't want to put any of us in that position.

But I can't keep the truth from Soph and Sarah anymore. I've been careful to evade rather than outright lie, but they've guessed that something is up; they've noticed me mysteriously leaving events early with a hungry smirk on my face.

The Friday after the weekend of the Airbnb trip, the girls and I have planned a classic basic bitch evening. Our group chat for organising such nights is called "Jeans and a Nice Top." We have different chats for different utilities—there's "Call Me Maybe" for all sex- and love-related content. There's "It's A No From Me" for bitching—discussion can be about anything from long voice notes to the prison industrial complex, it just has to be overwhelmingly negative. Sarah gets very tetchy when chat discussion does not fall within the specific chat remit. For tonight, we've decided on location: Soph's place. Drink of choice: rosé. Mission: get shitfaced.

We three sit on Soph's balcony, an elaborate cheeseboard balanced on a small table between us and bottles of wine in a cooler next to my feet, like soldiers ready to serve. The UE Boom blasts Caroline Polachek. We are in our element.

The chatter begins. Sarah reveals that she has started seeing someone new, an artist called Tess. She is gleefully relaying a tale of couples' strap-on shopping—a beautiful hallmark of any fresh queer relationship.

"And get this," exclaims Sarah, "before me, Tess had never used a double-sided dildo?? Like, what has she been doing??"

"Not perforating her vag, maybe?" Soph helpfully offers.

"Very funny, Soph. But that's actually homophobic." (Sarah and I believe that everything we take issue with is homophobic. Low-rise jeans? Homophobic. Post office lines? Homophobic.)

Sarah is happy. Anecdotes are spilling out of her with the ferocious speed of lust. Soph is encouraging the divulgence of sexy details, of course. And I am thrilled for Sarah, I am, but I am also jealous. She gets to start a romance and then just enjoy it, tell her friends about it, be gleeful. How fucking easy. And I know I'm being unfair, because obviously being in a queer relationship isn't always easy, but my god, imagine if I could just invite Arthur over to join us right now.

I need to tell them. I will tell them. I will tell them that not only have I fallen for a man (embarrassing), but a married one at that.

Soph begins to talk about her ex, Reid. She broke up with him because he was a douche but it's now come to light that he was also a douche who was cheating on her—she found out from a mutual friend this week. I assess that right now is not the perfect moment to bring up Arthur. I will bide my time. I will commiserate. I will drink more wine.

"Soph, my gal, my angel," I begin, "I know that sucks to learn, and I am so, so sorry, because being cheated on is awful. But is this not yet more evidence that you did the right thing breaking up with him? That man was scum. For starters, he only had one bedsheet, Soph. One bedsheet."

"I know, I know," Soph agrees. "But it's also just like, so galling. Like, that *he* would cheat on *me*?"

"It's like Jay-Z cheating on Beyoncé," adds Sarah. "It makes no sense."

"Not even!" interjects Soph. "It's like . . . if Beyoncé has a brain aneurism and started dating, like, Nick Lachey, and then Nick Lachey cheated on *her*."

"Soph?" I question cautiously. "Have you been re-watching *Newlyweds*?"

Soph downs the glass of rosé she is holding. She puts her hands up next to her head. "Fucking guilty as charged, bb. Guilty as charged."

"I fucking knew it!" I laugh.

"Jessica Simpson is just so endearing! I love her!" Soph is screeching now.

I raise my glass. Soph refills hers. Sarah is now drinking from a bottle. "To Jessica Simpson," I toast.

"To Jessica Simpson!"

Okay, they're getting smashed. So am I, but I also have a mission.

A few more bottles in, I leap into the breach.

"So, you know how a while back I slept with that guy at work, Arthur, who turned out to be married?"

"Yeah, I'm pretty sure we recall that, Hera," Soph deadpans. She squints at me. "Whyyy?"

"Well . . . the thing is . . . I haven't stopped doing that."

The two of them look at each other knowingly. "Jesus Christ, Hera," Sarah mutters.

Soph adds more drama. "For fuck's sake, Hera. Are you serious?"

Soph gives Sarah an imploring look now, like, *What has our idiot child done this time?*

I nod solemnly. "About as serious as climate change, unfortunately."

"And this has been going on for how long, exactly?" asks Sarah.

"About two months."

They're like a tag-team. "And you've not told us this because?" prompts Soph.

"Because fucking obviously! It's not like this is a fun thing to tell you guys. I get that it's like, morally dubious, or whatever."

Sarah now speaks like a counsellor, with a weirdly calm voice. "And how long do you plan to keep this up, babe? Is this a sex thing, or is this a feelings thing?"

I sigh dramatically. "Despite my best efforts, it seems to be Hayley Kiyoko–level feelings."

"Right." Soph opens another bottle. It is like a field after a festival on the floor of this balcony. "I guess, first of all, elephant in the room. You do know that like, statistically, he's not going to leave her, yes?"

"I am aware of the affair statistics, yes, thank you, Sophie."

"Okay, so, that in mind . . . thoughts?"

"Yeah . . . It's not like I planned to do this. And I know that cheating is bad. And I'm particularly sorry that I'm bringing it up tonight, Soph, re: Reid. But Reid was a jerk who didn't deserve you and I really hope you guys can believe me when I tell you that what I feel with this guy is—Well, he makes me laugh. And I make him laugh. That sounds really normie, probably? But it is so rare that anyone I want to fuck also makes me laugh."

Sarah interrupts. "Hera, didn't you briefly sleep with a comedian?"

"Exactly," I say. "I don't want to date people who don't make me laugh anymore."

They giggle at this, I have broken the tension slightly.

Sarah goes back into serious mode. "Hera, you know we are never going to tell you what to do. And I'm sure you've thought about his wife, what this would do to her if she knew. And I'm sure you've thought through the very likely possibility that this will end with you being fucked over."

"Is there another sentence there, or is that it?" I ask.

"I just . . . *we* just," Sarah looks to Soph. "We walk, sorry, we *want* you to be happy, and for you to be with someone who treats you well. If you think this dude is going to be that person for you, we'll support you. But as soon as he doesn't make you happy, he's gone, all right?"

I nod into my drink. "Yeah, that seems fair. That seems fair."

There is silence. I can't keep on with this conversation, because if I do I will get mushy and declarative and the girls need to be edged into this relationship bombshell. They've responded well so far, but I know they're not saying half of what they're thinking.

"Okay, can we talk about something else now?" I beg.

And they, good friends that they are, acquiesce. The evening goes on.

It's not that I haven't been on the other side of the situation, when friends have dated people I've had reservations about, and for years and years I've had to muzzle myself and even support these choices, because that is how it works. I supported Soph when she dated Brian, the guy who didn't "believe" in anti-depressants. I supported Sarah when she was obsessed with a woman who routinely dumped her on Wednesday nights so she could sleep with a random at the local gay bar's lesbian night and then get back together with Sarah the next day. I supported Ben when he kept fucking a guy who called blow jobs "lucky suckies."

You cannot tell your friends that their relationship is doomed because their partner is trash. You cannot even tell your friends that their partner, though they may not be trash, is nevertheless just not that good—like, they're fine, but who wants to be saddled with fine ad infinitum?

So I do see that from Sarah and Soph's perspective, Arthur is a two-timing cheater promising me love and in actuality giving me less than a few hours a few times a week. I do see that, from their perspective, he is not the most viable romantic option for me and for the durability of my emotional equilibrium.

But they don't understand! I can't explain to my friends that I seriously relish the prospect of having boring news people over for dinner at Arthur's and my future home, where I'll say outlandish things and pout about how I don't care for Nagorno-Karabakh and they'll say, "Oh Hera! We're talking about Iran and you know it!" and then I'll flounce off into the kitchen to eat the dessert I've made but now will not share. And then the boring people will leave and I'll have my own beautiful boring man, and the fact that he knows all the African nations off by heart is actually divine to me, the idea of him memorising them all from a map on the wall next to his single bed in his little bedroom growing up in a suburban house.

I want to tell this to Sarah and Soph, I do. But I am worried they would sound so silly, so dependent, these reasons of mine. And if they are dependent, then I don't want to know. Because I want him. So I determine to only bring Arthur up when directly asked about him. In the Uber home, at around 2 a.m., I message Arthur. I am drunk, obviously.

Hera: *Hey darling, you up?*

He is not up. I can see there is no green dot.

Hera: *Just wanted to say I love you. I miss your erect action.*

Hera: *But I also just miss you.*

Hera: *Okay good night mr sleepy man. Enjoy your ZEDS.*

The next morning he responds. He says, *I love you drunky.*

This is romance: this is love.

After that dinner with my friends, I find it harder to mentally compartmentalise the moments when I am disappointed with Arthur (he's unavailable, he's with his wife, he's given me no concrete plan about when this will change) from the moments I am happy with him. I still do it—it just requires more energy. Compartmentalisation does not seem to be a problem for Arthur. I am in awe of the smoothness of his emotional topography. While I have spent much of my life unable to claw my way out of reasonless melancholy, Arthur seems to be upset only when there is a chance he could be perceived to be underperforming at work or in life.

He gets tense when he's working to a deadline or there is the possibility that one of his staff has made a mistake and he'll have to reprimand them. He really does not enjoy confrontation—a characteristic that I notice the more time I spend with him, and the more he brings out his work laptop when we're in hotel rooms.

When he doesn't want to talk about whatever is bothering him as he's typing away, his shoulders will hunch and he'll become the tiniest bit snappy, and he'll say that he is fine but clearly he is not, and I love this. That is, I love the idea that maybe he actually is not conscious of his own moods; that maybe he truly does not recognise how transparent his irritation is to me. I am always so extremely, extremely aware of my own mood and everyone else's. Growing up with parents who hated each other, I have been trained from infancy in reading body language and intonation, in sensing the emotions vibrating in a room and then moderating relations between parties. It is kind of adorably cute to me, the little emotional trajectories Arthur will invariably follow when he is stressed by work—the eyes down, the lack of touching, needing me to ease him back into reality with gentle banter, with the lightest caress, until he eventually becomes himself again. His emotional rhythms seem like problems I can easily solve, and in comparison to my own existential quandaries, as well as the problem of him having a wife, steering him through these brief bouts of anxiety is kind of relaxing for me, like absentmindedly folding a paper crane from memory, or dissecting a mango with a razor sharp knife to produce bite-sized cubes.

For the first two months of our affair, I am so spaced out on endorphins and the prospect of my day job not being my only life, that I push aside the task of thinking about how to deal with the problems of our future. It's like putting off doing taxes, it's like not buying early bird flights for a holiday that you are definitely going to take. Let it all be simple: let him see only the carefree version of me, for now. I don't tell him about the unabating sadness I have always carried with me, or how I have now managed to assuage this sadness by using him as one would an emotional intravenous pump. I don't tell him what it does to me when I think about his wife, about him being with her and not me.

I want to take the good and reject the bad.

But time is passing. This is not a fling. And talking to my friends has only made this all more real, made the stakes higher. I am not callous, and it is becoming less easy to play the chill girl. As it is, I care all the time and not one bit of our relationship is a glamorous game to me. It is decidedly unglamorous, I am learning. The Holiday Inn is not glamorous. Always texting before you call to make sure your partner is not with his wife is not glamorous. Being kept a secret by the person you love is not glamorous. It feels like walking around in a midnight graveyard in Sunnydale without a stake. It feels like getting your period mid-hike with no tampons in sight. It feels like pretending you've read a book and then someone asks you a question about a specific plot point.

I am realising that I desperately need for Arthur to leave his wife. I want this man for myself. I want him to have one partner, and I want for that partner to be me. I hate it, but it is inescapable—I want to be the one who makes his smoothies. I want him to meet my dad, and I want for them to bond over their mutual love of me. I want them to make fun of me for not knowing about sport. I want Arthur to get drunk with the girls. I want Sarah and Soph to tell him about our schooldays. I want to snuggle him on the couch with Jude.

I want to ask him to leave her. But more than this, I want to not have to ask. Please, please, don't make me beg for you, Arthur.

TWO more months go by like this. At work, we message, and on weeknights and weekends, we fuck when we can. It feels like I could now map Sydney by its budget hotels. I know which hotels have last-minute deals. I know which hotels allow early check-in. I could also map Sydney by parks. I know which parks have secluded areas. I know which parks are home to trees whose leaves hang around them like hoods. I know which parks have the least bindies in the grass. Though he continuously says he loves me, Arthur makes no admissions about "the next step."

In a hotel room one evening, four months into whatever it is that we are, I take a risk. We've had sex and we're sated and this is the point in the evening when, if he didn't have a wife, we'd maybe take a shower and then huddle in for the night, falling asleep in the glow of what we've made. But he does have a wife, and he has to leave. So before we begin to go through the motions of getting dressed and calling Ubers, I summon the courage and I say, "Imagine if you didn't have to go. Imagine if we could just rest now."

The pain in his expression is real. He tells me he's sorry, that he knows this is all so unfair. "You deserve that so much, Hera," he says.

It's like when you fall over on the street and you're fine, you're holding it together, but then a stranger asks if you're okay and, with that shred of kindness, with that acknowledgement from another person that you've experienced a bad thing, you just start crying, you can't help it. It's like the first therapy session with a shrink when you matter-of-factly tell them every awful thing that's ever happened to you, and you do it professionally, you do it like you're reciting a grocery list, and then they say, "It sounds like you've been through a lot," and that's it, you're done for, you're a mess of tears.

Arthur's acknowledgement that this is unfair dislodges a block in my defensive wall for a moment, and I silently start to cry. He hasn't seen me cry before. Has he imagined that I don't?

He is grimacing, like maybe this is the first time he's really understood that this thing we're doing affects me, that I'm not just a butterfly of a young woman, chirpily pollinating before moving from one flower to the next. Or perhaps he's already aware, and he's just been hoping that I'll never bring it up. Either way, he is forced to reckon with it now.

"Hera," he says softly, "I don't want to leave this room either. I just. Well, I haven't wanted to presume that what I want is what you want. I sometimes can't figure why you would want me, to be honest."

I let out a laugh. Is he seriously suggesting that his reticence to plan for our future is because he hasn't been sure how committed I am? I recently turned down a weekend away with girlfriends because there was a small chance he *might* be free on the Sunday to fuck for two hours in a hotel with no air conditioning next to a train station. Have my feelings not been obvious?! Does he not realise I've been fantasising about sharing a mortgage with him? I must make him understand the gravity of my desire.

I say, "Look, I'm not saying that it makes perfect sense . . . or that—that I could have predicted falling in love with a man who thinks short-sleeved shirts are acceptable. But if that's what you're worried about—that I might wake up one day and be sick of you—put that aside, you idiot. I want you all the time. I've done the chaotic twenties thing and, to be frank, I'm pretty over it. I want to get coffee with you in the mornings and I want to do the Saturday quiz with you. I want to go to IKEA together. If you'll have me, I want to be boring with you."

"God, Hera, I really want to be boring with you."

"Okay."

"Okay."

I had hoped that, having established we want to be together, he'd outline a game plan, give me something concrete to go on, but no. It's up to me, again, to push the thing that neither of us wants to say.

"So, what does this mean for us then, Arthur? I don't want to make this crude but, like . . . I can't break up with your wife for you."

"No, that you can't." He breathes in, like he's mulling over a complex maths problem. "I don't . . . I don't know how this is going to work. But Hera, I want you, I want to be with you. So I will tell her. I don't know how, but I promise you I will tell her."

I allow myself only the smallest smile; I don't want to reveal how overjoyed I am at this. Finally he has made a promise. And yes, I had to coax it out of him, but it still counts.

But then he smiles too, a really, really wide smile. "So this is real, then?"

"Pretty fucking real, Arthur."

And he grunts an excited "Arghh!" and he lurches forward and wraps his arms around me, holding me in a tight bear hug.

We are two idiots, yes, and we've made a pact.

So now, when you question how I could have been such a fool, when you are tempted to chide me, perhaps, for my naivety, remember this. I knew that he was good, and I knew that he loved me, and I couldn't fathom why he would cause me and her and himself so much pain if he didn't at least intend to eventually get joy out of it, change his life, start a new one.

Our future together was simply the most logical option, as well as happening to be the one that allowed me to continue to have a stake in the world and in my own life.

Before Arthur made this promise, there was still a niggle of doubt in my mind as to whether I should be hedging my bets. I was still making sure to see my friends from time to time; I was keeping a toe in the water of the world outside of Arthur. But I feel no compulsion to do this now. All I can think about is when this waiting period will be over, when real life will begin. When I'm not with him, I'm thinking of him. I'm imagining what kind of house we'll live in. I'm picturing where we'll travel together. I'm reading recipe books for the first time, so I can make him dinner when the time comes. I was already doing my work on auto-pilot, but I have now realised that the bare minimum is even less than I thought. Before the promise, I would still half-heartedly banter with Ken. Now I respond to his remarks like one responds to a boring relative on the phone at Christmas: "Mmhmm . . . yep . . . yeah, for sure. Oh wow." Before the promise, Mei Ling and I would message back and forth about our interminable boredom. But to do that now would feel disingenuous: like yes, the job is boring, but I have a beautiful secret life ahead of me. I feel guilty that I will be getting out, whereas nothing has changed for Mei Ling. I never do ask her if she is a middle child. I am no longer curious. These non-Arthur office relationships seem immaterial to me now.

Most days, but not every day, Arthur meets me somewhere after work, usually a bar, sometimes a park if the weather is good. I invariably get there before him, reading a book and biding my time until he arrives, telling myself that this waiting is not pathetic because if I wasn't waiting for him I'd probably just be reading a book somewhere else. Sometimes the bars we meet at are host to lots of businessmen having after-work drinks, and I am always so clearly out of place, sitting there on my own with my bell hooks and my backpack. I can sense everyone looking at me and wondering what I am doing there. A young un-suited woman alone at 6 p.m. in a suits bar—I never foresaw that I would be her.

And then, when he strides into the space in his business attire and slides into my booth, I feel such a thrill, like, *Here he is, my own office man!* I am gleeful; I give him the biggest hugs, I crumple his shirt with my enthusiasm and energy. I say, "Tell me absolutely everything about your day!" And even though I know what has happened in his day, seeing as how I hear his phone calls and we message each other every few minutes, I still truly want to know. I want to know how he views his day, I want to compare it with my version of how he's lived it, and I want to offer up these comparisons to him. He does the same with me, recounting what he imagines I was doing and thinking on the other side of the Dell barricade. He describes my facial expressions, how when I type I look like I am attempting brain surgery.

He almost always has to leave soon after he's arrived. He has to go home to her, and for now I accept this. I am playing the long game.

On weekends the different tracks on which our lives run become more problematic. The suburbs in which I meet my friends and go drinking are not the suburbs near Arthur's or my father's house. This means that sometimes—on a Friday night, for example—I won't see him all evening, and he will get upset about this. He'll text me at 10 p.m. and say, *I've managed to slip out for a walk,* and unfortunately I am far away at that moment, in some other part of the city, and it will hit me that I've missed my chance to spend time with him.

To remedy this, I start going out less. I don't mind. He's going to leave his wife—this is a temporary situation. I stay home on weekends, waiting for Arthur's texts, waiting for him to tell me we have an opening, at which point it is go! go! go!!

Dad has adopted a no-comment policy about my change in lifestyle. He never asks where I am going when I leave the house at strange hours, returning an hour or two later in a better mood that quickly becomes a worse mood. Occasionally he'll mention that he hasn't seen Sarah in a while, or he'll ask me how Soph is doing, and I have enough information to reassure him that I haven't fallen out with them, so he lets me go on, living my ghost life, clearly figuring that I know what I am doing.

ONE weekend about five months in, a month after Arthur has said he will leave his wife, I am doing my usual waiting routine, having told Arthur I'll be around. Dad is out for the night, and I'm sitting at home with Jude, checking my phone and waiting for time to pass. I'm re-watching *Don't Trust the B---- in Apartment 23*.

It's 9 p.m. and I haven't had any update from Arthur yet about if or when he can see me this evening. I'm getting restless and lonely. So when Sarah calls to tell me to get in an Uber and come to an exhibition her now official girlfriend Tess is in, I am persuaded to leave my self-imposed isolation.

I have always derived an almost transcendent joy from such events: from observing all the fabulously self-conscious but performatively ambivalent hipsters wearing their mad little outfits, their expensive sculptural pants and their bizarre corset tops from Vinnies, trying to sell their spray-painted tree trunks, using the word "intermedial" again and again and again, pretending not to know their corporate parents who have turned up to support them and who have paid for their fine arts degrees and the materials for this show.

Sarah generously lets me make fun of Tess's piece, a "contemplation of textuality in a digital age." Tess has screenshotted every break-up text conversation she had with her ex-partner and screenprinted the collected writings onto a wall-hanging. I ask Sarah if she is concerned that her messages might suffer a similar fate if she and Tess ever break up, and she says, "Oh, to be honest, we don't really message that much. We're pretty much together all the time anyway."

Imagine getting to be with your partner all the time!

I haven't been out like this in ages, letting myself give in to the night, laughing with my friends, drinking stupid canned beer and vaping in alleyways, and I am rolling in it, it is like falling into silk. Sarah at her side, Tess introduces me to her art school mates and I ask each of them who their favourite artist is. They tell me Jenny Holzer, they tell me Marina Abramović, they tell me Nick Cave, Stanley Brouwn, Yinka Shonibare. And when they return the question, I deadpan: "Rupi Kaur."

The horror on their faces! My god, I have missed this. Sarah decides to join me on this journey.

"And weren't you saying just the other day, Hera, that you would argue Rupi Kaur is kind of like Christian Bök for the thinking woman?"

The art students are beside themselves, they don't know what to do. They are vaping ferociously, some of them texting—I presume they are messaging each other, bitching about this Kaur sycophant who stands before them.

"I was saying that, Sarah, yeah. I feel like Kaur has already built where Bök strives to go, you know?"

Tess rolls her eyes and grins. "You two are idiots. Please ignore them, everyone."

Sarah and I look at each other and declare, in unison, "That's actually homophobic, Tess." Sarah gives Tess a kiss and then we run back inside to the open bar to drink more terrible but free sauvignon blanc.

As Sarah and I are doing the rounds of the show, commenting loudly about the pieces we see—"This one is clearly an homage to early Ken Done" and "It's so interesting what the artist has done with texture here"—I realise that I haven't checked my phone in a few hours. So I take it out of my bag and have a look, and I see that I have twelve messages from Arthur, sent two hours ago, saying he can meet up in ten, then asking where I am, then bordering on the verge of rude, then backtracking and saying he loves me and hopes I am having a good night, then asking where I am again. I ignore Sarah for a moment, panicked, and I message him back and say how sorry I am, that I'm out with friends and lost track of time, that I can see him any time tomorrow.

But his green dot isn't there and it's late now and he's evidently gone to sleep in a huff. My high is gone, I now feel depleted and stupid and sad. I make my excuses and I get an Uber home. He doesn't message me back till late the next day, saying that it's okay, he was just upset because he missed me, and I had said that I'd be around, and he'd counted on that.

Now I feel guilty. What message was I sending him, being out of contact while I was out getting pissed somewhere on a Friday night? I need to show him that I can be responsible, that I can live an adult life with him. But then there's a rare spike of annoyance too, which goes like, *Is this guy for real? My entire life is on hold for him and he hasn't left his wife and now he's angry that on one occasion out of a hundred I was not immediately accessible when it was convenient for him?* And almost as soon as this feeling comes it is displaced by understanding: I too would be upset were he absent when he said he'd be around. I feel stuck. I am aware that a past version of myself, one who is not so embroiled, would likely see this all with much greater clarity—would likely stick up for herself more, would find Arthur's entitlement galling, or she would never wait around in the first place.

But this lucidity feels impossible to access now.

The next time I see Arthur is the Sunday afternoon after the Friday night. We meet in a park between our two houses, and we discuss the evening in question, how it made both of us feel. We sit on a blanket I've brought from home and we smile politely at people walking their dogs around us. It's chilly and I've not worn enough clothing. My teeth chatter as I explain to Arthur how on Friday night I felt trapped in waiting, and he explains that he guessed I must have felt that way and that it made him feel terrible and he is so sorry and he wants more than anything not to make me feel that way, but that he always misses me and he was counting on seeing me and when I didn't respond he felt stupid, abandoned, left hanging. And of course it is coldly amusing to me that he feels that he can say this, having experienced it one time, whereas this is how I feel most of the time and I do not tell him, I protect him from it, from the hurt he causes.

So, emboldened by my annoyance at the double-standard that is apparently invisible to him, I say, "Leave your wife, then." And he responds gravely, "I will, I promise, I will."

He goes on, "I just need to find the right time, I need to be respectful. She's really busy with work at the moment. But once her latest project is done I think it'll be a lot more viable. I don't want to kick her when she's down."

And despite this being a piss-weak justification—there is never a good time to tell your wife you are leaving her for a younger woman—the very fact that he's thinking about logistics and considering schedules is itself heartening to me. And that he's sharing his thought processes with me? That's good, that's transparency. We will continue our adulterous dance. But I will be like Sophie Ellis-Bextor in the "Murder on the Dancefloor" film clip. I will do what it takes to make sure we are the couple that wins.

In the weeks after this last "talk," I find myself constantly urging Arthur to tell her, in varying degrees of coolness and manic hysteria, as I become more and more infatuated, more convinced that he is the only path my life can take. He fobs me off with vague assurances. He tells me "soon." I give him questions that only have two possible answers, so he has to engage. Instead of "What kind of house do you see us living in?" I ask, "Do you feel we're more of a terrace couple or an apartment couple?" I cringe when I hear myself, the nag I am becoming. On the rare occasion when I do see Sarah and Soph, I am barely there, too engrossed in my phone, in the prospect of receiving a message. Their conversations do not interest me, I can only just feign casual investment in Sarah's relationship, and I laugh at the wrong beats in Soph's work anecdotes. So young, these concerns seem to me! So small, so trifling is the folly of their youth.

One weekday evening I return home after work and find that Dad is already there, reading his book on the verandah, with Jude at his feet.

"Skived off early, did you?" I say.

Looking up from his book, he appraises me. "I hope I have taught you, my girl, that sometimes the best thing you can do with a day is leave it behind and then start again tomorrow. On that note, fancy joining me for a G & T?" He raises the empty glass he is holding.

"Don't mind if I do—and another for you?"

"I'd be much obliged."

I head into the kitchen and mix us our drinks, and when I

return to the verandah I sit in a chair next to Dad's, and we take in the serenity.

"How goes the fast-paced world of news?" he enquires.

"A British TV star has been caught cheating on her husband and now people are calling for her to be fired from the show she's been on for, like, decades."

"Ah, nothing new under the sun," he muses.

"And how about you?"

"I'm not as young as I once was."

"Let me guess: you designed a residential foyer and today you realised you forgot to include a door in the plan?"

"That is precisely what happened, Hera. But I covered for it by explaining to the engineers that mine was a conceptual choice, a commentary on the futility of God's tendency to always open windows."

"I bet they loved that."

"Yes, we're all getting along very well. No, to answer your question, my day was completely average, and around three o'clock I thought, bugger this, and decided it would be far more enjoyable to come home and sit here instead, so leave and sit I did."

"Dad, you know I love you, but it's my duty to tell you that you're very much flagging your boomer privilege right now. Like, what I wouldn't give to just leave work when I felt like it."

Dad considers this; he is used to playing scapegoat for all my generational resentments.

"You're right, Hera. I am absolutely the economic enemy. Unrelatedly, how's the free rent treating you?" He gives me a moment to look chastened, and then he goes on, in a more thoughtful tone: "I wasn't totally speaking in jest before, Hera. I left work early because, as I hope you know, sometimes the most powerful thing you can do is leave, provided you've determined that what you might gain is more important to you than what you might lose."

"Okay, Confucius, have you seen my dad?"

He turns to Jude. "See how she treats me?"

We sit for a while in silence, during which I pick up Jude and place him on my lap, stroking him demurely, like an old dame with her Pomeranian in a period piece.

The conversation pivots to less philosophical territory, but I am unsettled by Dad's foray into existential advice. What does he know, or what does he think he knows? And what is he trying to say to me, on that basis?

It's not as if Dad is unaware of the vagaries of the world: he knows them more than most. Sometimes you do just have to leave.

THAT night we make curry, and we eat it at the kitchen table while watching a British crime drama on TV.

About halfway through the episode, I get a message from Arthur: *Rendezvous in 10? I can meet you at park?*

My heart swells and I type back in the affirmative immediately.

I put my phone down and turn to Dad. "If you can handle my absence," I say, "I might just step out for a bit, go meet a mate for a drink."

Dad tries not to show it but I can see that he is hurt: we were hanging out tonight, and I am unceremoniously cutting it short.

"Oh, right then, an abrupt exit. Jude and I will have to cope without you, I suppose."

"Sorry, Dad, just gotta live the nights of my glorious youth and so on, you know how it is!" I stand up from the table and give him a hug from behind.

I speed-walk to the park. When I arrive at our spot, the park is deserted, and I have two minutes to wait till Arthur arrives, so I sit down, scroll my phone, and let myself be warmed by thoughts of his arms around me.

Another seven minutes pass, so Arthur is officially running five minutes late. No matter, five minutes is fine. Arthur's green dot is not there, which surely means he is on his way.

I spy a drunk guy stumbling through the far side of the park. He is gripping a wine bottle by the neck and talking loudly to himself. I hunch over and try to make myself physically smaller, so as not to draw his attention. He might be harmless or he might be a rapist and in situations such as this (and in life in general, I guess) there is no way to know which, so best to err on the side of caution.

I stare intently at my phone, typing random letters into the Notes app, so if the man notices me it might appear that I am in dialogue with someone, that I am not just a young woman totally alone in a park at night.

Arthur is ten minutes late now, and the drunk man has taken a seat on a wet patch of grass in my peripheral vision.

Ten minutes after the agreed meeting time: after ten minutes you can text someone to ask how their journey is coming along, to imply that you're waiting, that you're sick of waiting. I'd really prefer not to message, I don't want to be that woman, but I can't help myself.

Am in park. You close?

His green dot is still not there, and there is nothing to indicate that he has seen the message.

I didn't bring my headphones so I can't listen to music, and besides, I probably shouldn't anyway, for vigilance and so on. Drunk guy is singing now, and I'd like to tell you that it's a sorrowful Irish ballad, or at least a downbeat Eric Clapton, but it's not, it's Avicii. I am listening to a totally tone-deaf man sing-yelling, "Heeeey, brother," over and over. And I feel for him, I do, they're the only words anyone can remember from that song, but it's also a little menacing, given the context.

I rest my phone on my leg and stare at the sky instead. My

thoughts return to Dad. I imagine him sitting alone at home, just a few blocks away, watching TV in our warm house, probably wondering what I'm doing, why I would leave him like that, so randomly, on a Tuesday night, after dinner. I think of all the dinners he's had to spend alone and my heart breaks for him and I hate myself. I am in a park waiting for a man who has a wife, and Dad was watching *Spooks* with his daughter but now he's just watching it with his dog, which is nice, but it's not the same.

Finally, after twenty minutes, my phone lights up: *So sorry running late, had to deal with something here. Leaving now.*

I don't click on the notification. I don't want to give him the satisfaction of seeing the read receipt, knowing that I am just sitting here, anxiously anticipating any message from him. I mean, he knows that I'm doing this anyway, but I grasp at what dignity I can. I don't reply, I just wait. I am trying to work out how I will camouflage my irritation when he arrives. Will I make light of it, tell him I was reading a *New Yorker* long-form and barely even noticed the time? Will I rib him for it and play it off as a joke?

I receive a text from Soph: *Yo, ended up at Mr. Moore's tonight. Wanna join?*

No, Sophie, I think to myself. I do not want to "join." I am busy sitting by myself in a public park for an indefinite amount of time.

No, but really, though, where is he? I make myself wait another five minutes, taking it to a grand total of forty, and then I message him again.

Arthur, no offence, but where the fuck are you?

He's green, the lights are on! I see him typing, deleting, typing, deleting. A message appears.

Hera, I am so sorry. I'm not going to make it. I can't get away.

A moment later, a second message: *I thought I could, I'm so sorry.*

It's only when I feel a tear on my cheek that I realise I am crying. I feel, in this moment, pathetic. And I have felt many things with Arthur thus far, but pathetic has not been one of them. All the other times I've waited for him, I've had things to occupy me: books to read, people to watch. I've had distractions to assure me I am not waiting, not really. I've been young, I've had options. I've had some modicum of power. But this, this absolute aloneness, the dark and quiet of this place. Avoiding the drunk guy who may or may not assault me. I thought we weren't doing this. I thought we had an unspoken deal that he wouldn't perform the clichés favoured by adulterous men on TV, and that accordingly I would not treat him like one. But getting your mistress to wait for you in a park at night-time and then abandoning her there because you can't think up a good enough excuse for your wife? I thought we both knew that there was a line.

I stand up and brush myself off, and this alerts the drunk to my presence. He is upright again, stumbling around only a few metres from me.

I look at him directly, almost daring him to confront me. He doesn't, though. He gestures to his wine bottle—offering it to me, I think—and he slurs, "Cheer up, love, it can't be that bad!"

I can't think of a reply, so I half-smile, half-grimace, and I salute him as I turn to leave the park.

When I get home, the lights are off. Dad's gone to sleep and the house is dead quiet.

How long can this last for, you ask? How long can two people be falling in love with each other, having sex in hotel rooms and kissing in the stairwell at work, messaging every two minutes of every day, before one of them gets fed up that the other isn't leaving his wife?

I can only speak for myself, of course, but for me, I do have a number. It's six months. Six fucking months, if you will.

PART · THREE

On the six-month anniversary of Arthur and me beginning to do whatever it is we were doing, I got on a plane for England— leaving Sydney and Arthur behind me.

I'll explain. That night, sitting pathetically in the park, had changed something for me. I spent the half-week and weekend that followed going over and over it. I made a manic decision. I didn't want to leave him, but I could not stay. Arthur was so rooted in Sydney, so sure of his place, so tied to his life. And I'd been tying myself to it too. But it now felt that continuing to live and work here would be like holding on to an anchor that was attached to nothing. I was twenty-four. This was not supposed to be my life.

At work the week following the park betrayal, I sat at my communal desk and I sensed Arthur's presence on the other side. While the Dell barrier used to be titillating, a metaphor for our forbidden romance, it now seemed to me to be a much simpler metaphor: we were divided, and we could not see each other. And he was not standing up to make eye contact over the barrier. He was making no effort to dismantle it.

As Alison lectured me on incorrect colour coding, as Mei Ling sent me Moira Rose gifs—*Oh, God. I'd kill for a good coma right now*—as Ken drawled on and on about negative interest rates, I felt myself spiralling. Every recurring thought, every plan I tried to devise, it came down to this, to the seed in my mind that I could no longer ignore: I could not keep living like this.

I told myself that if this was love—if this was real—it would work out, Arthur would leave his wife. But for now I needed to go. I needed to show him what living without me was like. He had to understand that I was not going to wait for him forever. That without him, I could do whatever I wanted. The world was mine, if I so chose, he had to see that. And I had to believe that.

I had a British passport. I had a little money saved from working and living at home. I would resign, and my ostensible reason for doing this would be career-related. I'd get a job in the UK, doing what didn't matter. Toggling between browser windows whenever Alison looked my way, I started spending my office hours looking up other jobs on Indeed, applying for roles in the UK. Anything could feasibly be seen as a step up from the job I currently had. I was an independent woman, I would follow my own path. I would build a life without Arthur, just for me. I would not wait in parks.

The job search this time round was more straight-forward. I knew the lingo, I knew the buzz words. Plus, I now had experience working at a reputable news company. On Indeed I found many, many terribly paid freelance content producer jobs. The UK was heaving with them, it seemed. I constructed and fired off cover letters with the zeal of a Dominos flyer delivery person. By Wednesday I had procured an interview for the Friday. I took a half-day off work and at 8 a.m. Sydney time I did a twenty-minute Skype interview with a manager in the UK. During the interview I was basically told I had the job and that they'd send the paperwork through on Monday. I was to be a freelance "feminist content producer" for an online marketing company. And they say living the dream isn't real.

There was, admittedly, an undercurrent of ulterior motive in the decision to trade my Australian life for a British one. Arthur was from the UK. Was there a part of me that secretly hoped he would be tempted to follow me, tempted to return to his home country to be with the sweet, young love of his life? I cannot say this did not cross my mind. We would live atop a little shop in Soho. He'd write and I'd work out what it is that I wanted to do with my life. We'd eat full English breakfasts. We'd drink gin in a tin. But I would not tell him this. He had to work this out for himself. My reasoning to him would betray none of my hopes and dreams for us. He had to think I was pulling the plug on us. He had to be coerced into action.

So that weekend, on the Saturday, before I'd even been sent the paperwork for the new job, I met Arthur in a café halfway between our houses. I'd been cold to him all week—he knew something was up. He looked desperate, and I liked seeing that expression on him. I felt that usually I was the one with emotions smeared all over my face, no matter how much I tried to hide them.

Over a smoothie (him) and a flat white (me), I told Arthur that I loved him but that I was leaving, that he needed to sort his shit out, that I could only be with him when he'd proved to me that he was serious, when he'd left her.

"What are you saying?" he asked. "You can't. You can't just leave me, Hera, without even discussing it first."

I'd never been in this position with him before. He was begging. It felt good.

"I'm serious, Arthur. I wish I wasn't, but I am." I took a sip from my flat white, and resolutely I looked at him, like he was somebody I was firing, someone in a redundancy meeting. I'd managed to dissociate. I'd made a choice and I would not be swayed. It was his turn to feel things as I had been feeling them. It was his turn to feel powerless.

"But Hera, I love you. I know things have been hard, but we'll work it out together. We can't work it out together if you're not here. Please don't leave me."

I paused, determining the right words to use. I said them slowly. "That's just it, Arthur. I've been here, waiting, for you to leave your wife, like you promised. And you haven't done that; you haven't even planned how you're going to do that. I love you,

you know this—but that's not enough. I need you to step up. So I'm going to go, and you're going to stay. And if you leave your wife, let me know. But apart from that, I don't want to talk to you. I don't want you to message me. If you won't leave her, I need you to let me live."

For the first time, I saw Arthur cry. His tears were silent and intense. His body was heaving, his eyes were glassy. Here was a man who, for the first time in his life, maybe, was not getting what he wanted. I stood up from the table, walked round to his side, and touched his shoulders. I kissed him on his left shoulder. I went to the counter and paid for our drinks, and I exited the café. I needed him to sit in what he'd done, needed him to feel the weight of the hand he'd forced me to play.

I was devastated, but proud of myself too. Maybe I could even do what I threatened—maybe I could make a new life.

On the Sunday, when I told Dad of my plan, he did not seem surprised.

"You've never been one for settling, Hera."

If only he knew! All I had wanted was to settle. Flight is what you do when you can't settle, I wanted to tell him.

"Well, I'll find comfort in knowing that my home country will benefit from my loss," he said.

I began to tear up at this. Why did he have such faith that I was a good person? I did not deserve it.

He gave me a hug, and I cried, though not for the reasons he likely thought I was.

The next Wednesday evening, after work, having signed the new job paperwork I'd been sent, I emailed my resignation to Alison. At the office on Thursday morning, Alison took me aside, into a small conference room, and told me she'd received my notice. She said this without visible emotion. Her primary concern, she expressed, was that I remember to return my head-set to IT on my last day, as "people always think they can take them." I thanked Alison for her mentorship and she looked at me like she wanted to murder me.

Now I had to break the news to Mei Ling. Back at my desk, I IM'd her.

Hera Stephen: *buzz buzz bitch*

Mei Ling Chen: *go on*

Hera Stephen: *what has two tits and is getting the fuck out of here?*

Mei Ling Chen: . . . *???*

Mei Ling Chen: *pls don't tell me you mean what I think you mean*

Hera Stephen: *I'm sorry bb. I'm out. Your strength is an inspiration but I am weak.*

Mei Ling Chen: *Are you srsly leaving me alone with alison? Hera I am going to die*

Hera Stephen: *Well then you should quit too! Come on, it'll be fun! Imma move to the UK. We can get weirdly invested in football and spend our days snorting cheap coke?? Tell me that doesn't sound appealing.*

Mei Ling Chen: *Obvi it does but Hera, I can't. My family is here. I live with my mum. She needs me.*

I had no idea Mei Ling lived with and cared for her mum. I realised I knew almost nothing about Mei Ling. I had never asked.

When the company-wide email went out, telling everyone I was leaving, I got responses from people I'd never talked to, never met, telling me *good luck* and *we'll miss you*. Arthur did not respond to the chain. Ken emailed back, *Sad to see our pretty lady flying the coop.* Killara came over to my desk and gave me a hug, said she'd wished she'd gotten to know me better. I was moved by this. I don't think she really meant it but it was nice of her to say.

On my final day in the office, I was presented with a Coles

mud cake and a card, chosen by Ken. Ken could not control his laughter as I opened the envelope. The card's cover read, "You are dead to us." Inside were a few signatures I could not decipher, a message from Sally that read, "You will be missed"; a line from Mei Ling—"Stay gold, ponyboy"—and a stick figure drawing of a woman drinking a pint, signed, "Get lit, Ken." I looked and looked for a note from Arthur. There was none. Eventually I found one from "Doug." It read, "Don't go."

His note made me sad and then it angered me. Who was he to tell me not to go? He had the power to make me stay, and he was choosing not to exercise it. I dug into a slice of cake and got crumbs all through my keyboard. I did not clean them up.

I'd told Soph and Sarah of my plan to leave almost as soon as I'd come up with it. Over the next few weeks they'd cycled through different emotions—disbelief, hurt, excitement. I think overall they were oscillating between jealousy and concern. Jealous, because I was extricating myself from a life that wasn't serving me. And concerned, because clearly mine was not a well-thought-out plan.

Sarah, being practical, expressed some worry that I might be attempting to solve a huge problem in a rather melodramatic fashion, and that moving to the UK, where I had no friends and very little family, for a job that had no office, might not be the best idea I'd ever had. I assured her that she was wrong and that, as it happened, it was actually the best idea that I, or indeed anyone, had ever had.

Soph did not try to talk me out of it. Some things never change. Instead, she made me promise to do regular FaceTimes with the pair of them. I promised her that I would be in regular contact.

I can tell you now that I absolutely intended to ghost them. I intended to ghost my entire life.

And so, and so I left.

Unfortunately, although you can relocate your life, it will still be your life. I learn this swiftly.

I don't really know what I am hoping for. I am hoping, I suppose, for transformation. In books, when people move to new cities they become part of new stories, the narratives of their lives are entangled in new webs, they form unexpected textures, they wrap around city structures like scarves, they find their chosen family, or they at least find a mirror in which they can see an altered reflection of themselves. They see that they can be different here, they can break their old patterns, they won't watch the same two Netflix shows before bed each night as they attempt to fall asleep, they won't think the same thoughts that keep them up, unable to detach from reality into dreams.

I suppose my thinking is that as I am relatively young and female and not totally unattractive, I will be swept up in a surprising new current, a new life, and maybe I will stop loving Arthur and start loving someone else, preferably someone single. Or, alternatively, I will live a life of pleasant distraction until such time as Arthur leaves his wife and comes to me. I want both of these things at once, even though they are fundamentally incompatible. I will try to live life here like I am not in love, even though I am.

It rains a lot in the new city, and the job I am doing could really be done anywhere. As this job has no office, my days consist of waking up, logging on, adding empowering words to press releases from sex toy companies and vape delivery services, working out how to insert the empty lines between Instagram captions and hashtags, and editing the exposure on matte still-life photographs of jade eggs. I tell myself that this is good, that this is me living my life without Arthur. I wear lipstick sometimes and I go to the pub with my new flatmate, who seems to have even fewer friends in this city than I do, despite her having grown up in it. Her name is Poppy. I found her on a flatmate-finding website. On the website she listed her main hobbies as "music, wine, and working out." In reality, I am learning that her main hobby is being extremely fucking loud. Nevertheless, when I cannot stand being alone of an evening I deign to drink pints with her as she goes on and on about her high school friends who now live in other cities. When the pub closes, we stumble back to our crappy two-bedroom flat, knowing each other no better than when the night began.

I join a choir, I quit the choir. I join a feminist book club, but when I get to the first gathering I realise that the meeting place is a twenty-four-hour teashop rather than a pub or bar, which I think speaks to its overall vibe. Who wants to drink peppermint tea in a public space at 8 p.m.? Fourteen barely discernible white women with short fringes discuss the intersectional merits of Roxane Gay's *Bad Feminist*. I quit the book club.

What do you do when you're in a new city and you're by yourself and you have no one to talk to about the affair you've been having and how now you're heartbroken because he didn't leave her? Even the possibility of having that kind of conversation requires years of friendship. Someone needs to really like you before you can take the next step and tell them how shit you really are. If you are trying to make a friend in a new city, you don't want the potential friend's first piece of knowledge about you to be that you are an unsuccessful homewrecker. A homewrecker is bad enough—but one who did all the bad things and still didn't get the guy? That's not only morally bankrupt, it's pathetic.

I make a playlist of sad songs, obviously. In breaks from my corporate writing, I put on my noise-cancelling headphones and head outside, and I listen to Kate Bush's "Running Up That Hill" again and again and again as I walk. The city I'm in is pretty much flat so that makes the symbolism hard to actualise, but I find inclines from time to time, which is something. Even now when I hear those opening beats I get flashbacks to depressed promenading, to eyes straight ahead, hands in coat pockets, tears streaming down face.

I haven't worked out how to dress in this city, as it is colder than what I am used to. Consequently I wear either far too many layers or not enough, so each walk leaves me either shivering or sweaty as hell, sometimes both. On my walks I try to discover unexpected scenic delights near my flat, and this does not happen. I find a lot of alleyways, I find a lot of abandoned crack spots, I find a pretty good kebab shop.

Occasionally, if it's the weekend and she's not at work, Poppy attempts to join me on my walks, saying casually, "Ah, a stroll would be well nice right about now, wouldn't it?" And I'll say, "God, ain't that the truth. Anyway, see you in a bit!" and then stride blithely out the door, as if I am completely oblivious to her hinting.

I start out attempting to do my work from cafés, reasoning that this will tie me to the urban landscape and make me believe that I am really here. Each day I set down my laptop at some frustratingly angled table, drink a disappointing flat white (British coffee is trash, no matter how cool the café), and scroll Twitter, and type. Like with job applications, it is scary how I can disassociate. Three hours can pass and then I'll look down at my screen and see that I've written four pages' worth of content about a product I don't remember ever having been conscious of, let alone knowledgeable about. I send the copy I write off into oblivion, to Sue, to Sara, to Amanda, to Emily, and I await instructions for the next urgent five hundred words on feminist candles.

Each day just past lunchtime my stomach growls and I buy

an overpriced sandwich from whichever hipster establishment I am gracing with my presence, rather than walking the twelve minutes back to my unit and my sandwich press and the unlikely but terrifying possibility that Poppy will be there. I tell myself I am saving time. What I am not saving is money or myself.

I am trying to forget Arthur. I am trying to move on. But working in these cafés, walking miles each day, knowing no one—all it does is give me yet more time and space to daydream about him.

You can exist on two planes at once, have two guiding motivations, even if these motivations are together a self-defeating combination. I want Arthur to leave his wife and come to me. But I also know he's not doing this. So I decide to fast-track falling in love with someone new by sleeping with British strangers.

I sign up to two dating apps and craft myself two generic personas. On the first app I am straight, Australian, here for a good time and not a long time, etc. I say my favourite movie is *Crocodile Dundee*. On the second app I am queer, into far-left politics and craft beer. I say my favourite movie is *The Babadook*. All bases covered; I now quickly fuck a cross-section of characters.

Rather than feeling like the beginning of a new journey, these dates feel like exercises in misanthropy. It is alarming how simple it is to make certain men think that they are in love with you. As soon as I decide I might care what a man thinks of me, as soon as I doubt myself for a second, the power is gone. So I have to choose my targets wisely; I have to date men I don't see as people. This is pretty easy.

Here is what I learn.

Most men are ready to read into the first three character traits you present them with, and if you just pick the right three for the corresponding man, bam, you've got him.

They all love eye contact. They love a woman who does not look away and who makes them feel observed, like they are being truly seen for the first time. I have perfected my penetrating gaze since my time with Max. You must turn his eyes into a double-glazed mirror; only look into him to see yourself. He thinks it's him you're captivated by. Let him think this.

Generally, most guys like it if it's clear that you're smarter than them, but only if you temper this with some playful idiocy, some display of down-to-earthness to suggest that what you really are is fun. Make a nuanced remark about the American healthcare system but then say that you learnt about it from *The Simpsons*. You must convince him that being in love with you will allow him to be in on every joke, on all the jokes he's never noticed were being made. Obviously you should never let him know that it is actually him you are laughing at; but you needn't worry too much about this, as chances are he will never consider this possibility. He might even think that it's you you're laughing at. How wrong he is, but how charming the idiocy, like watching a child who is blithely unaware that their drawing looks nothing like what it attempts to represent.

The third thing: let him explain stuff to you. That they like to do this is common knowledge, thanks to Rebecca Solnit, but unlike Rebecca, I think: why not embrace it? Let him go on and on and on about how supermarket marketing is all about psychology as if this is news to you. Let him reveal to you that the label on a jar of mayo might make you inclined to choose that mayo over another based on what kind of person you'd like to be, even though all the products are qualitatively the same. Then, when he finally stops talking, make some witty comment that shows you've known this all along and you have just been indulging him. Make this remark kind, not cutting. Make it so he isn't sure to what extent you hate him. Make it so he thinks he might have misread your remark at first, and, maybe you really are impressed. Then kiss him on the lips and stare into his eyes once more. Ask him when he last truly felt happy, and wait for him to tell you. He will tell you. No one ever asks him this. Boom, it's done. You have him. You don't want him, but you have him.

I fuck a gynaecologist called Kieran in a back alley after a

rum bar, then go back to his apartment. It is furnished with a
fridge, a bed, and a very large gaming station. I tell him that I
love what he's done with the place and I genuinely don't know
if he understands my sarcasm: he thanks me and tells me where
he bought the bed (Argos). He wants me to meet his mother the
next weekend so I ghost him.

I fuck an anthropology grad named Paul, who says he just
can't ever figure out what I am thinking and how hot that is.
After we have sex, we sit and smoke in the lounge room, and
Poppy comes home and she and Paul talk. It soon becomes clear
that they are trying to mine each other for information about
me, but I've not revealed enough of myself to either of them for
it to be worth their while. I bid them goodnight and retreat to my
bed. Eventually Paul comes into my bedroom and slides under
the sheets beside me as if any of what just happened was normal.
I let him pay for breakfast the next day and then I never return
any of his increasingly frequent calls or texts.

Women are more complex but similar rules apply. I fuck a
woman who makes bronze tampon necklaces. She's straightfor-
ward: I tell her I love the musical episode of *Buffy*, the philosophy of Hannah Arendt, and the songs of Willie Nelson. She tells
me she loves me soon after this. And it's not that I don't love
these three things; I do. It's just that I immediately know which
three things to tell her about. I like so many things.

There will always be a Venn diagram crossover of three of
your things with someone else's things. Present them like jewels;
like jewels that promise intimacy. Wait for the other person to
pick them up, and act surprised and delighted when they do. Act
like it is you who feels that you are being seen properly for the
first time. *Let them think that the discovery is theirs.* Show don't
tell, etc.

As you can see, my romantic entanglements leave no room

for feelings to grow. I'm self-sabotaging every date, picking people I know I will hate. And if it happens that they seem nice, then I play a version of myself that is so far from who I know myself to be that it is guaranteed we will never fall in love. How could we, when I'm pretending to like *Crocodile Dundee*?

I stare at my phone even more in this country than I did in Australia. Because the thing is, while I told Arthur not to message me anymore, I didn't tell him not to *not* message me. And so even though I have left him, even though I've made it clear that our relationship is over unless he leaves his wife, we are still engaged in an international game of messaging chicken.

He waits till I'm online (which is pretty much all the time), and then he type type types, then deletes without sending. He knows I can see this. He knows I am watching. And I do the same thing back. Sometimes I type actual messages to him before deleting them. I write all the things that I envisage doing with him one day when we are together; and sometimes I just write gibberish, holding down the "l" key for minutes at a time. I wonder if he can tell which of my ellipses are masking real messages and which are masking absolute nonsense. I feel that I can guess with his—something about the speed with which the ellipses flash up then disappear, something about the length of pauses. But either way, I am still holding his gaze to his phone as I type, and this is enough of a connection with him to get by. I am like a smoker subsisting on Nicorette patches; like a smoker subsisting on Nicorette patches, with increasingly painful RSI.

I understand that it is pitiable, how my stomach plummets when there is no green dot, because this means his attention is not on me. Every time I read a funny line in a book I take a photo of it, just in case there is a moment in the future that I can send it to him. Whenever I see couples sitting happily together, I want to push them apart. My concentration is wrecked; I constantly miss my train stop.

Back in Sydney, Soph gave me wisdom from her diplomatic experience. She said that it is natural when one moves to a new place to hold on to things and people from one's past at first, but that eventually as you put down roots, you begin to let the old stuff go. I nodded as she told me this, as if agreeing that yes, my electronic dedication to this man would soon waver and I would be freed of the endless cycle of checking my phone for his messages. A real part of me did want this. And another real part of me did not. The longer I stay in the UK, the more terrible people I have sex with, the lonelier my days become, the more I realise that I have no intention of giving this dream of Arthur up—even as I can feel this limbo sucking the life out of me like a Dementor's kiss. I know that he has made his choice. But maybe soon he'll come to his senses. Surely my absence will grow so torturous that he can't stand it. This is the hope I hold and protect like a votive candle at a women's march in the rain.

Two months into living this new half-life, it is my birthday. I do not tell Poppy that this is so, as I am fearful of what kind of bonding activity she would attempt to orchestrate if she knew. Sip and paint, probably. Or like, an escape room. I shudder at the thought.

At 9 a.m. UK time, my dad FaceTimes me. He's finished dinner and he's at home with Jude on the couch.

"And what fabulous plans do you have in store for you today, birthday girl?" asks Dad.

Imagine if I told him the truth, which is: sit in this flat, write some content, buy two bottles of wine from the nearest off-license, and drink them alone in my room.

"Umm, I'm probably going to do some work, then head to an art gallery and meet up with some friends for drinks. Nothing too crazy."

"That sounds lovely, Hera. Jude and I miss you. And I ran into Sarah the other day at the train station—she says it sounds like you're loving it over there."

Bless Sarah. I have barely talked to Sarah, or Soph, since I've been here. She's a good egg, covering for me like that.

"Anyway, Dad, I've got to run. I've got a deadline this morning and I can't afford to miss it. But thank you very much for calling, and I love you."

"I love you too, Hera, always. Happy birthday, my girl."

I press the button to end the call. My phone screen freezes on Dad's earnest, perpetually worried face before I am greeted again by my background picture—a selfie I made Arthur take with me back in Sydney, after one of our park sex sessions.

I spend the day as predicted, not leaving my room except to buy alcohol. By 10 p.m. I am red wine drunk, and I am scrolling through old messages with Arthur on Instagram. It's his morning. He's awake. It's no longer my birthday in Australia. I thought that maybe my birthday would compel him out of his silence, but it appears not.

I'm listening to Spotify on shuffle from my laptop, and of course the algorithm decides to taunt me. "The River" starts playing, and I'm right back there in that karaoke room. I miss Arthur so much. Surely sending him one message would be okay? It's not like I'm moving home. Just a little message, as a treat?

I see his typing ellipses. I watch them disappear.

I fear I am about to fold. I type *Hey stranger*. My finger hovers above the send button.

Before I have a chance to do this, however, his ellipses transform—they become words. Arthur has sent me a message.

I know you told me not to contact you, but I couldn't not say happy birthday.

The serotonin that immediately floods my body is intense.

My fingers start to type before I even know what I'm saying. This is a bad idea and I am actioning it.

Are you going to say it, then? I reply.

Happy birthday, Hera, he responds.

And then, a second later, he adds to this: *I miss you. I miss you so much it hurts.*

If I were sober I might have the strength to not respond to this. But I am not sober.

Fucking same, obviously. I press send.

I'm going to tell her everything darling. I'm going to end it, he writes.

And even though he's made this promise before; even though there is still no timeframe for when this leaving will occur—I can't help myself.

It's back on.

Except this time, I am living halfway around the world.

Almost immediately, our chat rhythm reverts to what it was like in Sydney, except for when the time difference between us means that one of us is asleep. I tell him about my day, he tells me about his. We message on Instagram, we begin to FaceTime whenever it is viable.

My late night is his early morning. My morning is his evening. He can't call me when he is at home with her, and he can't call me from work when not on his lunch break. So my late late night and my mornings are when we FaceTime each day. This means that when we talk I am either drunk or tired, and the morning session eats away at my day, eats away at the hours of my life in which I have the potential to be productive for money. We are living on opposite continents and his schedule still dictates mine.

Every morning, I wake up and check my phone. If it is 9 a.m. in England, it is 6 p.m. in Sydney. He's either hanging around at work waiting for me to wake up, or he's on the commute home. He sees my green dot and messages: *Good morning sleepyhead, ft?* I reply, *Give me five.* And then I brew some coffee and wander over to the couch in the lounge room. I plop down on the brown pleather and arrange three cushions behind my back, reclining lengthways, back against couch arm, and I place my laptop on my knees, and then I click the FaceTime symbol and he accepts the call, and then there he is on my screen: my love, on my screen.

And I say, "So what's the news of the day? Any changes in Chechnya?" and he laughs because I make this joke every day, and on not one of these days do I know any more about Chechnya than Bridget Jones did when she rehearsed, "Isn't it terrible about Chechnya?" as a line to impress Salman Rushdie–types at the launch of *Kafka's Motorbike*, the greatest book of our time . . . probably.

He tells me the Chechnya situation is a mess, he says it is his main priority, he says his boss has asked him to put all other reportage aside and to cover the Chechnyan beat exclusively.

I smile, but it is a tight smile, because I do not know when I will see him again and not one thing I do here is real, apart from talking to him.

The city I am in is a city full of *events*: of poetry readings; of music; of esoteric talks on punk bands whose single remaining relic is a sliver of poster on the back of a pub toilet door; of guided historical walks around parks that camouflage the graveyards of children. The more I get to know it, the more it seems to me that it is a place built on the premise of distraction. This is something Sydney does not have enough of. Perhaps Sydney is good if you are happy. But if you are lovelorn and melancholic and you need to be constantly surrounded by noise and ideas in order to forget yourself, you can maybe only find events enough to satiate this need four nights a week. Well, four nights a week is not enough: I need all seven.

Sometimes, in this city of distraction, I won't look at my phone for a full hour, and I congratulate myself when this occurs. Look at you, Hera! So independent. Inevitably, though, I now walk home from every event looking down at the phone in my hands the whole way, messaging Arthur about the places I've sat that day, the interactions I've overheard. Sometimes we FaceTime as I walk home, my head bobbing in and out of frame, black night behind me, my face pixelated and barely visible.

One evening, a few weeks after Arthur and I have resumed contact, I go to an exhibition opening—no one has invited me, as I do not have friends, but I see a flyer for it in a café I'm working in, and I decide to brave the unknown. At the gallery, after drinking enough free booze, I boldly enter a cluster and try to talk to some harness-wearing British art students about their work. Art students look the same everywhere, which is comforting. After some stilted conversation, I decide to do the Rupi Kaur bit. It speedily becomes clear that this is the wrong move, but too late, I'm in it now.

"Sorry," one woman replies, in an accent I've now learned means *I went to Oxford*, "you're saying the Instagram poet Rupi Kaur is your favourite artist?"

". . . Yes?" I decide to dig in, but the shock is already lost, and without it I can see how I must appear to this woman: an uncultured Australian, a fool to be pitied.

She smirks, looks me up and down, then concludes, "What an interesting thing to say." She walks away, leaving me to try to re-engage in the cluster, whose members have already moved on to chat about how one of their girlfriends had recently had lunch with Grayson Perry.

I silently shift back from them and locate the nearest piece of art, which I feign intense interest in. It is an abstract sculpture made of nangs. I turn to a man next to me and say, "What do you reckon, shall we each steal a nang and get out of here?"

"Sorry, a what?" he asks.

Kill me. There must be a different word for nangs here? Either that or this guy does not go to art school.

"Oh, ha! Never mind . . ." I trail off. "Ignore me." He does.

By 11 p.m. I have faced as much of this crowd as I can. I slink out of the gallery and am immensely grateful for the onslaught of cold air, for the anonymity. Out here no one can judge me. Out here in the dark my aloneness is not socially suspect. I light a cigarette and smoke as I stride away, and I message Arthur: *Ft?* It is 8 a.m. his time; he's usually on his way to work by now.

He calls a few minutes later, and I stop on the footpath. I need to make him laugh; I need to remember that I can make people laugh. Not bothering with a hello, I say gravely, "Arthur."

"Hera," he counters in the same mock-serious tone.

"I've noticed something, Arthur. I've noticed—and hear me out, because I'm aware this might be a controversial observation—but . . . British people *love* going to the pub."

"Hera," he replies seriously, "you can't just go around saying things like that. You can't unstitch the fabric of the universe in a sentence and then expect non-geniuses like myself to just go on with our days."

I exhale. Here is my person. As I walk, we talk about him moving here with me—this is a conversational development that has begun in recent weeks. He even brought it up first. We talk about how he might feel being back in his home country after so long away, about me being his convict transplant. I try to paint my picture for him—I describe the little apartment we'll rent, in which I'll cook and dance to Robyn in the kitchen. How he'll be hunched over his laptop but then close it abruptly when I pull him up to dance with me. How I'll make him come to all my silly little events and we will laugh at them together. Arthur is always saying that he never has the time to enjoy things like I do, and I tell him tonight, as I have told him before: Arthur, time is everywhere, it is in everything. Time is literally all there is.

One morning four months into me living in the new city, ten months into me loving him, we FaceTime as usual. Work is boring, the weather is bad, and I've been allowing myself to entertain the prospect of returning to Sydney before reminding myself, "No, no, you left for a reason. He has to leave her first!" But I also know that talking to him every day and sending him nudes probably isn't the smartest way to convince him of this necessity.

We talk nonsense for a quarter of an hour, more banter about news events, my review of a Greggs sausage roll ("It's like . . . average? I'm sorry, but it's average, Arthur, someone has to say it"). He laughs along, but he is a little subdued, less defensive about Greggs than I anticipated. Quiet settles between us.

Something always happens.

On my screen, Arthur inhales and there is a shift in his face and even though he's been laughing, smiling, as I natter on, now he looks serious; now he looks like he is going to cry.

"I have to tell you something bad."

And you might not believe me now, but it's true nonetheless, that even before he tells me I know what it is; I know from the way he is looking at me. I shift on the couch, feel my spine stiffen with resolve.

"Kate is pregnant."

Kate. Kate. Kate. Kate. Kate.

The name I have been studiously avoiding; the name I have not dared utter this entire time.

Arthur's wife has a name and her name is Kate, and Kate, Arthur's wife, is pregnant with their child.

I grip my coffee mug, determined not to drop it like people do in films when they are shocked. I will hold on to this mug, and somehow this will make it okay. I will hold on to this mug, and it will not shatter, and neither will I.

I don't say anything, I don't know what to say. I don't cry. I will not cry.

But he does. He breaks down, and suddenly I am the one consoling him.

"I don't want to be pregnant," he says. "I'm so sorry," he says.

He absolutely doesn't want this, doesn't want to hurt me, to hurt her, to hurt anyone. "I don't know what to do," he weeps. And he doesn't. He clearly does not know what to do. I am looking at a man who feels he is being faced with a decision that will make him the baddie either way. I am looking at someone who is deciding between bad and worse. And even as I see a life I imagined for us disappear before my eyes, even as it dawns on me that Kate will always be in our lives now, that there is no easy extrication from this; at the same time all I can think is: please let him think that I'm bad, and not worse. Let me be bad. Let her be worse.

We cannot move overseas now. I will always, always be reminded of the relationship I destroyed, and this reminder will be in the form of a small human being who will likely detest me because of what I have done to their mother. All signs point to—I should end this.

Because obviously, if you've been having an affair with a married man who won't leave his wife and then you move cities to start a new life and then he tells you on FaceTime that his wife is pregnant, what you do is you immediately say, "How interesting for you, I'm done. Good luck." You thank your lucky stars you got out of that situation in time, before it could truly fuck you up. You amputate that bit of your story. You move on and you find someone single, someone ready to throw themselves into building a life with you.

What you don't do is what I do.

"Okay," I say. "Okay. I'm going to ask you some questions, and I need you to respond truthfully. I really need you to be straight with me, even if it hurts."

"Okay." He looks at me, as he has so many times before, like I hold all the answers. He looks at me like he did that first night out in Sydney, asking me to pick the restaurant. He looks at me like he did outside that first hotel, putting his faith in me to work out how to open the gate. Once again, it is on me to be his guide.

I ask what needs to be asked. "Does this change how you feel about me?"

"No."

"And do you still want to be with me?"

"More than anything."

"Do you realise that she is going to fucking hate you, but that nevertheless you have to tell her the truth, and the longer you avoid doing that, the worse it is going to be?"

He stares at me in silence for a few seconds, then he crumples again. "I do. I do know that."

I exhale.

"But not yet." He looks down, then up. "I can't tell her yet."

I inhale.

Here it comes. Will this be yet another moment in which I accept that my fate is his to decide?

"But I will tell her. When the time is right, I will tell her. I promise you, Hera. You are what I want."

His reasoning is that he can't tell her now, when she's pregnant. He can't jeopardise her health. And when the baby is born he can't exactly leave Kate immediately. He can't make her single parent to a newborn, can he? He owes her more than that, he says. He is a decent man. I wouldn't want him to abandon his child and the mother of his child while she is still breastfeeding, would I? I play with different reactions in my head. I test them out. Am I so selfish as to ask him to leave her now? God, I want to be, but I am not. If all works out as I hope, then I will be taking enough from her in time. I can give her this, I tell myself. I can wait for him to leave her until after she's had the baby, until the baby's on formula and sleeps through the night. I can stay here in England until then. I can destroy myself awhile longer to maintain her innocent happiness. Or, can I? How much more is there left to destroy, I wonder.

I am saying very little as he splutters for words.

"The baby is an accident!" he reiterates. He's only had sex with her twice since he's fallen for me, honestly, he cries. As if this is supposed to make me feel better about his wife being pregnant? Like, oh, you only fucked twice. Well, that's okay then? But it will not pay to dwell in resentment right now: I must face reality as it is. I must decide if I can live with this, or not.

He launches into a new line of reasoning. He isn't in love with her, he repeats to me. But before he met me, they'd been trying for a child for so long, and then they'd stopped, and now—he can't deprive her of this opportunity; it will already be considered a geriatric pregnancy. He owes her this baby, do I see? He's taken her childbearing years.

I observe him doing the mental maths, trying to find the solution that will ethically exonerate him. He is trying to convince himself that giving Kate this baby is like a fair trade for leaving her. He wants me to agree with him on this.

I think back to the song he sent me all those months ago, about the woman whose friends are all having children. Should I have predicted this? Was there a part of me that knew this might happen?

Surely not. Surely I would not have continued had I foreseen this.

He's still talking, and, abruptly, I cut him off. I need to think.

"Arthur, I love you. I just need a beat to process this. I'm going to call you tomorrow, okay?"

He looks meek. "Okay, okay, that's very fair," he allows. But I can see the fear on his face. His face mirrors mine. Is this the thing that will force me to stop?

"I'll talk to you soon, darling," I promise. And I end the call.

I sit on my couch in silence. I have more conflicting feelings than I know what to do with. I must decide on a course of action, but everything is a blur.

I will work through my emotions the way I know best, I resolve. I will get rip-roaringly drunk.

It's still only mid-morning at this point but I live in the United Kingdom: the pubs are open. I button up my coat, I do up my laces, and I make my way to the nearest watering hole.

I start as I mean to go on: with pints. I sit at a bar stool and drink slowly, one beer after another. I have a book with me that I look at from time to time. I cannot tell you what the book is about, I do not know.

By the time 5 p.m. arrives, I am not sober, and the after-work crowd begins to trickle in. This is perfect. I will ingratiate myself with them. I will lose myself in their small problems.

A group of colleagues is drinking pints at a table behind me. I wait until they're on to their third round, and then I make eye contact with one of the men. I smile. He asks me what book I'm reading (they always do).

"The pages may as well be blank for all I'm getting out of them!" I respond.

"And what's a little Australian lass like yourself doing in a place like this?" the man asks.

Usually I would take issue with this, but for right now, I'll allow it. I tell him I've recently moved to this city for work, that I don't know many people here.

"Well, then you must join us!" he cries.

Hook, line, sinker, etc.

Soon I am one of the gang. I reveal nothing about my life. I do not tell them, for instance, that my married, long-distance partner has just divulged that his wife is pregnant. I do not hint at the likely imminence of my breakdown. Instead, I ask these drunk strangers about their days, their lives, and they tell me.

I say, "Wow, it sounds like Sandra really has it in for you. Maybe talk to HR, is that viable?"

I say, "That sounds difficult, Rob. But have you ever considered that your brother-in-law's tendency to say 'That was yummy' after every meal might be the product of insecurity? Him trying to ingratiate himself with the family, and all that?"

I say, "Gosh, and I thought Jeffrey Epstein had problems."

And in my head, throughout all these exchanges, through all the pints, there is a constant hum, a chaotic spiral. Because here is the thing: I know that I will wait for him. Despite this pretence of taking time to decide, I already know that I will agree to it all.

This does not bode well for my mental health. But the immediate problem is this: how can I possibly sell this to my friends—and then to my dad, when the time comes? The people who love you do not want you to self-exile halfway around the world as you wait for your married partner to have his child and leave his wife. How to frame it?

But again: I am drunk. So instead of erring on the side of caution and waiting until I am sober to broach the topic with my friends, I message Soph on my way home from the pub: *Can we ft please? Need to talk to you.*

I've FaceTimed her only once since I've moved here, about a week in, so she is aware that if I am wanting to call her, it means crisis.

She writes back immediately. *Yep, gimme a sec, I'm at work. Will go to bathroom to call you.*

When Soph pops up on my phone screen, I can verify that

she is indeed sitting on a toilet. The light is bright, she's wearing make-up, she looks harried. Meanwhile, I am lying on my stomach on my bed, phone resting on my pillow in front of me like a crown on a ceremonial cushion. My mascara is smudged and only my lamp is on. It's dark in my room and my face looks grainy on camera. I see myself as Soph must see me: a fucking mess.

"Hey." I smile, attempting to keep it casual. "What's up, bb?"

Soph's response is clipped. "Hera, you asked me to call. What's wrong? I've got to be in a meeting in five, so hustle."

"Um, yeah, look, it's just that . . . hmm . . . how to say this? *How to say this?*" I ask this last bit in singsong.

Soph seems underwhelmed. "Hera, are you fucked right now?"

"It is true!" I exclaim, and then I grimace like the bared teeth emoji.

She sighs. "Okay, my little wasted wench. Just spit it out, what's wrong?"

"Yeah, all right, all right. So . . . the thing is. You know how Arthur has a wife?"

"I am extremely aware of that fact."

Again I attempt to undercut the devastation I feel. "Well, in an interesting turn of events—"

Soph interjects. "She's pregnant, isn't she?"

She must have read it on my face. "Um, yep. Yep, she sure is."

"Fucking dickhead," she says under her breath.

"What was that, Soph?" I ask brightly.

"I said he's a fucking dickhead. And let me guess, now he says he's going to leave her but only after the baby is born?" Raised eyebrows from Soph here.

"Umm . . . yes."

"Uh huh. Okay. So what's your plan here, Hera? Are you

going to come home and hang out in a little pied-à-terre while he takes his wife to pre-natal classes? Are you going to give him gobbies when time permits? Or are you going to madwoman in the attic yourself, until he leaves his wife—if he ever does?"

"That's not fair, Soph."

She softens a bit at this. "I know, I'm sorry. It's just, I love you. And this guy keeps fucking you over." She pauses. "Do you really still believe he's going to leave her?"

My voice cracks a bit. "I have to, Soph."

I can't tell her what I really feel, because I think it will be too sad for her to bear. She still thinks I can opt out of this. I am young, I have a job, I can just say no to the conditions I am living in, surely, she reasons.

But my whole life I've felt that I am acting out emotions with the people I sleep with. My whole life I've felt that I could leave whoever I am with at that moment, and that though it might be difficult for a time, I'll be fine. And now I deeply love someone. So what if his wife is pregnant. If I leave him, what else will I be going to? More of the numbness I've always felt? More dates with people who'll love me while I'm completely unmoved by them? More men called Clemens? More women called Clem? More drinking, more time passing, more coming up with ideas for things to do on a Friday and then a Saturday night, and then all the hours in between and after? There are so many hours. If I end it with Arthur, what will I do with my days?

I settle with saying the following instead: "I can't end it, Soph. It'd be so much easier if I could, but I can't. Because otherwise I'll be walking around for the rest of my days wondering what would have happened if I'd just tried harder."

Soph smirks. "And do you feel proud to be actualising the sunk cost fallacy in the year of our lord 2019? Do you feel like enacting it now is retro?"

I let out a short laugh, because I can see from this response that though Soph does not agree with what I am going to do, she will not disown me for it.

"Soph, I feel pretty similar now to how I felt waiting in line with you at Homebush all those years ago, trying to get T-Swift tickets even though the website said they were sold out: if doing this is a sunk cost, then let me go down with my ship."

And so, and so I stay. I stay in love with Arthur, and I stay in England. I commit to remaining here at least until after the baby is born. And then, *then* my life can begin.

For the next two months I continue going through the motions in the new city. I sleep with more people, to tell myself that I am still living even though really I am waiting, only waiting. I don't discuss these dalliances with Arthur, but surely he presumes. I write more content. I have a loyalty card at Pret A Manger, and a favourite wrap (meatball). I start calling fish and chips "chippy tea." I stop assuming I must seem upset when British people greet me with "All right?" I talk to Arthur every day. Since I have confirmed that I will wait for him, we now message each other pictures of hilarious baby outfits from terrible Etsy shops, emblazoned with slogans like "GIRLBOSS" or "MARXIST KWEEN." We talk about what kind of stepmum I'll be. We talk about what I'll teach the baby, how my parenting style will complement his. Occasionally Poppy is around when I'm FaceTiming Arthur in the lounge room, and though she is clearly dying to know what is going on, even she seems to know better than to ask.

I go to queer club nights and I use my accent to differentiate myself from all the other dykes in crop tops who look exactly the same as me. I sleep with a woman who works in care. I sleep with a woman who sings sad songs about being sad. I go to her concerts and drink with her friends afterwards, and like the night after Arthur told me Kate was pregnant, I tell the people I am with precisely nothing real about myself. It appears that I have now mastered the art of mysteriousness, something I never thought I'd be able to pull off. Turns out that to be a mystery you just have to truly, truly not want others to know you. Here in this new city I want to disappear until such time as I can re-emerge in Sydney with Arthur as my loving partner.

So I try to stay away, I really do, to give Arthur time to have his baby and leave his wife. But it is only barely possible to live in a new city when the person you love is still online on Instagram, his little green dot staring at you like an eye you can't see yourself reflected in.

And a new city becomes frankly impossible to live in when the person you love is still online on Instagram, his little green dot staring at you like an eye you can't see yourself reflected in, when there is also a global pandemic. But as usual, this takes me some time to work out.

In hindsight, I wonder whether Arthur didn't let me in on how bad he thought this whole thing was going to be because he didn't want to worry me, or because he didn't want to sway me into coming home. It was easier for him, I think, to imagine that I made choices for myself; to imagine that every decision I'd made since falling for him was unrelated to him. If I was my own woman, he could not be to blame.

THE virus seeps into public consciousness and then into our lives seemingly overnight. If I were still being paid to be invested in the news, if I listened more when Arthur talks about work and what he is covering, then maybe I would have picked up on the gravity of the situation sooner. Maybe it would have occurred to me that the world is about to change. People stop hugging at pubs, then fewer people are in the pubs, that is about my level of cognition.

He does not say this, but I know that my coming home will

make his life harder—the increased number of lies he'll have
to tell while fitting me around doctors' appointments—and he
doesn't want to outright ask me to exile myself during a global
health crisis. That would make him a selfish person, which he is
not.

These middle days of March 2020. In interactions with supermarket cashiers, in my few FaceTime conversations with Dad, in
the sporadic interactions I have with Poppy, the virus isn't that
huge a topic of conversation, until it is the only conversation, and
then it is too late, we are in it.

Lockdown commences in the UK, and the Australian government recommends that citizens overseas return. When Dad
asks over FaceTime if I'll come home, as there are rumours of
border closures, planes being grounded, I say, No, no, I am making a life here in the new city. I'm sure my voice wavers; I doubt
I sound very convincing. I am trying to make myself believe
it. And surely the pandemic will be over soon. Poppy is not so
hopeful; she returns home to her parents' house. She is still paying rent, however, so I can afford to stay on.

The weeks of lockdown stretch into months and still no freedom in sight. The spring days are long, and there are no pubs open
in which to commiserate with strangers. Depressive thoughts
flourish, wine is my only companion.

I take to walking three hours each day, one and a half hours
each way to a sub-par workers' café that is doing takeaway coffees and toasted sandwiches. I dare not sit in the nearby park to
eat said sandwich, as police patrol all public spaces, telling anyone who isn't exercising to move on—so I eat as I walk, my own
personal black parade.

In the supermarket near my flat, half the people wear masks
and half do not. There is no prospect of a vaccine yet. Schools are
closed, universities are closed. People on Twitter preach mutual
aid, which is useless to me, as I know no one here.

I am not good at being on my own, without distraction. There are no events. Just me, and my head, in my flat. I write my copy. I go to the shops. I go on my walks. I drink. I wait to hear from Arthur.

He sends me flowers. He sends flowers to my flat in the new city while he is in Sydney with his pregnant wife. He gets the florist to type out little notes referencing our exchanges, showing me that he's memorised everything we've ever said to each other. The delivery guy leaves the flowers on my doorstep and I am so thankful for him, for my married man who is doing this for me. I put the flowers in a vase and then I won't message him. I wait for him to message me, until eventually he breaks, and he asks me if I've received anything in the mail.

Oh, well there were some Dominos pamphlets?

Um, there was a toilet brush I ordered?

Some mail for the guy who used to live here, I think?

And then, when he types and deletes, types and deletes, I'll say: *Oh, and there were some flowers too. I think they were from Soph?*

And he'll type: *!!!! YOU KNOW THEY WERE FROM ME!!!!*

And I'll type: *I know, sweetheart, I know. Thank you.*

And he'll say: *I love you so much*

And I believe him.

I last three months before I crack. My mind is unravelling. I am sleeping at odd hours, I am crying at pop songs. I am drinking too much. I need something to change. *I cannot keep living like this*. Without consulting Arthur or my father or my friends, I book my flights home.

PART · FOUR

On the two flights back to Sydney the flight attendants are in hazmat suits. Matte red lipstick and contouring are concealed beneath the white hooded shrouds of virus protection. The airport silently reverberates with fear, everyone having taken their first taxi or Uber ride in months, experienced their first contact with people outside their homes. This is not the initial exodus; it is the desperate crawl of those who have ceased to manage.

The only store open is a chemist, and I purchase a bottle of water because I can't bring myself to reveal to strangers that in this terrible, terrible time, what I really long to buy is lip gloss and a trashy mag.

I feel the thrum of *soon*. I want to be in Sydney. I want to see my dad, and my friends. But most of all, I want the hours between Arthur and myself to disappear. I want to smell his neck.

There is something about moving that allows the mind to override what it knows: that none of the circumstances which forbade happiness prior to this moment have in any real way changed. But when you are in love you just think: I need you close; you are getting closer. I am coming.

When I finally land in Sydney, I am tired but also exhilarated. I am back: back where things makes sense—or, at least, back where I can try to make sense of them.

Although Sydney is not locked down, all arriving passengers have to spend two weeks in quarantine. The airport is like a military zone, police and army officers everywhere; this virus is the crisis they've been waiting for their whole lives. A lot of them look like kids, probably because they are. Little boys (of course they are mostly boys) with acne and hats with chin straps, very important for the first time ever and not quite believing their luck.

I stand in a queue to have my temperature taken. Around me, my fellow queuers compare their journeys, compare the awfulness of the lockdowns they've endured. Like, sure, the couple in front of me shared a twenty-three-square-metre studio in London, and that was bad, but the guy behind me was in a two-bedroom house with seven family members in Tel Aviv—and his aunt decided to learn to play the violin. Raised eyebrows to the swarm; it's hard to top that. He looks satisfied, and then sad.

I am bussed to a government-commandeered hotel from the airport. The guards will not tell us which hotel we are going to— all will be revealed when we arrive—and I know this should not be my main concern, but I am crossing my fingers that we end up at more of a Hilton than a Travelodge. When we pull up at the Park Hyatt, an expensively dressed woman seated in front of me audibly sighs with relief. She quietly asks one of the guards if it would be possible for her to stay in her usual suite. He replies, "Not fuckin' likely." I have missed Australia.

Inside, I am escorted to a room in which I will pass two weeks of my life either drunk, asleep, or on FaceTime to Arthur. So, not so different from how I have spent the past ten months, and the last three in particular. The room's windows do not open, but I have a good view of a construction site across the road. A note slid under my door (presumably by a guard, as we inmates are not allowed to leave our rooms) invites me to join a Facebook group for lockdown residents in this hotel. I do so, and I am delighted by what I find. There's a thread asking what we've missed most about home. One guy, Tommo, whose profile picture is him with a fish, has written, "Not me fucking mrs!" and five people have liked it. Nora, whose profile picture is a baby, has answered, "the bush." Tommo has replied—"urs or mine?" I screenshot all the responses and send them to Arthur.

Dad is the first to visit. He can't come up, obviously, but he brings a box of books and a jar of Vegemite to reception, which is then left outside my room by a guard. Dad calls me when he is standing on the street opposite my window, and I wave down to him as we talk.

"How goes it, kiddo?" he asks.

"Nice outfit," I reply. He's wearing my favourite shirt of his—even from this distance I can tell it's his Mambo "Dial-a-dump" monstrosity.

"I thought I'd dress for the occasion," he explains.

"It's weird," I say. "I can see people outside just like, walking around—and they look fine? Like they don't look totally harrowed and broken? It makes for a nice change."

"Mmm . . . and remind me why you resisted coming home for so long?"

"Shhh," I chide. "I'm here now."

THE day after Dad visits—Day Three of Quarantine, officially—Arthur manages to get away from his place to come to see me at lunchtime. He's been working from home, as has everyone who is legally allowed to. When I see him on the street, it is so bizarre. He looks so shy; I forgot how apologetic his normal posture is, like he's sorry for taking up space. It's so cute. He's standing next to a construction fence and he's a bit hunched, even though he's looking upwards, trying to find which window I'm in. We're on the phone: I'm attempting to describe my location to him, but I have no idea where I am in relation to the rest of the building.

Finally, he sees me.

"Hello," he says. His voice sounds like a smile.

"You look like a bird's-eye view of a businessman in the Matrix," I respond.

"And you look like a very beautiful ghost, haunting the hotel like it's a gothic mansion."

At this point I flash him my tits from the window.

"Would a ghost do that?" I challenge.

I can see him laughing on my screen and in real life, and both visions are gifts from above.

"Hey, Arthur?" I prompt.

"Yes, Hera?"

"I bloody love you."

I can see him grin to himself. He looks at me as he says, "I bloody love you too."

About an hour later, Soph and Sarah visit. They call me as they stand on the street where Arthur stood just before, waving up at me. I fantasise about them all running in to each other down there, realising they're gesturing to the same person: the truth out in the open.

This does not happen.

When my fourteen days are up, I am released from my hotel prison. Leaving my room feels illegal, but no one stops me as I walk down the hallway and take the lift down to the lobby. I sign out at reception. I exit the building and breathe fresh air for the first time in two weeks. Dad is waiting out front. When he gets out of the car to help me put my bag in the boot, I hug him so tightly I think I might asphyxiate him.

When we're seated in the front seats, Dad asks, "Now, what would you like to do, Hera? We can do whatever you like."

"How about we drive to the beach, get a coffee, have a walk?"

So we do just that. He doesn't quiz me about my time in the UK, he doesn't ask that much about hotel quarantine. Instead, we sit in amiable silence. We park the car next to a coffee shop at the beach. They're only doing takeaways but this is still like heaven for me. A long black for Dad, a flat white for me, and a brownie to share: some things never change. Dad pays, and I almost cry. I have not had anyone buy me anything—unless it's a drink because someone wants to fuck me—for so long.

We meander along the promenade, past the pool where Dad taught me to swim.

"Do you remember how angry you used to get when I was teaching you breaststroke?" he asks.

"Duh!" I exclaim. "Because you'd tell me to swim towards you, you would *promise* that you weren't moving, and then I would see that you were absolutely moving. Like, that's why I have trust issues with men, I'm pretty sure."

"Uh huh, of course it is." He smiles. "It's very good to have you home, Hera."

"Cut it out, loser." I give him a hug. "It's good to be home, Pops."

THAT night, instead of spending time with Dad or my friends, I meet Arthur. I've persuaded Ben to let me use his apartment for sex while he isolates for seven days with his current squeeze. He dropped his key off at the hotel for me on his way into iso; I promised him juicy details and his thirst for gossip outweighed any moral qualms he might have.

In the Uber to Ben's place, I am full of adrenaline, hope, and worry. I cannot wait to see Arthur, but at the same time I'm anxious—will the feelings all still be there? We've spent so much of our relationship apart, pining. A small part of me is concerned that yearning is where we have become comfortable.

When the car pulls up I see Arthur standing on the footpath outside Ben's apartment block. He is not looking at his phone; he's just staring blankly at the street, waiting for me to arrive. I see my own feelings on his face; a combination of exhaustion and need. Dusk is falling, the suburban road is quiet, and when I step out of the car into this sublime stretch of normalcy Arthur sees me, he strides towards me, I'm in his arms. We don't say anything for now. As we hold each other, my head on his shoulder, his on mine, my mind is quiet for the first time in so long. I can feel him crying a little, small heaves, and my eyes are wet too. He kisses my shoulder, I kiss his, and he squeezes me like he's making sure I'm real, that this really is the body he knows. We stand like this, silent, for a long time.

I needn't have been worried. This emotion can't be faked. I need him, and he needs me.

I hear a cough and see that my Uber driver is still in his car next to where we stand, waiting for directions for his next ride. He's just been watching us this whole time. I give him a wave.

"Hey, Arthur," I whisper, "what do you reckon the Uber driver thinks of us?"

We observe ourselves. Both our faces are wet from tears and we are clinging to each other like baby monkeys.

"I think he thinks we are absolute sops."

"If we fuck right here and now, do you think he'll give me a five-star rating or a zero-star rating?"

"It depends," says Arthur, "if we've still got it."

I let out a gasp. "Well, fuck you then!"

Finally the Uber driver leaves, and we are alone on the street.

Arthur brings me close to him. "I'm kidding, I'm kidding. Come here."

He leans forward and he kisses me, softly at first, but within seconds it is passionate, intense. I feel the indent of his spine through his shirt, I feel his shoulder blades, and all I want is to feel that back, claw that back, throw that back onto a bed. He breathes me in.

"You still smell like you," he says. "I was worried your scent might have changed. But it's exactly the same."

"You still smell like you too," I reply.

It feels like there is too much to say, I don't know where to start. It's not awkward as such—it's just, a lot. We need to get back to each other fully: we need to make love.

"Shall we go inside?" I ask.

"You've always been the smart one in this relationship," he says.

So I take his hand and lead him to the front door. I consult my phone to find the code to get into the building, and I punch it in wrong not once but twice. On the third try, we are granted entry.

"Ben's apartment is number six, so I guess—up?"

"Again with the brains," murmurs Arthur.

We walk up the stairs, hand in hand, and as he's taller than me our steps are out of alignment. But soon he modulates, and we climb in rhythm.

We get to Ben's door, and I fumble around in my bag for the keys. I get the right key on the first try, thank god, and we are in.

Ben's apartment smells like male deodorant and Chinese food. He may be gay, but he's still a man: this place is messy. There's a giant Tom of Finland poster above the couch, and empty water glasses on every surface.

It doesn't matter.

We find the bedroom, and in the bedroom, our bodies know what to do.

We wordlessly take off our shoes, and once this chore is done, Arthur reaches up under my skirt, pulls down my underpants, and throws me back onto the bed. He begins eating me out immediately.

It feels so good, but it also doesn't feel quite right: I need to see his face. I've spent too long without him to not see him now. I grab him by the shoulder and drag him back up.

"Not now, Arthur—I need you inside me."

He does not need telling twice. He kisses me hungrily, then gets up off the bed and swiftly removes his clothing. While he does this I take my own shirt and dispose of my bra and skirt, throwing all garments onto the floor. He comes back to bed, and with his strong arms holding his body above me, with his eyes on mine, he enters me. I feel the sweat on his back as he pushes; my legs splay out, out. I want him in me as deep as is possible. The fog clears in my mind: no thoughts, just ecstatic pleasure.

I understand why people start wars, I understand why people blow up their lives. If the choice is this or not this, I will destroy everything else every time.

AFTERWARDS we lie in bed, legs entwined, my breasts pushed up against his chest.

It is 9 p.m.

At 9:30, he has to leave.

I stay in bed after he lets himself out, wrapped in the sheets that now smell of him. And there is sadness, yes; there is loneliness. But he is so close now, compared to what has been, and there is comfort in this. I will have this man. He will be mine.

I meet up with Soph and Sarah the following night. They greet me with much fanfare, much talk of my miraculous return from the plague continent. We sit on Soph's balcony with a few bottles of wine, like we did all those months before, before the world changed. The girls update me on what Sydney's been like during Covid—"People were not chill for like two weeks and then everything went back to pretty much normal."

"So what's it like being free?" asks Sarah.

And I know she's referring to me being out of hotel quarantine but it also feels like maybe it's a dig? Is she trying to chastise me for still being in an affair? Or is that just me, twisting every harmless comment into a critique of my romantic situation? I decide to respond like Sarah's question is innocent.

"It's pretty wild," I reply. "Like, I was saying this to Dad too—just walking around here feels different, like the energy in the streets is different. In the UK it just felt like death was everywhere, which sounds dramatic—but also, like, death *was* everywhere. And here it's like the world has just kept on going and I'm happy for everyone but also I kind of want to shake the smiling people I see in activewear and be like *Do you know what's happening out there?? Shit's fucked, babe!"*

"So you're feeling like, survivor's guilt, basically," observes Soph.

"Oh absolutely. I'm basically a war veteran."

"Hera, one day you are going to get cancelled," says Sarah.

"Oh god, I fucking know," I sigh. I pour myself more wine.

"Anyway," Sarah says chirpily, "what did you get up to last night? First night of freedom. Did you and Papa Stephen cook that ravioli thing only you guys like?"

Ah, here it is. I was wondering how long we could get into the night before I am compelled to bring up Arthur.

I take a sip from my glass. "Umm, no, actually. I hung out with Dad during the day—he took work off which was very cute—and then in the evening I saw Arthur."

Sarah and Soph make knowing eyes at each other, and then Sarah says, "Well, there's the least surprising thing we've heard in a while."

Soph chimes in, "Yes, there are three things we can count on in life: death, taxes, and you being a fucking idiot."

I doff an imaginary cap. "Pleased to be of service."

I intimate that I would prefer this topic be abandoned, and they acquiesce.

We drink into the night, and I message with Arthur the whole time.

THE next day, I start looking for a room to rent in a share house. I can't keep living with my dad, I can't go back to how it was before, leaving the house at odd hours, knowing that Dad senses something is up. I decide that I can't be in love with a man who has a pregnant wife and still be living at home.

Over the following week, I interview with several share house "families" whose ads I've found on Facebook. Everyone wants "someone tidy" and "someone who is up for a chat over a glass of wine on a weeknight, but who enjoys their own space." Everyone is a "mid-twenties young professional." Everyone is keen to highlight that theirs is "not a party house." Where have all the party houses gone? I wonder. Where is the household that says "we welcome messy, slutty debauchery"? Where are the hedonists, where are the people who unashamedly crave fun? I wish that just one ad would specify that its members eschew the gym in favour of getting shit-faced.

As established, I am not a natural interview subject, and though I've gotten better at interviewing for jobs, the idea of being interviewed to live in a share house still terrifies me. I am literally being judged on my personality and perceived coolness by a bunch of strangers who don't even want to fuck me. If I am rejected, it is one hundred per cent because they don't like me as a person. In one interview, in an attempt at bonding, I make fun of an Australian web series that it turns out one of the housemates works on. In another, my jokes about mental illness (even though I'm referring to my own!) are poorly received.

Potential Housemate: "What do you like to do on a weekday evening?"

Me: "Um, probably just try not to off myself, am I right?"

From the look on his face, no, I am not right.

Finally, I find a place that will do. Unlike the others, there is only one person interviewing me. Ivan is a late-twenties engineer who is wearing a *Big Bang Theory* T-shirt, and he says he and the other housemates couldn't manage to coordinate their schedules to interview people together, so he's taken it on because someone had to. He seems aggrieved by this, but also used to it. He reminds me of Alison. Ivan makes no concessions to sociability; not so much as a glass of water is offered as we sit at the shitty kitchen table. All he asks is whether I have a job and can pay the deposit immediately. I answer both questions in the affirmative, even though I am lying about the job. I will have to borrow the deposit money from Dad. I figure I'll get a job soon enough—Ivan need not know this.

The house is a terrace that was probably nice once but now resembles a large-scale teenager's bedroom filled with empty pizza boxes. There is mould on the kitchen ceiling, and the array of unwashed mugs next to the sink tells me that I will fit in just fine here. I am offered the attic room. It's draughty and dusty and some of the floorboard nails glint out like shy hellos. I imagine that I will live like Jo March here, writing into the small hours of the night as my candle wanes beside me.

DAD helps me move my stuff in the next day.

As we lug boxes of books from the car into the house, Dad glances at the dead plants on the verandah and says, "You've always enjoyed a fixer upper."

He resists further comment as we trudge up the stairs to my room. He's loaning me a mattress until I can afford to buy my own. He is also loaning me sheets, pillows, and a desk. I arrange it all in what I hope is a charmingly bohemian fit-out, though a casual observer would be more likely to assume I was a squatter.

I see Dad off, then go back inside and sit on my mattress. When it gets dark, I go to sleep, because I don't yet have a lamp to read under, and Arthur is not free.

It is a strange, out-of-time life I am having, with Arthur. Back in Sydney, but still waiting for his wife to have their baby; she is seven months pregnant. Bears can hibernate while they wait for time to pass but humans cannot: we must keep going.

It is June and everything feels unreal; I've been living in lockdown far away and now here I am in the city where my friends and family are, even though the pandemic is still raging across the sea. Shops and restaurants are open, people are running around in dresses and light coats, and while the water is still cold, the sun is bright.

I need to pay rent, so I get a job in a shop that sells overpriced matte ceramics. I've always resisted retail unless I am really, really broke, because it has seemed to me the apex of capitalism, but after so much time moderating and editing content online, it now feels like there is something honest about shopwork. No one here is bullshitting, no one pretends they really enjoy the job they are doing, and no one buys in to the corporate buzz words we have to recite. Here on the shop floor with our name tags and unpaid lunch breaks we are selling our time to sell people objects, and I find myself enjoying the camaraderie.

I am experiencing the same pleasure in routine I once felt entering the school gates: walking through the shop doors, waving hello to my colleagues behind the counter as I bound upstairs to the staffroom to dump my bag and grab my lanyard—this is what it felt like arriving at school every morning, seeking out my friends in the playground, greeting teachers and younger students chirpily, because this place belonged to all of us.

In the shop, my colleagues and I have a boss who cares as little as we do; she is trying to make it as an electronic musician and selling matte pottery is just her day job. She lets us do whatever we want unless management is present, in which case we all put on eyeliner and talk very seriously to customers about handwashing valuables and the Pantone colour of the year (Inner Self, it is called, I shit you not). My favourite colleague is a guy called Harry who is twenty-two and really into rugby. I have no idea how he landed this job, and no idea why he stays. Whenever he makes a sale he'll catch my eye from across the store and mouth, "Goalll!!!!" over the customer's shoulder. Harry enjoys my lack of sports knowledge as much as I enjoy his excess of it. Our banter pretty much consists of me using incorrect metaphors about touchdowns and then looking confidently to him for confirmation—"Crushed it, right?"—and him saying, "Oop my gal." We teach each other our words, and delight in hearing them out of context.

So yes, everyone hates working retail, and so do I, in theory. But in person what it means is that I get to go to a place each day where I have things to do that are easy but require attention, and other people like me are going through the same motions, and intimacies develop over the most mundane things. I hear about colleagues' miscarriages, and break-ups, and their hopes and dreams, and I tell them some of mine back, and all the while we are rearranging window displays, and taking online orders for someone who wants seventeen "incrementally different" vases. I only have to tell them the bits of my life that I feel like sharing. Our friendships, if I can call them that, are based on the immediate; how what a customer said has brought back a childhood memory, or how our mutual hatred of the stock manager reminds us of a *Broad City* episode. I feel myself laughing in a way I haven't for a long time, because, as it turns out, people are very funny. That nothing-looking guy you passed on the street just now? He might be really fucking funny. Or he might be an anti-vaxxer. You just never know.

Whenever Harry and I work a shift together, we make up weird challenges for the day. Sometimes it's like "only talk to patrons in a French accent," and sometimes we decide on certain subjects that we must bring into small talk with customers. It's infantile, sure, but it truly kills me to watch Harry segue every conversation into a consideration of Dennis Quaid's best roles. He'll be at the counter bubble-wrapping a mint green bookend and then he'll pause, look the customer dead in the eye, and say, "Is it just me, or are you also thinking of Dennis Quaid's performance in *A Dog's Purpose* right now?" Another day, Harry tells me that I must utter the phrase "God, this reminds me of that summer in New York" whenever I'm ringing anyone up at the cash register. Like, "That comes to two hundred and twenty-three dollars. God, this reminds me of that summer in New York." And then I'll laugh quietly to myself, as if lost in memory, as the perplexed customer tries to work out how to respond.

Not one of my new colleagues knows about my romantic situation, because I really don't want to have to explain to everyone that my partner is someone else's partner. They all think I'm single and so are constantly trying to set me up with their housemates, lauding Bill's pasta-making prowess or Tina's bouldering strength.

Bisexuality is a curse in this way: you must fend off double the terrible set-ups.

Harry insists that I will get along with his friend Josh. He says it so often, with such certainty, that eventually I put down the forty-nine-dollar thimble I am holding and say, "Harry, precisely *why* do you think Josh and I would get along? Like, what was the moment where you thought, 'Ah, peas in a pod, Hera and Josh'?"

And Harry considers this for a second, then says, "It's because you want to save the world but you pretend all the time that you don't, and Josh works for a union."

And I think, Oh okay, after like a month of working with me, it may be that Harry knows me pretty well. This is an interesting revelation.

I don't agree to a date with Josh, though, because I don't want to cheat on my married lover.

I work in the shop, I see my friends occasionally, I read books and wash my underwear, and some evenings Arthur makes up an excuse and we'll get to spend the night together, renting weird Airbnbs and eating at restaurants nearby, discovering the city afresh based on where last-minute accommodation is available.

One night Arthur has told Kate that he is having a business dinner, and so we are to have (six!) hours in each other's company. I'm at work during the day, and I'm in a good mood because of the love I'll be getting and the sex that I'll be having and the tenderness I'll be feeling come close of business. I've told him to book the place; a little challenge for him, I am curious to see what he can achieve.

Usually I book the place, and I tell myself that this is because I have better taste than he does (this is true), and not because he doesn't want our jaunts to end up on his credit card bills for her to see. Sometimes he transfers me money afterwards—sometimes weeks later, because he'll forget, and obviously I don't want to remind him, I don't want to ask him to pay me back for the weird Airbnb we fucked in.

Occasionally he'll bring cash to our rendezvous, and he'll hand it to me so tenderly, and he'll say, "I'm so sorry that this is how it is for now," and then we'll not speak of the cash again; we'll not speak of how it makes me feel like someone he needs to pay off. We'll not speak of the money he has and the money I don't, and how this creates an invisible charge in all our interactions with shopkeepers and waiters. How there is a pause when we buy coffee together and the barista says, "Together or separate?" and then we'll say, "Together," and Arthur pays and I always say, "Thank you," because I was raised to be polite, but how I resent saying thank you, because he earns a million times more than I do and also we both know that if his wife or a mutual friend of theirs ever saw us he'd probably push me into a nearby bush and pretend he didn't know me and then, when they are out of sight,

I'd climb out of the bush and brush the dirt off my knees, and we'd keep walking together arm in arm, and I would accept this, my martyrdom, because I am in on the joke. If I express that I am not in on it, or that I feel excluded by it, then the joke will be over, and I will no longer be able to justify being with the person I love. It is very important that we pretend I have power in the joke we have made.

But this day, this day he has booked the place. I am thrilled. At work, my manager asks me to redo a window display and "use my imagination." Over the course of the next eight hours, between unboxing new products and selling pastel toothbrush holders, I create my masterpiece: a matte ceramic homage to *Romy and Michele's High School Reunion*. Of course, this theme is not made known to management and is not printed anywhere in the display, but I figure that no one who has seen the film will fail to recognise the inferences connecting the purple feather boas I've draped around the garish yellow ceramics, and Alan Cumming whispering, "Michele." I play "Time After Time" on repeat through the shop's speakers and make Harry slow-dance with me around the aisles. I smile, thinking of the lace underwear sitting beneath the lunchbox in my canvas bag in the staffroom. I tell a customer that the best thing about the candelabra she is purchasing is that it is "such a good day-to-night transition piece" and she fervently agrees, and my colleagues and I wait until she leaves the store before we burst out laughing.

Arthur texts me the address of where we'll be staying around 3 p.m.; I see on Google Maps that it is a very sterile-looking building opposite a hospital, extremely close to where my mother lives and therefore to where I lived before my dad was awarded custody. I feel a bit sick when I notice this. I really do not like the area. It reminds me of a lot of hurt that I have never shared with Arthur. I think I've told him before that my mother lives in this area. But why would I expect him to remember that—and, even if he did, how would he know to avoid it? Lots of people are fond of the place where they grew up, the place where their mother still lives. Lots of people like their mothers.

I decide that I will not let it affect me. No, it will be good, it will be fine. I will be with him in this place, and it will be ours and not hers. I don't even know if my mother still lives there, I remind myself; I am just assuming she does. Maybe she's moved far away. But I have no way of knowing for sure, so when I catch the bus to her suburb after work I think every middle-aged woman I see on the street is her.

Passing the familiar supermarket, the butcher, the greengrocer, I remember how I was obsessed with my figure back then, would pause to observe my reflection in every shop window, sucking in my stomach so I could see my ribs through my shirt; how I wished I could be free of this body, and free of this mother the universe had cruelly tethered me to. As a young teenager juiced up on *Nylon* I decided I could still call myself a feminist if I only hated *one* woman.

Snap out of it, Hera! You are no longer that girl, I say to myself. *You are on your way to see the man who makes you feel human, and these shops have no hold over you: they are just shops.*

And they are just shops, but everything is just something. And I am weirdly vulnerable, ill at ease, in this one small corner of Sydney I have not returned to for many years.

I get off the bus at a stop near the hospital. My calico bag is hot against my side, and I am reminded of how in my early high school years, before I moved in with Dad, I used to get off the school bus just a few blocks from here, with my heavy school backpack digging in to my shoulder blades, sweat patches blossoming at my underarms through my polyester uniform. Today I still see schoolgirls wandering around in clusters, and I wonder whose party they are going to this weekend, which fact from history has today impressed itself upon their open minds. I think back to Soph, to Sarah, to the cafés we used to sit in after school, to not knowing what the future held and thinking that was a hopeful thing. I smile at the schoolgirls and they do not smile at me, as I am old and irrelevant. I want to yell, "Stop! You don't understand! I was once one of you, I understand you, I love you!" but I know better than to do this, and besides, I have a sterile hotel bedroom to get to.

Arthur is still in the office at this point; he always works late, even when he says he won't. I figure this will give me a chance to scope the joint, move some things around, make it less awful. I'll put on my lingerie and I won't laugh at myself when I do it: I am a woman with a body who wears lingerie seriously. My body is strong and it has curves and I used to feel repulsed by it. I used to feel that my flesh enshrouded me, that it obscured my essence. But I am beginning to accept that I am my flesh, and that when there is more of it, there is more of me. I like my hips, I like the way they sway. I like what they can do. I like what they can do with Arthur.

I'm in the room now. It's awful. It even feels like a hospital, which is bizarre. The bright lights, the lack of décor. It has the energy of being like, a waiting room for death. So not the most romantic vibe. Arthur is running late and I'm annoyed. I feel the potential in myself to be shrill, to be that woman, and I hate it, I resist it. I have allowed myself to be an active participant in the secrecy, so what right do I have to anger? I hate my brain, the twists it makes in any mental scenario. My mind is basically one hundred per cent mental scenarios at this point. Working at the shop does provide solace: in silly moments with Harry I do remember that I used to be fun, that my brain used to get giddy on a regular basis. But it feels impossible to access that version of me now; in the Mariah Carey voice: I don't know her.

When Arthur eventually arrives, yes, I'm wearing the sexy underwear, I've arranged myself on the bed. I tell him to hop on, we make love. It's not the same as it was at the start, but it might be even better, because we know each other's bodies now, and we know each other. I know the faces he makes; he knows when to touch me, and where, and for how long. I know about his mother, I know about his father. I know his favourite band, his favourite song, his least favourite foods (there are three), the drinks he enjoys, the drinks he hates; what he thought he'd be doing with his life now, what he spends his lunchtimes thinking about. And he knows my dreams; well, he knows a lot of them. The more I tell him, the more I realise that there is so much more to say; this is something that makes me happy, this discovery that I do have these little kernels inside of me of things I might want to do and feel and achieve. He tells me he has no doubt I will do all of them, and when he says this, I don't doubt it either.

My self-belief isn't because he believes in me, it's not that simple; I believe it because I have voiced it to him, and I only tell him things that are true, otherwise what would be the point of being in love?

We eat dinner at a nearby restaurant, and just like the first time at the Chinese restaurant, I still love it when he orders; I love how bad he is at it.

We drink wine. I love wine but he might like it more. I can drink it whenever I like but I have a feeling that when he's with her he does not drink as much.

She's very pregnant now, while we're having dinner. The baby is a girl—at least until she tells us otherwise. He talks about the baby like she exists outside of her mother, and I do the same. The baby this, the baby that. Like the baby is not inside her womb, where she sits at home, unknowing.

We talk about what they might name the baby. He lists names that I know must come from Kate, because they aren't to his taste—Meg, Nell, Judy—and in these names I find myself unwillingly at an entryway into understanding Kate's personhood. I do not want to think of her as a person with tastes and desires, as this will make it impossible for me to destroy her life. I resent the fact that I now know she is clearly a fan of Ethel Turner's *Seven Little Australians*.

I suggest Maisie, as an in-joke to myself. Arthur hasn't read any Henry James so he doesn't understand the reference, and I don't explain it to him, it would be too cruel. He really likes the name though; he keeps rolling it over on his tongue: "Maiiiisiie." It does sound good with his accent, I must admit.

We talk about the house we'll live in. We talk about the influence I'll have on the baby. We talk about how I'll interrupt his Zoom meetings. We even talk about how we might manage co-parenting; how hopefully, in time, the three of us adults will develop a relationship, not necessarily good, but not bad. How we'll manage for the kid. These kinds of conversations have become standard for us since he told me Kate was pregnant and I didn't leave him. I hope if we repeat them enough they will become real. We talk about the children he and I will have too. How they'll all be siblings; how they'll all love each other. I feel myself getting caught up in the swell of this possibility, that I might be a person with a family of my own. I am twenty-five years old, living in a share house, working in a shop. The fact that motherhood is now an imminent prospect should terrify me, perhaps, but it doesn't. I will have Arthur, I will have our children, I will have purpose.

When we leave the restaurant, it's still relatively early; he doesn't have to be home for another few hours, so we make our way back to the Airbnb. We walk arm in arm through the high street of this suburban enclave, and I'm tipsy enough and in love enough that I've forgotten, for a moment, to remember where I am, to be vigilant.

And so of course it is at this moment that I happen to glance across the street and there she is, my mother, talking with a friend outside a restaurant. She has aged since I last saw her, but the hand gestures she makes in conversation are exactly the same.

I feel red anger snaking up my neck, but also, I am ashamed to admit, I feel scared. I feel an urge to duck behind a postbox so she won't see me. I feel like a child. Instinct kicks in and I grab Arthur's hand and I pull him forward with me, making us both half-run down the street, and I don't look back or say anything to Arthur until we have turned a corner.

We are stopped, both panting for breath a little. I keep my head down for a moment, as I know that my face right now will betray my fear, my hurt. I cannot tell him about my mum, not now. I want to, I do—and this is maybe the first time I've ever wanted to tell someone I'm seeing about her, about what she did. But I push it back. Because Arthur needs to see me as an adult woman ready to be a parent—not as a scared little kid with mummy issues herself. So I just hug him really tightly for a second, I collect myself, and then I look at him.

"Sorry," I say. "That must have seemed really weird."

"Um, yes? Hera, are you okay?"

He is, obviously, confused by what has just happened. How do I explain it away? Think fast, Hera.

"It's just . . ." I say, willing myself to come up with something. "It's . . . I just saw my ex on the street. And I didn't want her to see us. I didn't want to put you in that position. I didn't want us to have to lie. So I panicked. Sorry."

His expression breaks into understanding. "Oh darling, I'm so sorry. I'm so sorry you felt you had to do that. This really isn't fair, is it?"

"No, it's really not," I confirm.

How have I managed to turn the situation around like this?

If I were in a less frantic state of mind maybe I'd try to push my advantage here further—get him to agree to a specific deadline for leaving Kate, or something like that. But I'm too frazzled to think strategically. I let it go. I'll just let him stew in guilt for now. I'll play the bigger person.

"Come on, let's go back to the Airbnb. We've still got a few hours before you have to get back to Kate."

His face twinges with hurt—it is rare that I explicitly mention how he always leaves me to go to her. But for now—let him feel it. Let him feel bad.

When we get back to our room, I tell Arthur that all I want is to fall asleep with him. He looks overwhelmed with guilt. He says, "Of course, Hera, of course we can do that."

So we snuggle in and fall asleep, my head on his chest; and then about two hours later, at eleven thirty, the blare of his alarm wakes us, and we are jolted back to reality. Still half-asleep, we gather our clothes from where they've been carelessly flung around the room, and we shimmy into them. We put on our socks, we tie our shoes, we check that we haven't left anything behind. Arthur orders an Uber, which will make two stops. The first one is at his place, which is closer. I duck down in the car so she won't see me if she's looking out the window. The second stop is at my place, where I exit the car alone.

LATER, lying in my attic bed, I let out the sobs I've been holding in. I want so, so desperately for Arthur to tell Kate. I want to wake up with him, and I want to tell him all about my mum. I want an ally in my life, I want him to be on my team. I want to have his child with him, and then I want to have more of them. I want us to be a family. And I don't think I can wait anymore for him to be ready. I don't know how, but I will have to make it clear to him that I'm not asking him to leave her, I'm telling. I need a specific timeframe, I need a date. Not just "when the baby needs less night-time feeds," or some other vague variant of that. I'm going to have to be *that* woman.

While I wait to be brave enough to issue an ultimatum, I continue to live my life.

At work my mind wanders back to school times, back to when I had so much fucking verve. Now I box up expensive cups and sell customers their $200 soup bowls, and I horde all my verve for interactions with Arthur.

If I were a proper member of my generation, I might describe how my housemates and I become fast friends and spend hungover mornings on the verandah drinking tea and talking about gentrification. But the truth is I am alone a lot of the time, and so are the people I live with. It's not the seventies, plans don't just come together: you have to book in a date and a time to see people, and then hope that none of you have to reschedule or bail—it is amazing to me that people ever see each other. It is so, so much easier to cancel than it is to get public transport. And cancel I do. I am ashamed of myself, of what I am allowing myself to become; of the lack of agency I am exhibiting in my own life, *my life*. I don't want my friends to be any more privy to this than they already are.

But I cannot avoid them entirely. It may be easy to cancel plans with some people, but not with Sarah. That girl is organised and tenacious. A week after the mother encounter, Sarah has organised a dinner party at her place with Tess, Soph, Ben, Ben's current paramour Tim (paramedic, hates garlic??), and John and Angela (John of "I love sex work" fame). She's made it clear that my attendance is mandatory, so here I am. Sarah does not have enough chairs for this dinner party, despite having asked her housemates to find somewhere else to be for the evening, so the lounge has been placed next to the table too. I somehow end up sharing the lounge with John and Angela, and as a result we are far lower than everyone else, just above eye level with the table top. Soph's across the table, and she motions for me to check my phone. Surreptitiously I read the text she's sent: *Wow babe, that seat sucks for you. Good luck tho xx.* When I look up at her, she's giving me an evil little grin, and then she turns to Tim and says something amusing, I suppose, because he laughs.

In front of us is an Ottolenghi spread, pomegranate seeds everywhere, cauliflowers like edible floral arrangements, wine glasses and bottles arranged haphazardly. *What did millennials do before Ottolenghi?* I wonder. Did we just not eat?

I try to make conversation with John and Angela, I really do, but it's like trying to coax a facial expression from someone who's just had Botox. When I ask them about their weekend, they tell me about the nice walks they went on. People say that it is boring to hear others describe their dreams, but people's dreams at least tell you something about their inner lives. Tropes falling into non sequiturs, teeth falling out, running late to the airport—talking dreams means acknowledging the crazy that resides in every mind. Describing a coastal walk you went on with your partner, however: this is the stuff of my madness. I can see Soph and Tim engaged in a more interesting-seeming conversation on the other side of the table, and Sarah's wrapped up with Tess and Ben. I hear the word "futch" being used and it calls to me, but I cannot actively break from John and Angela in transparent pursuit of better discourse, and besides, the couch we are on is so low, and so deep, that we are essentially in another world to the rest of the party.

I turn myself to face my couch fellows, my back at an awkward angle. "Oh yeah," I say. "That is a really lovely walk."

"Isn't it!" John and Angela are smiling at me encouragingly, silently urging me to speak the line that will enable them to utter theirs.

I repress a shudder. I consider refusing. But their faces are so full of expectation, of hope. I fold. "But it's a bit busy on weekends though, isn't it?"

They are thrilled. "Oh, we *know*! So many people on the weekends, it's insane—and no one wearing masks, of course, and you're shoulder to shoulder!"

Repress it. Repress it, Hera! Do not bring up that you know from John's Instagram story last weekend that neither he nor Angela was wearing a mask on this walk.

I take a big gulp of wine. I am drinking steadily towards oblivion. I decide the best way to live out this conversation is to play dead, offer nothing. "That is so true," I say without any hint of inflection. "You are so right."

I scooch forward on the couch until I am perching on the edge of it and I concentrate on my plate, to signal to John and Angela that this part of the conversation has ended. Let's have an interlude, let's regroup, let's then attach ourselves to other conversations. I allow myself a glance at my phone, and I can see that Arthur has messaged.

How goes the soiree?

The soiree goes like shit, Arthur, I want to type back. *I am once again alone at a dinner full of couples, and I don't like tahini, and I fear that very soon I am going to break and just stab John straight through the eye.*

Instead of responding, I turn my phone around on my lap so I can't see the notifications.

The table is getting louder as more is being drunk, and people are beginning to throw out lines directed at the whole party, not just the little clusters we've formed based on proximity.

"Okay! Okay!" screams Sarah. "Let's go around the table, and everyone has to say the worst thing they've done this week."

There are groans from John and Angela, while Ben exclaims,

"Ooh, yes!" and poor Tim just looks confused. *Is this the kind of people you're friends with?* I can see him wondering at Ben.

Soph, Sarah, and I developed this game many years ago, in a bar after a dinner we'd been at where the host asked us to go through our "highs and lows" of the week. Usually I love this game, but not tonight. What have I done recently that *hasn't* been bad?

Sarah is baiting me, that much is clear. We have an unspoken agreement that she and Soph don't address my mistress status when in company.

Ben clears his throat, starts the game. "This week I was at the gym and I wanted to use the treadmill, but they were all being used, and I saw one that had a sweat towel on it, which means someone had claimed it, obviously, but I just threw the towel across the room and stepped on. And then a few minutes later, the guy comes back, sees what's happened, gets his towel from the floor, and he confronts me, yeah? He asks if I moved his towel and stole his machine. And I looked at him stony faced and I said, 'Nah, mate, I don't know what you're talking about,' and I kept running."

Soph responds, "Oh, for fuck's sake, Ben, that is not that bad. You're just a bitch, and we all already knew that."

Ben shrugs almost proudly. "It's true, it's true. What can I say?"

"Okay, okay, my turn!" Angela exclaims as she enters the fray, like she's trying to get it over with. "I fucked up a thing at work. I cc'd someone in an email chain that I absolutely shouldn't have, but I'd been using an assistant's laptop because mine was broken, and I'd sent it from her email account because I couldn't be bothered signing in to mine to just forward this one thing, which she also had access to, so then when I realised what I'd done I just logged out of her account and used my own for the rest of the day, and no one's picked up on it yet but if they do, she is fucked."

Oh no, Angela has misread the game. No one is saying anything, too aware that this is not the kind of thing we laugh at.

I pipe up; I have to. I'm drunk and I'm angry. I try to couch my comment in diplomacy, but I don't do a very good job. "Okay. But Ange, the thing is, someone *is* going to notice, and you *are* going to have to come clean. Like, that will weigh on your conscience big time. Wouldn't you prefer to deal with it now, even if you have to cop the consequences?"

And she goes, "Yeah, but if it's a guilty conscience or me getting fired . . . like, I refuse to be fired."

There's tension in the air, it seems that Angela is cottoning on to the fact that even though the rest of us are proudly bitchy, we aren't into actively blaming innocent people for our mistakes. John's looking at his hands, and Angela is now getting defensive as other people avoid her eyes.

She cracks. She looks for a new target, in order to redirect the room's derision, and she finds one. She finds me.

"Oh my god, Hera. Don't act as if you wouldn't do the same thing. We all know you're fucking a married guy who's about to have a baby with his *wife*. I think that takes the cake for worst thing any of us has done this week, wouldn't you say, guys?"

There is silence except for Ben wheezing out, "Noooo," under his breath. I am frozen. To hear that my moral turpitude is up for discussion is one thing—it's not that these thoughts are new to me—but to hear it from Angela? From Angela, who has just freely admitted to sabotaging an assistant in order to cover her own arse? From Angela, one of the most boring people in the world? Up with this I will not put.

I begin to speak, but before I can get it out, this response I haven't yet fully mentally formulated, Sarah interjects. She stands up from her chair. There is a steeliness about her, her diction is precise, clipped. "Angela, I think you'd better go. John, can you take Angela home, please?"

Angela stares at her. "Are you fucking serious?"

Sarah gives me a subtle wink, then says to Angela, "As serious as climate change, unfortunately."

And with this, Angela is ousted from the group. It's like a scene from *Real Housewives*, except none of us are rich.

The evening continues, stiltedly, after this episode, and no one brings up Angela's accusation except Ben, who judges that Angela was being "way harsh, Tai." Tim is clearly uncomfortable and I can see him trying to catch Ben's eye, willing him to inform the table that it is time they head home for the evening, and wasn't dinner lovely, and so on. I can see Soph and Sarah looking at me worriedly from time to time, as I contribute sporadically to the group conversation. Tess is telling Sarah how delicious everything was, in damage control mode.

After an hour or so of this, of the play-acting we are all doing, Ben does get the hint, and he and Tim say their goodbyes. When they go, Tess makes the tactful call: she's going to head to Sarah's bed; she's exhausted from the studio, she says.

And then it is the three of us, and now I cry, just a little, just for a moment. Sarah and Soph call Angela a frog-mouthed cunt who will never set foot in this house again, which cheers me up somewhat, but not enough.

They're like Christine Baranski and Julie Walters in *Mamma Mia!*, offering platitudes. I know that they love me, and I know that they believe me when I tell them I'm in love. And I know that they know that telling me to break up with Arthur is not going to work, so they've just got to ride it out with me, despite their reservations.

As I do not want to give my friends an opening to suggest that he may not leave her, or that he has not been treating me respectfully, I do not tell them that now, when I wake up in the morning,

I do not think of what I want out of the day, only of whether I will get to talk to Arthur, get to see Arthur.

So, I make jokes; jokes to convey to them that I am okay, that they don't have to worry—that they don't have to stop me.

We pour more wine, and I drawl on. "The thing no one tells you about being a mistress," I say in an American accent, "is that day use hotels are rarely available from 8:30 a.m., and isn't that just crazy, when the average man's fake workday begins at that time?"

Perhaps a year ago this would have been amusing to them, but now I see their ill-concealed shudders.

Nevertheless, Soph attempts to maintain light-hearted conversation. Adopting the same Midwestern accent, she says, "And the outdoor sex! No one tells you how much cramping is involved when you're just fucking someone up against a tree!"

I laugh: this is funny because it is true.

The first time Arthur and I made love in public we were both shocked afterwards by our own audacity, messaging about it for days and weeks afterwards—*Can you believe we did that?* and *People could absolutely see*, and *That was insane!!!*—but there are also only so many places you can have sex if your partner is married and your share house is a cesspit, so public fucking becomes normalised quite quickly.

I give some sage advice to Soph and Sarah. Always wear a skirt; you might think that you can just whip your pants down to your knees but if you don't take them off all the way, leaving yourself butt-naked in a national park, then they'll loop in the bottoms of your legs like a harness, restricting movement and pleasure for everyone involved. Also, always bring a picnic blanket. People emphasise that grass stains are hard to get out and this is true, but what we don't talk about is the amount of actual dirt that accumulates in your underpants and crevices if you're just going at it on the ground.

The girls laugh along with me, but again, there is a wariness to it all, like this conversation is occurring on a fault line, and at any moment it could split and I could fall in. At any moment I could say something too real, too awful, and then none of us could play our roles properly.

And I don't really know what reaction I am looking for from them; what I hope to achieve by spitting out these comedic, unhinged lines. I suppose I want to paint it all like it is purely conceptual to me—like it's performance art and I'm the artist. But if my romantic life were Yoko Ono's *Cut Piece*, then I am clearly Yoko's shirt and not the scissors. The problem is that Soph and Sarah care about me; they think that I deserve better than being a cut-up shirt. And so I continue doing bits, making gags, until eventually Soph leaves, Sarah goes to bed, and I fall asleep on Sarah's couch, because I don't want to sleep alone in my own bed tonight.

The next morning, I leave the house before Sarah and Tess wake up, before the other housemates are awake. I feel icky from the night before, I feel the uncomfortableness of Sarah asking Angela to leave. These decisions I have forced my friends to make in my defence, they feel gross to me: they make me feel gross.

Two months have passed since my return to Sydney. Kate is due within the week.

It is a sunny Sunday and I've spent the day at work, trying to delete thoughts of Kate from my mind, unsuccessfully. I've only just gotten home when I receive a call from Dad. Jude has died.

I'm living only a fifteen-minute drive from Dad's place, and so I don't quite believe it. I guess I thought that if Jude was dying he'd at least have pitter-pattered over and told me? I don't know what I thought. I don't know what to say to Dad, all I can do is cry, and Dad cries too. He asks if I'll come over, and a hardness comes over me. Arthur has said he might be free later tonight. My dog is dead but, instead of going to comfort Dad, I know that I am going to wait in my room until I can see Arthur. I tell Dad that I can't get away right now but I'll be there first thing in the morning. Dad sounds confused, because surely we would want to mourn this together. But he doesn't push.

"I'll see you tomorrow then, Hera," he says. "I love you." And he ends the call.

I sit on my bed and think about Jude. When Dad and I first got him, I held him close and whispered into his silly, floppy ear that he would always be safe with me, a little schoolgirl in a green uniform.

Jude has known me through it all, and he's always loved me, no questions asked. He never, never asked why I was so often home on weekend nights during my early teens. He never commented when I went through my black hair dye phase. He made no remarks when I would only listen to Missy Higgins.

Dad let me name him, and I chose Jude, because I'd learned

at school that St. Jude was the patron saint of lost causes, and I just loved the image of my dog leading a bunch of stragglers and no-hopers on to better things. Before I met Jude, in my head he was a golden retriever. When Dad brought him home from the pound, he was in fact a schnauzer-cross. Nevertheless, he had gravitas, and he was very, very good. He was Jude, and he led me onwards many times. It turns out I was the lost cause he'd look after. I sound dramatic, yes, but also I named my dog after the man who betrayed Jesus, so it checks out.

So now, alone in my share house, waiting on my married man and ignoring my grieving father, I feel like someone has punched me in the throat. I am lying in my attic bedroom, surrounded by ashtrays and empty plates, and I just think, at least Jude didn't see me like this. And then I think: I'll never see Jude again.

And as you know, I don't show Arthur my sad emotions all that much; I couldn't even tell him about my mother; my role is to be the emotionally together one. I am the free one, I don't have to wear the guilt of destroying a family! I am younger, I have the world! But right now all I want is to curl up in the arms of the person I love, and for him to just care for me. He's been weakening me; it turns out I need him very much. And maybe this one time, if I ask, he'll come through.

So I message him on Instagram. *I know you probably can't, but if you could, I'd really appreciate it if you could come over now instead of later. Jude died and I'm very sad.*

As I type this now I am moved by myself as I was then; even in my moment of grief it didn't cross my mind to call him on his mobile phone, as this was a privilege I was not afforded, and I didn't demand it. One time I called him accidentally and he answered the phone then hung up immediately. I could sense his stress so intensely. I also couldn't help but laugh, because didn't he know that if you have an iPhone you can just reject the call? You don't have to answer it to then hang up. He hung up on me so as not to alert his wife to my existence. Why did I find this endearing?

My head has become so good at warding off resentment before it can even percolate. I do not hate Arthur for how long it takes him to get back to me. I don't hate him for the situation I am in. I don't hate him for likely being at some boring barbecue with his pregnant wife and not able to check his phone.

And then, my screen lights up: an Instagram notification. He's responded. He's made an excuse; he'll be with me within the hour.

The elation! The sweet, pure surprise of it! He will come to me, because he loves me and I need him. It's not all in my head! I mean, I know it isn't, but, at the same time, this is proof to placate the voices in my mind, if not my friends, who will need more evidence than this. His baby is due any day now, and he is still making himself vulnerable to being found out, because he doesn't care about the consequences, because spending a life with me is the best consequence.

Even as I am experiencing this joy, I am disgusted with myself—how can I feel such glee while also being devastated about my dead dog? How can I be so happy when what he is doing is, in the scheme of things, so paltry, such a small gesture, really the least he can do? I know this and I don't know this. I want to hold Jude and I can't. I want to cry but the tears won't come. So I sit cross-legged on the floor next to my bed and beat my foot with my knuckles again and again like a snare drum until my married man arrives.

Finally I hear a knock on the door. I make my way downstairs and there he is. He looks so gorgeous, with that little curl falling on his forehead. I step onto the verandah and throw myself into his arms and the sobs begin and they don't stop. He whispers, "I know . . . I know, darling . . . I'm so sorry," as I cry and cry.

I hate myself in this moment, because I know that I am

allowing myself to cry for tactical reasons, even if the tears are real. Since he is not the immediate cause of my distress in this situation (dead dog), like he usually is (won't leave wife), my crying won't make him feel guilty. That's why I let myself do it. He can be the hero of this crying. I want to give him this. I want him to comfort me over hurt that is not of his own making. I want him to feel good about helping.

That said, it's not just a tactical manoeuvre: I do want to be comforted by him. It's a game and it also isn't. If he left me at this moment I would break, and I don't know when it happened exactly, when it slipped from lust to love to *love*. Is love just when you decide that having power is less important than having your person? This is what Angela could not understand at dinner, this is what upset me—what Arthur and I have is true, it's pure, it's good. It's in no way comparable to blaming an assistant for your mistake. It's not sordid, it's this: it's loving each other.

Arthur steps over the threshold. My housemates are not home, so I lead him to the couch in the front room and for a while we just sit there. I tell him about when I first met Jude.

I'd been at school all day, and I did not like school very much at that point. I liked learning, yes, but I did not have the social ease that other people seemed to possess. I never knew what to say, I tell him. At the bus stop that morning, I announced that I would be getting a dog that afternoon. For three minutes or so, the spotlight was on me in a good way. People asked what kind of dog, and even the popular girls had opinions about what I should call him. A girl from an older year suggested "Oliver!" and this was the first time she'd ever spoken to me.

The problem was, though, that as far as I knew I was not getting a dog that afternoon. I mean, I wanted a dog, as every sane person does. But there had been no indication that I would get one. There had in fact been many conversations about how impractical it would be to get a dog.

In that moment at the bus stop, however, I just decided to say it, to make it true for a moment—to be the girl who was getting a puppy. I marvelled at the power of my words: I said I was getting a dog and then people believed I was getting a dog.

But then the awful realisation dawned: what would I say the next day when the other girls asked about my new dog? I would have to say that my dad had changed his mind, or that the dog had been run over, or that the dog had been abducted. Or could I just google photos of dogs and continue the ruse? On the bus trip home I was spiralling.

I pause for a moment here and look up at Arthur's face. He is enraptured and there's a look I don't usually see in his eyes which is: surprise. I can see the cogs turning in his head. You were unpopular? he's thinking. You lied to get people to like you? You're not an entirely mysterious, buoyant, irreverent woman who has sprung out of nowhere to be what I want? He didn't have many friends in school, I know this. I've just not let on before that in late primary school and early high school I was the same. He doesn't know that I was the kind of person who would destroy a boarder's image of her dad so I could feel popular and powerful for just one moment.

I go on: it's too late to stop my story, and I'm curious to see his reaction to it, how he will take this new information and gel it with the version of me in his head. How will he spin it to make me even more delectable than before? Because I know that's what he will be doing; that's what we all do when we want someone. Every new nugget of information is a testament to their brilliance, humility, humour, kindness.

I continue my tale. The bus pulled in at my stop and I got off, and I walked down the street to my house. My schoolbag was heavy with folders and highlighters and a huge calculator I never used but always carried. It was humid, I felt ill.

When I opened the front door, I could see Dad in the kitchen at the back of the house, which was odd, because he was never home at this time, he always worked late. He was gesturing to something, there was a manic energy in the air. He was stage-whispering, "Go on!"

There was a pause, in which nothing happened.

And then a puppy came stumbling out from behind the counter, unsure where to go, staring at me quizzically with his big eyes.

He didn't come any closer; he looked scared. So I walked towards him. And that's when I first met Jude, I tell Arthur. Jude was the lie that came true, just to save me.

Then I start crying again and I'm not doing it performatively, it's not calculated at all, I just can't stop. I'm thinking about that gorgeous silly dog. And then I feel Arthur's arms around me, and he's pulling me into him, and I think maybe he understands. This is what love is, I think again: I'm crying, and you're here.

We stay on the couch together for a while, not speaking, not moving. Eventually, though, I stop crying, and he's still there, he hasn't gone. He begins tracing his fingers down my back, in spirals and shapes that get more and more elaborate, until I find myself shaking with silent giggles.

"What is it?" he asks softly, his voice full of concern.

"It's just . . . Arthur, are you tracing a swastika on my back?"

He bursts out laughing, my favourite sound.

I jump onto him, straddling his lap. I'm kissing his lips, his shoulders, his forehead. I look into his eyes and they see me just as they did the first time we had sex—that is, they actually see me. I feel his body change beneath me, I feel mercury coalescing into amber, I feel every mixed metaphor there is because I dropped science after year ten and I'm not bound by rules.

After we've made love, we order pizza. I am thrilled that he isn't leaving immediately, and I wonder what lie he's told to secure this pocket of time. I put that wonder aside.

I tell him more stories about Jude, we drink wine, I tell him about the time Jude pissed on our mean neighbour's briefcase, because Jude was an evil genius. I tell him about how my ex-girlfriend had never warmed to Jude, and how Jude used to peer up at me when she left the house, big all-knowing eyes, like, *Oh Hera, really? That's your choice?* I tell him how my dad loved Jude with his whole heart; how, despite his initial reservations, it was only really when Dad sat patting Jude that he seemed truly content. I subtly introduce the topic of my mother. I tell Arthur how when I broke up with my ex, Dad said, "She never really seemed to connect with Jude, did she? Your mother didn't like dogs either," and how this made me grin—that this emotional intelligence had been swishing around in my gruff dad's mind, and the only way he could voice it was through Jude; he would never tell me that he didn't like my partner, but now the relationship was over he would acknowledge that her unease around canines reminded him of my mother, aka the person he distrusted most in the world.

I see Arthur glance surreptitiously at his phone.

The familiar feelings arise—the feeling of dread, knowing that he will soon leave my arms to return to hers, to do their dishes, to make their bed. I rarely wait for him to tell me he has to go, because hearing these words is always enough to make me want to cry, and I hate being the mistress who cries when he leaves. Until now, I've always given him a way out. I'll say, "It's probably time you were off, isn't it? Miles to go before you sleep."

But this time—this time I can't do it. Him being here, comforting me as I grieve, and me beginning to tell him about my mum; these are real things, serious things. I cannot go on with only the most nebulous idea of when he will be fully mine. I will break the cycle for both of us.

He's gathering his keys, his phone, he's putting on his pants, his socks. I am naked, sitting on the couch.

"Arthur?" I throw it out into the room, the seriousness of my voice, the discussion it is preamble to.

"Hera," he responds, with a mock solemnity I suspect he will soon regret.

"Arthur, I think I have to say something that I really, really don't want to say."

He looks at me like he knows exactly what that is, but then his face twitches, he kind of flinches, and it occurs to me that he might be thinking I am about to end us. It's a strange sensation I feel. I feel hurt that he could think I would want to end it—have I not signalled with every action I've ever taken that what I want is him, no matter the cost? But I also feel—and I hate that I feel this, for how clichéd it is—but I feel powerful. And this power gives me the courage to go on. Imagine if this was a relationship I had power in.

I say, "I don't know what words will make this better, so just, here: you have to tell her everything. You have to give me a date for when you are going to tell everything." I have become cold, my face has become unreadable. I am forcing myself to get it out.

And instead of evading, which I thought he might do, instead of saying, "We have to wait till the baby is born before we think about this," he looks . . . relieved.

He looks terrified, but he looks relieved.

He looks at me very seriously, and in a small voice he says, "I know."

Without me prompting him further, he offers: "How about the end of the year? I'll tell her by the end of the year. I can't do it while we're both sleep-deprived zombies, but by the end of the year the baby will be four months. I'm told they sleep better then. The end of the year. Is that okay? Can you be okay with that?"

It is August. I can be okay with that. I have to be okay with that.

I nod. "You're sure about this, Arthur? Please don't say this if you aren't sure."

He comes over, still only half-dressed, and he lies on the couch next to me. He says: "The promise of having you, *you*, as the person I get to hang out with forever—that is the only thing that makes all this doable. I wouldn't . . . I couldn't have done this if that wasn't the end goal. So yes, I'm sure. I'm not sure how any of it is going to go. And it is going to break Kate's heart. But I am sure of you. So: by the end of the year. I promise."

"Okay, okay! You don't have to be so intense about it!" I feel high with success, like I've just successfully negotiated a terrorist situation.

It feels like getting home and seeing that someone else has cleaned the kitchen. It feels like trying on an expensive, impossibly soft cashmere jumper in an intimidating store and then going up to the bitchy sales assistants and buying that jumper like it's nothing. It feels like sitting down with your friends on the deck at school, knowing that they've saved a spot for you.

I snuggle into him, I kiss his silly cheek. We lie like this for a few minutes, before he really has to go.

The next day I go see Dad. He is ashen with grief, but he smiles when he sees me. Jude is already at the vet, and from there his body will be taken to the pet crematorium. Sitting at the kitchen table with cups of tea in front of us, I tell Dad I'm sorry I couldn't come last night, and I'm crying as I say this, from grief and from guilt—because I know where I was instead, I know what I was doing.

He gives my shoulder a squeeze and says, "That's all right, Hera. We've our whole lives to remember him."

And at this injunction to remember, yet more tears well in my eyes, and the room goes cloudy. Dad is referring to a world that Jude is no longer in. Yesterday he was in it, and today he is not.

It's a Monday morning; Dad would usually be at work. It's a Monday morning; usually I would be at work or in bed, pining.

"Do you have anything you need to do today?" Dad asks.

"Nope. I reckon I just need to hang out with you, if that's all right?"

He smiles. "I thought you'd never ask."

We revert to gnome mode; we revert to what we used to do when I was too sick to go to school, but not that sick, really. I get out a packet of brownie mix, and Dad shuts the blinds. He's rifling through a drawer in the sideboard, and as I'm cracking an egg into a bowl of chocolatey, sugary chemicals, he asks, "*Indiana Jones* or *Lord of the Rings*?"

"Oh, *Lord of the Rings*, for sure," I reply.

Dad's on his knees, slipping the DVD into the player. "And will you be asking me to fast-forward through every scene with Sméagol, as usual?"

"One hundred per cent, babe."

Brownies in the oven, blankets procured, we proceed to watch just over eleven hours of Middle Earth adventure, pausing only for bathroom breaks and/or to take the brownies out of the oven and eat them. Dad observes several times that Samwise is uncannily like Jude, and he is right every time. When the final film ends, we get up, we fold up our blankets. I wash up the brownie pan and the bowl, Dad dries. And after a hug, I get on a bus and return to my attic bedroom.

The baby is born. The baby! The baby I intend to step-parent, whose mother doesn't know I exist! That baby!

Covid restrictions still apply, even if the city is not locked down, so hospitals are strict about who can visit the hospital: Arthur is essentially locked inside the maternity ward for five days. Since I issued my ultimatum, I have had a terrible, terrible churning inside myself: a fear that once the baby comes Arthur will fall back in love with her mother. I have no way of controlling whether or not this happens, so I try to push that thought aside.

He sends me photos from the hospital. None have the mother in them, thank god.

And he tells me they have named the baby Maisie: Maisie Jones.

I almost choke on my own breath. Oh Arthur, you beautiful fool.

I feel guilty. And at the same time, I feel victorious. In naming his child according to my suggestion, he has sent me a message. He is telling me: you are part of this, even though it's not public yet.

I cannot tell him what I meant by proposing Maisie, so instead I tell him it's a lovely name, graceful, sweet. He thanks me; he tells me he loves me.

In the photos, Maisie is angelic. I was worried I'd hate her, resent her, want to smoosh her little face for what she's putting me through. But of course I can't. She has no control over the situation she's been born into. All I can do is love her.

The day Arthur told me Kate was pregnant was the day I realised and accepted that I would always be his second priority, which I know might seem odd, because he already had a wife—but up to this point I knew I could best her. The baby, though: you can't best a baby. You can't try to get a father to love you, his mistress, more than his newborn child. And you wouldn't want to, because that would be evil. And I may be a mistress but mostly I am a nice person, and I like babies. I will love his baby. The way I make it work in my head is I think of her as my baby too.

I send Soph and Sarah a photo of her, saying isn't she sublime. Sarah responds by love-hearting the photo, no text. Soph texts, *Oh yep, that's a baby! Sorry, Hera, you know I don't really get babies.*

And I can read the unspoken messages in this exchange. I understand the questions not being asked. How could I engage in this, sharing photos of the baby like she's my own, when the baby's mother is in hospital, unaware that she is being betrayed, unaware of my existence, unaware that I intend to step-parent her baby, unaware that I fully intend to hold her baby in a park ten minutes from her house while her partner kisses me and we coo at the baby. I know that this unsettles my friends, perhaps even more than all the other stuff.

I don't see Arthur much over the next few weeks, but eventually, eventually, he is able to leave the house a bit more. And one weekday lunchtime, on a day when I'm not working, I'm just sitting in my share house reading a book about lesbian taxidermists, he drops by. And with him—with him is Maisie. We sit in my diabolically messy front room. I wish that I'd had the foresight to relocate the pizza boxes.

But you guys? You guys, she's fucking gorgeous.

People always say this about newborns, but she's just so bloody small. She is a borlotti bean of a human. Arthur's holding her in this little fabric strap thing that's tied up at his back, so she's facing his chest, all cuddled in. She's sleeping. And is it weird to say he's looking at her like he looks at me sometimes? Like he's so proud of her just for existing? I see in the tenderness he has for her everything I love about him.

I haven't had much to do with babies, so I'm nervous around her, assuming she can sense my neonatal amateurishness. I ask Arthur if I can touch her head; I don't want to assume anything, I don't want to move too fast. He tells me that of course I can.

And when I am stroking her perfectly perfect, soft, angelic little head, he whispers in her ear, "Darling, this is Hera. Hera is a very special person."

Maisie does not respond to this, as she is a baby, and asleep, but I am pleased with the calibre of my introduction. It's like getting a good report at school: "Hera is a diligent worker. Hera has a vivid imagination. Hera is a very special person."

Arthur undoes his sling, and he places the baby in my arms. This is a pivotal moment; I have to get it right. I know that newborns' necks aren't formed, I know I must support her head. I hold her in a pose that seems uncomfortable for both of us, but once she is in my arms I am too afraid to rearrange them. I look up at Arthur, and I'm sure he can see my nerves, but he is smiling, like he is happy to see us together, happy with the image it forms in his mind.

After a minute or two of this perfect peace, however, she wakes. She looks me resolutely in the eye, sees into my soul, and she beings to wail with a ferocity I thought only Claire Danes was capable of. Fuck. I am supposed to be demonstrating my maternal calm, my ease. I attempt to shush her, to bobble her in my arms a bit. I begin to speak in a voice I've not heard myself use before. It's hushed, it's high-pitched, it's singsong. "It's okay, it's okay. It's okay, sweetheart, all will be well. Shhhh, Maisie, you're okay." Do women just have this voice inside them all the time, ready to emerge the first time they hold a newborn? Or have I simply imbibed this from television, from films? What is the natural way for a woman to calm a baby? I feel extremely unnatural, and like the baby is calling me out on it.

After a minute or two of letting me struggle—perhaps recognising this is a challenge I want to face and win—Arthur gives in. He takes Maisie back, and begins to march with her around the room, bouncing her, singing a song I don't know. I trail him like a useless addendum, like a broken Dyson. Eventually, after what seems like hours but is probably only a few minutes, she falls asleep on his chest again. He looks at me with tired eyes, and confirms my other fear: it is time for him to go. She needs a nap. Before he leaves, however, he notes my disappointed expression and reads it correctly. He says, "It's absolutely not you, Hera; she gets like this all the time. She's just tired, or hungry, or something else I haven't worked out yet. Promise me you won't take this personally. She loves you, I promise. I tell her about you all the time."

I tell her about you all the time. I wonder how much of all of this is settling itself on the seabed of her subconscious. And just for now, can she do me a favour? When she gets home, can she tell her mother, with her eyes, that I exist?

Sydney gets sunnier and brighter as we crawl towards the end of the year. The days I am not at work I spend alone at the beach, reading books and messaging Arthur, who is working from home not too far away. Some days he'll surprise me with a beach visit on his lunch break; he'll wrap Maisie up in her sling and tell his wife he's going for a walk. Then he'll wander down to where I am, baking on the sand in my bikini, and he'll sit with me and we'll play with Maisie. Other families with babies will nod at us; sometimes their little toddlers will even waddle up to look at Maisie, who'll be in my arms or Arthur's, and I'll tell the toddlers to be gentle, that she's still little. The toddlers' parents laugh knowingly, looking at me like I am a sweet, protective mum, and I love this. When Arthur is not at the beach with me, I am just a lonely young woman without a job to go to on a weekday.

"What are you reading, darling?" he'll ask me. And I'll tell him, "I'm reading about phenomenology, one of us has to." And he'll laugh and shake his head like he is in awe of me, in awe of my brain. And then I'll read out dense passages to Maisie, and Arthur and I come up with her responses. We have a running gag that she can't stand Heidegger, and every time she makes an unhappy face, we attribute this to her anti-fascism.

One day in this endless summer that is only just beginning, Kate will be out for hours at a postnatal class at the hospital with Maisie, and Arthur invites me over to his house. This seems reckless to me; I feel a sense of unease. Entering her house, with her things, where she sleeps and eats and does not know about the other life her husband is leading, does not know about the feral woman metaphorically beating down her doors, now literally walking through them. I have imagined the inside of this house so many times. I have seen screen-sized packages of it on Face-Times when she is not home, I've seen the wall behind Arthur's bed, I've seen a sliver of his lounge room in grainy night-time light. I have seen the house from the outside, from the Ubers in which I crouch. It is small, nothing fancy, but it looks safe, domestic, the kind of place you'd be happy to return to after a long day's work. It's red-brick, there are plants on the small porch, and I wonder if he gardens or she does. I can't see him having a green thumb, so I surmise it must be her.

So on one level it feels wrong to be entering the house—yes, I've been fucking her husband, but so far I haven't invaded her personal space. I'm an ethical slut, etc. On another level, how-ever, it feels like progress, one step closer to their inner sanctum, one step closer to procuring my own. I wonder what is going on in Arthur's mind, why he's chosen now to admit me into his pri-vate sphere. I don't press him on it, don't ask questions, I simply agree. And at the arranged time, I stand at his front door, and message him to let him know that I've arrived. I hear movement inside, and a part of me hopes that there's been some fuck-up, that Kate is home, that she'll have to greet me, that it will all come out. But no, it is him. He opens the door, smiling like it is a miracle to see me standing at this precipice, and then he glances around to see if any neighbours are watching before, satisfied that there are not, he lets me in.

The décor is nondescript, but the house looks lived in, like the people who reside here have made their indents in the couch, like they have a favourite faucet. There's baby stuff everywhere, blankets and bulky paraphernalia whose purpose I can't iden-tify. Arthur is watching me take it all in, and I want to appear casual, like I don't want to read every greeting card on the mantelpiece, like I don't want to scrutinise every photograph in every frame, looking for signs of Kate, of how they are together.

But I'm not very good at appearing casual. I immediately vector towards the bookshelf and try to determine which books are his and which are hers. I know the crime thrillers are his, and I make fun of him for them.

I pick up a tatty James Patterson tome and gesture with it as I turn to Arthur. "See, babe," I say, "this is why I fell for you. It's because you're so cultured."

He laughs and replies, "Just wait until you see my Peter FitzSimons collection; I'm sure you'll want to undress immediately."

I don't need to see the dad-core history books to want to disrobe. In one motion I lift my dress up and over my shoulders and drop it onto the floor. I'm not wearing anything underneath. This has become habit. Arthur's eyes widen and once again I'm in it, in this blissful feeling of being the person he wants. My body is powerful, strong, and it undresses his quickly, with purpose.

We are so close now, so close to not having to do this in secret anymore. I kiss him with fury, I bite at his lips and his neck, I want to mark him, cover him in traces of me. As we move together I fantasise about having a bed of our own, I imagine this is our bed, our house. When he comes he is staring into my eyes. Face it, Arthur. Face what this is.

When it is over I walk to the bathroom to take a shower. I close the door, turn the shower on, and use this time to see what I can learn from the cabinet above the sink. I discover that Kate uses three different kinds of moisturiser. Kate wears nude-coloured hair elastics. Kate looks in the mirror I am now looking into each day, and assumes that she knows what her life will look like.

I step into the shower and let the water rain down. I use her shower gel, I use her shampoo. I use more of it and more of it; my hair is already clean but I'm lathering and re-lathering, watching the shampoo in the bottle go down. Notice this, Kate, notice the deficit. Notice this and confront him. Learn the truth and leave him, so I can have my life.

I hear a knock at the bathroom door and Arthur asks if he can join me. I tell him of course.

Afterwards, we lie together on the couch, and I bring up the deadline. I try to entice answers out of him, with softness, with longing. We agreed on the end of the year, but when, Arthur, what date, what time? December is fast approaching. Soph and Sarah are already making New Year's plans and asking me what I am doing. I've been telling them no, that I'll be busy. I will be with him, free, when the clock strikes midnight on that insufferable night. I say, Isn't that right, Arthur? Tell me that I'm right.

I feel so silly, caring about New Year's like a teenager. But it's not the day, it's what it represents. I have only ever asked one thing of him, to have it done by then, and my heart is clenching, holding it together, keeping the faith.

He tells me yes: he promises me that we will toast the new year together. We'll eat dinner, we'll make love, we'll be together then. Everything will be out in the open.

As the weeks of December go by, closer and closer to the deadline, my vision narrows. There is no space for giddiness, even at work. I have only one goal in life, one purpose. I am urging Arthur over text, over FaceTime, in person, over WhatsApp, in Instagram messages. I am trying every single avenue I can think of to persuade him to put me out of my misery.

He just has to find the right time, when it will hurt her the least, he says. I do not see that such a moment is likely ever to exist. Arthur, I reiterate: any time is a bad time to tell her. I am not cruel; I have never wanted to hurt her any more than is necessary. But *I* want to stop hurting. I am trying to force myself to consider my own pain as commensurate to hers, which is challenging, because I am a secret, and I am younger, and I can never get over the sense that when people call me a woman and not a girl they are teasing me somehow.

Occasionally I hear mothers in the ceramics shop telling their children to "mind the lady" and it never occurs to me that I am the lady in question. A lady probably does grocery shopping with a list. Sometimes, when it occurs to me that the man I love has a beard with grey in it and legs with thick hair and shoulders defined by years of supporting the weight of collared shirts and a laptop bag—I am taken aback. How have I tricked everyone into thinking that I too am an adult person?

I am a child, Kate is a woman. Kate works for a charity, I've learned. I sell cups.

But I have to start thinking of myself as someone who deserves things. I must.

I'm playing a grown-up game.

Since the night of Angela's outburst, I have barely seen my friends. I cannot stand the way they look at me now, with a mixture of sympathy and revulsion; what started in their minds as an honest mistake, a lapse of judgement, has fallen into an abyss. They see me eyeing my phone, they see the waiting game my life has become.

I used to be renowned for my ability to sleep. I could sleep in people's lounge rooms for whole mornings after house parties, through vacuuming, hungover chatter, doors slamming. I would not wake up unless someone shook me. I used to be able to fall asleep easily too. Head on pillow, whirring thoughts turning to nonsensical visual metaphors, and I was gone, into the tunnel of light that would bring me to my morning muesli. I have not slept this way for a very long time now. I come alive when I see him, I wither when he leaves.

I bring up the deadline with Arthur, again and again. If we are to be together for New Year's Eve, then he must tell her before this. When will you tell her, Arthur? What is your plan? He will tell her literally on the final day of the year, he says—the last possible moment he can do it and still keep his promise to me.

It is December 31.

I have spent the day cleaning my room, making it habitable for a man who's just left his wife. I have baked a packet cake, smothered it in frosting. It sits on the kitchen table on a plastic chopping board, as I do not own a cake stand. I have arranged an Aldi cheese selection on a dinner plate. Sarah and Soph are at a house party in the inner west, and as afternoon fades into evening they send me increasingly drunken selfies. My housemates are out, no doubt celebrating with their friends, their lovers if they have them. I am not drinking; I am too stressed to drink. I need to be steady and clear-headed when he comes, I need to be the stable partner who can look after him.

His green dot has been absent for twenty-two hours. This is it: he is telling her.

I sit in the lounge room staring at my phone, willing a message from him to appear. The people next door are having a party, and their music thumps through the wall we share, disturbing my otherwise silent vigil. It's hot and sticky, that summer kind of heat that stultifies the air. I turn a floor fan on full force and sit cross-legged in front of it, on the floor, near the door, ready to open it when he knocks.

It's a sick-making cycle of checking my phone and throwing it onto the couch facedown, only to retrieve it and check again moments later. It is like waiting for HSC results to appear on the Board of Studies website, that anxiety, knowing that one time when I flip the screen over it will display a result that decides my future. I've put in the work, I've put in the hours; I should receive the return I deserve.

I know he has told her today, because he knows what it means if he doesn't. He will knock on the door and I will let him in and we'll start our lives.

It is 10 p.m. by the time I hear the knock, hard and fast.

I jump up from the floor and go to the door.

He looks like a ghost. I wrap my arms around him and hold him tight. He has done it, he is here, he is mine.

I step back, preparing to lead him inside—and now I take in the expression on his face.

He sometimes gets this look in his eyes when there's something he doesn't want to tell me because he knows I'll be upset, because it is going to be yet another betrayal that I'll be forced to accept. He gets this look when he tells me that he can't stay for dinner. He gets it when he has to cancel plans. His jaw will clench, and he'll look so pained I almost forget that it is him doing this to me, not some mysterious malevolent force neither of us can control.

Now, as we stand here at the door, when he should be saying, "I love you," or, "It's done," what he says instead is this: he says, "I have something bad to tell you. I couldn't do it. I didn't tell her." And then he suggests we go inside so that he can explain. And I am speechless, my body frozen. A second ago I'd thought it was all over, that I could finally exhale. But it is not done.

I do not let him in just yet. I am trying to decide what to do. In this moment of abject pain, I am still strategising. The game cannot be lost. I will not lose. I steady myself. I will give no indication that I think less of him right now. I need to position myself as the option he should take if he wants to have integrity. He loves the idea of having integrity.

I cannot allow him to see that he has been breaking me, that I will now always be a bit broken by him.

I decide to let him in. Because I know in my gut that I can

talk him around, I know that I can get him to see what is right: I know that he can't really not keep the one promise I have asked him to make, the one that has kept me sane but also living half a life for so long. He is not that kind of man; he is a good man. He is scared, that's all. We just have to talk it through. I will debase myself one last time. I will beg him to see that he has to tell the truth, for all our sakes. I will beg the man I love to do the thing that will allow him to love me properly. Beg him to take me seriously, even though I am not the mother of his child. *I could be!* I will say. *I want to be!* I will argue. *Don't deny all the children we will have for the sake of the one child you already have.* These are words that will actually come out of my mouth, and I will mean them.

I turn from him and step inside, motioning to him to follow. He goes to take my hand, but I pull it away.

"You can come in, but please don't touch me, Arthur," I say quietly. The touch I craved just a second ago seems like a violent affront now.

The front room of the house is large and we seem very small inside of it.

I keep having a vision of us from above, from the perspective of the house itself, the house observing my hunched shoulders and his imploring eyes and jittery knee-tapping and the house just thinking to itself, "What sad people I have inside of me." I feel sorry for the house, and for him, and for myself. None of us will get out of this well. I know that soon enough, no matter what comes to pass, it will just be me in this room because he will have left, temporarily or permanently, to return to his other life, to deal with the things that matter more than me. And then, when I am alone in this room, I will just be staring at the spot where he has prostrated himself—but to what end?—and at the spot where I've felt so little regard for myself that I've cried and begged a man to stay, to choose me over someone else. To choose me or I don't know what I will do. Choose me—choose me, so I don't have to.

IT'S hard for me to describe to you the feelings that were running through me when I led him into my lounge room after he hadn't told her. It's hard because it still hurts, despite my best efforts to get over it, and it's also hard because this is for the most part a realist novel, and I want to make this scene believable for you, and what I did and the way I approached the following four hours is so fucking small (and I mean that as in what I did was small—I made myself smaller) that it might be hard to make you understand why a character would do that. If you can't relate to total desperation, I'm hoping you'll approach this scene like you might consider deleting someone from your list of possible suspects when watching *SVU* because surely no one could actually be so stupid as to leave so much incriminating evidence when committing a crime. If he was actually the baddie, he would not have committed the murder in broad daylight with CCTV while wearing a T-shirt emblazoned with the slogan I AM THE MURDERER. I don't see why I would be telling you how pathetically I handled this situation unless it is actually just the truth— otherwise, what would be in it for me? Why would I degrade myself in this way? Then again, people lie for strange reasons. People lie all the time, I've learned.

Maybe I'm the murderer.

But. Maybe you've been in just as dire a situation as mine before: maybe you too have known that you would say anything to make a person stay, even though obviously (even to you!) the smart thing would be for you to walk away, to close this chapter of your life.

Perhaps we're all pathetic, and maybe all my caveats are

superfluous. Maybe you too have begged a man to leave his wife and child while sitting on the floor of the lounge room in your share house on New Year's Eve, hoping that your housemates don't decide to bring people back for New Year's drinks at this moment, because that would really not help your case.

HE sits on the couch, and I sit on the floor facing him.

His main concern, he says, is what leaving Kate will do to the baby—how it will ruin the baby's life. "I thought I could do it, Hera. I wasn't lying to you when I said I would tell her today. But then this morning, I was watching Kate with Maisie, and Maisie needs her so much, and I just—I couldn't."

So I have to try to convince him that leaving his wife is the best thing he can do for the baby. I tell him that parents who stay together and don't love each other are worse than parents who live apart. I tell him that staying with someone because they are the mother of your child is not a valid reason, and that it traps her as well as him. I try to get him to see that I am the viable solution, that ultimately this means Maisie will get *more* love, not less. I remind him of the children we will have together, the siblings I want for Maisie.

All of this negotiation is interesting to me, from a distance, because while I do believe the arguments I am making, it is also insane that I have to pretend some kind of detached objectivity— like I am only spelling out these arguments because I want what is best for Maisie.

To retain an air of rhetorical equanimity and level-headedness, I do not say the one thing that I feel most strongly, which is: *Leave her because I love you, and because you love me, and because I matter more than the other things.*

He tells me again he doesn't want to ruin Maisie's life. And it is fair that he harbours guilt about perhaps fragmenting the person he's made before she even has a chance to make herself whole, before she's even got to have a go at it. But Arthur, I think to myself, your split was never going to be civil. The blood was always going to be bad. From the moment you told me you hated Doug, the blood didn't even have a chance to be good.

Am I the murderer.

I've never owned a slogan T-shirt but I've repeatedly doused myself in perfume before fucking a married man, hoping the smell will rub off on him, and then on his wife. I've never owned a slogan T-shirt but I have fixated on how I wanted so, so much for a seemingly very nice, blameless woman to just: cease to exist.

I lied. I have owned a slogan T-shirt. I've owned so many.

We sit in silence for a while as I wait for him to speak. His phone is vibrating, she is calling, and he does not pick up. I have a logical comeback to every misgiving he voices. And for every comeback he has another garbled version of the same reason. ("I can't do it, it's too much to bear. I can't be the person who does this to her.")

I try to fathom what is going on in his head as he clenches and unclenches his jaw, as the vein in his forehead pops; he is trapped in a circle of anxiety that I am familiar with. I can see that he is manic, and although mania is usual for me, it is not for him. I can see his mind trying to understand the churning going on in his body, like he's never lost control over the pit of his stomach before.

Almost two hours have passed since he arrived. We have reached a stalemate. We are made aware that a new year has begun when the sounds of cheers and fireworks fill the street; when the music next door gets even louder; when the chorus to Lizzo's "Juice" starts filtering through the walls. Arthur and I do not acknowledge this, and it's all so pathetic, so sad, that I can't even see the humour in this moment.

I ask him, "Arthur, where does Kate think you are right now?"

And he looks at me, totally blank, like he cannot fathom one thing that is happening in his life right now. He responds, "I don't know. I don't know. We were at her parents' house. I told her I had to go somewhere, I told her I'd be back soon." He cries a bit at this.

"Arthur . . ." It is time to play my trump card, the one that I really, really didn't want to have to play. I play—finally—for myself. "You have to tell her, and you have to tell her tonight. You cannot have done this to me. I love you, and you love me, and I have waited, and this is real. Not telling her now does not make it unreal. Just practically, even, you're going to have to explain where the fuck you've been. And it's going to come out. So please, please choose the option where I can let myself stay with you. Tell her because you choose to, not because you have to. Be brave, Arthur. I am begging you. I cannot be a secret. I am not a secret."

He is essentially imploring me to let him fold, and I will not. I will not do it. I feel like I am holding him hostage, making him promise to do violence. Again and again I am pummelled by the unfairness of this.

But women have been forced to harm themselves in the process of making men accountable for millennia. I have been in training for this moment. I will not be quitting, and I tell him as much.

It is late, it is so late. I say, "If you're here because you want me to give you a way out, I'm not going to do that."

Eventually I break him through sheer perseverance.

He cedes. By 2 a.m. he has no fight left in him. He says he'll do it, and I know he means it this time. I've crushed his spirit.

It does not feel like victory.

When he leaves, I am exhausted. I go into the kitchen and eat a fistful of cake. I ignore the cheese plate. I don't put anything away and I don't wash anything up. I climb the stairs to my bed. I plug my phone into the charger and I lie down on top of the sheets, fully clothed, and I drift in and out of sleep, waiting for the notification I know I will receive.

I wake from a fretful doze at 11 a.m. on New Year's Day to see that he has messaged. He's told her. This is all the information he gives me.

I do not feel the relief I thought I would.

For so long, all I wanted was this. And now it has happened, it does not seem like confession is the end, or the beginning. In all my previous imaginings, this was the turning point. Once this was done, we would be fine. It would be terrible and hard but finally we'd be on the same team, us against the world. But it's difficult to be on the same side as someone who is only sporadically responding to your messages. It's hard to be on the same side as someone who has forced you to force them to break up with their wife.

But I still want it.

ON the third day, sex. He comes over to my place and tells me how badly she's been taking it, how she can't speak, how she can't do anything. He looks like a broken person. He looks how I feel.

We make love quickly, me trying to imbue the act with every ounce of love I feel, to remind him what this has been for. Afterwards, he tells me he loves me so, so much, but that he has to get back to her and the baby, that he'll keep me updated on her progress, that it will all be okay.

It doesn't feel okay.

* * *

OVER the next few days, I barely see the green dot at all. This means he is talking to her, and that he is talking to her but not reporting back to me. I fear they are having discussions he does not want me to be privy to: discussions that are against my interests.

And I know that he loves me; never once have I doubted this. But I also know that people who love you can do things that would suggest otherwise.

My friends force me to come to an evening get-together at Soph's house. It's a Saturday, everyone's in high spirits. It's January—people have been at the beach today, they've been drinking beers on scorching sand. Everyone else's lives are going on as normal, and I cannot compute that we are all living in the same world in this moment. I feel abstracted, ripped from time. I've been spending my days staring at my phone, calling in sick to work. I know I am at this party right now, like literally here, but every moment I'm not spending peering at the Instagram app feels like a moment wasted.

I summon the girls away from the throng to the balcony. I smoke cigarettes with alarming speed as I tell Sarah and Soph what has transpired.

First of all, they're gobsmacked that he actually told her.

Sarah says, "I know you always believed it, babe, but I gotta be real: I can't believe he's actually confessed to the wife. That's, like, big shit."

"Yup, yeah, that's some big shit right there, for sure," I deadpan, not with humour but with exhaustion. "But now he's being all evasive," I continue. "I feel like he's withholding something, and it's making me crazy in a new and different way." This is the first time I've admitted to them that this relationship has made me feel batshit. It's been obvious anyway, but saying it feels both awful and good.

"Well," Soph begins, "I guess now he's told her, it's no more keeping up with the Joneses for you, bb."

I laugh. "Sophie," I say seriously, "I have been waiting for you to make that joke for the past year and a half."

She winks. "It's all about timing."

The girls ease me back into the party, and I have slightly more energy now. Sarah whispers to me as we head inside, "He's actually fucking done it, babe! This is not the time to mope. You're like, the mythical mistress who actually gets the guy. Let's drink to that!"

She's right, they're right. I believe it. He and Kate are probably having long talks in which he explains to her that he does not love her anymore, he is going through every time we've had sex, every time he's lied to her about where he is, every time I've been in the car outside their house, every time I've kissed him as he's held Maisie, every time I've held Maisie. At this moment, Kate is probably gathering her things, gathering the baby, trying to work out the most economical use of her time before her Uber arrives and she leaves him.

I drink into the evening, and when "I'm on Fire" starts playing through the UE Boom in the kitchen, I dance.

On the eleventh day, he messages me, he says we have the day to ourselves, I can pick where we meet, he just misses me so much. A family friend has been called in to look after Maisie. This must mean Kate is not there anymore.

And just like that I am buoyant, I am floating. We are okay. Everything is going to be okay.

I go to the shops and buy ingredients to make him a smoothie. I meet him at one of our favourite spots, near the beach. I bring the smoothie in a drink bottle. I am light, I am shining with light. He holds me and he kisses me so hard, and I know that every part of this struggle has been worth it. I was right to put my heart on the table, I was right to go all in.

We sit down on some grass. I pour his smoothie into a glass I have brought from home. I present it to him like an offering. He thanks me, but he doesn't drink from it. He places the glass down next to us. He's tense, but that makes sense. He's been living a nightmare in his home. I rest my head on his shoulder, I let myself breathe.

I move my head to face him, and I begin to speak, to ask how he is, but he interjects before I can get the words out.

He says: "I am going to hurt you very much right now, and I am so, so sorry."

She has asked him to stay.

He isn't going to leave her.

You were right; you predicted it. Everyone was right but me. There you have it. I'm a fool.

Now would be the time for me to get angry, make a statement, speak my mind, throw a fit, yell. Or I could try to talk him round again.

I don't have the energy. I am so exhausted. I tell him he is making a mistake and that if he doesn't know it now, he will know it in time. And it's true, he will know it in time. I tell him calmly, slowly, that he has broken my heart. He is crying but I am not.

He's saying sorry, I'm so sorry, over and over again, and I'm not responding—just looking at him. A dog runs up to us and starts lapping at the smoothie I have made, knocking over the glass. Neither of us shoos the dog away; we cannot acknowledge that this is what is happening right now.

I cannot stay here, I cannot watch this dog.

With a lot of effort, I stand up. I consider whether to retrieve the glass. No, I can't do it. Let Arthur sit with that. I look down at him. I tell him not to contact me again. I walk away.

PART · FIVE

During the immediate days and weeks following the annihilation of my heart, my capacity to cry is mind-boggling. People make this observation frequently, but every time it's like a medical marvel: you would think that the tears would eventually run out. Ariana Grande's did, why not mine? The truth is that tears don't *have* to do anything. Like with a retail manager who makes you work on your birthday, I have no power in this dynamic. My tears fall as they please.

For a while I can't tell anyone what has happened, how it went down down down. I can't tell them because I do not yet believe it; I can't fathom it. I mean, I know it has happened but, like, in the same way that I know management consultants are literally speaking words when they explain their jobs to me, even as I cannot hear them. Consultants speaking and heartbreak dawning: both are Schrödinger's cat actualised, things that simultaneously are and are not.

I also can't tell anyone because I am in no fit state to open the doors to the inevitable shivers of unsaid but vibrantly evident *I told you so*s that will be coming my way. Even if my friends have the grace not to say it out loud, I know that I will be able to hear it in every comforting phrase, see it in every glance they exchange with each other.

Thoughts aren't coalescing. I am stuck on a question, on a question which is a word: how? How could he do that?

Over and over in my head, infinitely regressing spirals of how. It is impossible to square the two versions I have of him in my head, pre and post "I'm not leaving her." I cannot believe that

I am sitting in my room alone, not knowing how I will go on, when he is twenty minutes away, with her, going on.

She knows, and he knows, that he is in love with me. And yet they are still choosing this life for themselves regardless.

Maybe one day when I'm older I'll understand why a person would do that. But I hope that I won't. Because that will mean that I've joined them: that I'm willing to betray the future in order to relive a past that cannot exist now; a past that, conversely, will only become smaller each time it is unfaithfully re-enacted. I don't know what I want but, by god, I don't want that.

A few days after it happens, I turn up at Dad's house weeping. I tell him someone has broken my heart, and he knows enough not to ask questions. He looks at me like he looked at me when I was a teen, when I was very sad, too sad to do anything. Back then I had to put all my faith in my dad, who said that I would get through it. I have been trying to avoid that dependence as I get older, but maybe now I just have to accept it.

Dad hugs me and tells me that I am not going back to my share house for a while, that I'll be staying with him, and that things will be all right. I am so relieved to have him make this decision for me. None of my friends seem to need their parents, whereas I need my dad so much.

He also says I'm not going in to work for a bit, that I just need to rest. Again the relief: someone telling me that I can rest. Nevertheless, I counter, "Dad, you do realise that they'll just stop giving me shifts if I take even a week off? I'm a casual."

He looks genuinely surprised by this idea. He says, "Surely they wouldn't do that. Your boss will understand."

He doesn't mean for this to be the effect, but for the first time in days, I laugh.

"Sure, Dad, my boss will understand." And I give him a big hug, like I am the one protecting him, the silly good fool, which makes me feel better. That he can have faith in the kindness of a retail employer after all the bureaucratic shit he's been through in his life, after the system tried to stop him from seeing his kid because of someone else's lies. For him, disappointment in one system doesn't mean cynical disbelief in all systems. I envy him this, even as I patronise him for it.

FOR a few weeks, I sit and I cry, and I do little else. I don't have the energy to eat and, more alarming, I don't have the energy to drink. I have a small amount of savings that I am paying my rent from. But as the weeks turn into a month, I realise that unlike the other break-up I've experienced, the pain is not going to pass within a familiar timeframe.

There is a large part of me, a part I try to hide, which hopes Arthur will just rock up at my door one day and say he's made the biggest mistake of his life and beg me to come back. I've told my friends by now what has happened, and they've each made me promise that if he does come knocking, I'll rebuff him. Every time I have made this promise I have crossed my fingers behind my back. Murderer, murderer, serial killer.

I stop paying rent, I break my lease. I move back in with Dad.

I do start working at the store again. My boss says he doesn't have any shifts for me, but then another Covid wave hits and I am one of the last women standing, so there I am back behind the counter. Masks, antiseptic, check-ins, angry people, sad people—rarely any happy people. I spend a lot of time in the staff toilet crying. The slightest rudeness from a customer can reduce me to tears.

For the next five months, I get on with my life, but I do not fall out of love with Arthur.

I take baby steps toward disentanglement, at the urging of my friends.

They force me to block him on Instagram, on WhatsApp, on Facebook, on Twitter.

But I can still see his Twitter likes and they are all tweets about love, and about being sorry. He knows that I'll be looking and, like an idiot, I am. I wish I could tell you that I laugh at these tweets, at these boomer-style attempts to communicate, but alas I am reading them all like secret code, searching for answers.

Soph and Sarah and Daisy and Ben take me out and tell me I'm worth more, tell me what a grot he is.

Dad and I eat a lot of ravioli. We watch old movies after dinner. After some months of me being back in his house, he buys a new dog. He names it this time; it's his dog. But I'm proud to be in the dog's family.

Dad names the dog Ash. He says it's because ash is what's left after a fire, but it makes the ground fertile.

I laugh to myself. I always think I'm the one who feels things the most, but Dad's been through more than I've ever dealt with, and he has more of an ear for the poetry of life than I give him credit for.

Dad has a partner now, but he doesn't call him that. He just calls him Daniel, because that is his name. Daniel is gentle with me, kind. Sometimes he stays over and watches old movies with us. Sometimes, when Dad thinks I'm not looking, he nuzzles up to Daniel on the couch, and he's smiling. Daniel pats Ash.

From time to time, I get drinks after work with the subset of my colleagues who are not avoiding all venues and we call this mutual aid. I listen to them talk about their housemates, about their problems, and I chime in occasionally when the situation demands.

I listen to the conversations going on around us, which bring me solace in their reassuring mundanity.

Two men I presume to be brothers: "It's just that Mum is such a nutter anyway . . ."

A woman on a date with a man who has been talking at her without pause for twenty minutes: "You're right, it is confusing when two people have the same name."

A couple of gregarious gays drinking cocktails, wearing activewear: "I just don't get people who are obsessed with Mickey Mouse. Like, do I want to meet Mickey Mouse? No thank you! I didn't grow up with Mickey Mouse, babe, I grew up with domestic violence."

And on and on, ad infinitum.

Some things are starting to become clear in my mind after a long time of being fuzzy. There are moments—swiping a credit card, exchanging pleasantries with a customer, eating dinner in a familiar restaurant—when I sense the edges of a remembered feeling: a desire for a future that is larger than the life I am living now, and larger than the life my friends seem content with. I am reminded that all this disquiet, this disquiet I have long reckoned with as my most permanent companion: it comes from a place of *wanting*. And to want is a hopeful thing. It's the most hopeful thing, really. The pain that follows me from house party to work to drinks to the beach to my bed at night, it is a pain that whispers of imagination—a pain that cannot and will not forget that the whole world exists, and I am in it, and I will not be sated by settling for a small part of it, at least not yet, before I've seen more. I have to at least see more.

I've stopped checking his Twitter feed as regularly. I grieve for him, and for the me I might have been with him. But I am also beginning to see, now that time has passed and the claw-like grip of lust is weakening, that the me I might have been with him might not have been the me I truly want to be. I mean, I still don't know who I want to be, but I am now willing to entertain the prospect that a forty-year-old man who's addicted to smoothies might not be the best person to decide for me.

That evening in the Chinese restaurant, I was looking for a way to stop it all, to stop the want. I saw him as a circuit breaker; something that could put my big, unmeetable desires on pause. I had wanted to funnel all that wanting into him, into something that seemed manageable, immediate, tangible. I had hoped that falling in love would make all the disquiet go away.

And maybe it would have, for a while. But probably not forever. I know myself. She is not that easily gorged. There is always a second stomach.

One afternoon, I am walking on a path by the beach, head-phones on and scarf wrapped around my neck against the cold. I walk with purpose to no particular end, as I have always done. I peer at the ocean not looking for an answer, just to see that it is there (it is).

A very little girl wanders up to me. She is proudly showing me her empty plastic cup, like it's a much-loved toy. I smile at her; she's very cute. I bend down to say hello. Something about her is familiar.

She looks around and I follow her gaze, to where she is likely looking back to her parents, showing them she's made a friend.

And then there he is, of course he is. He's standing up ahead on the path, watching me. He's sent his daughter to me as a Trojan horse.

"Hello, Maisie—you've grown."

She giggles at me and begins to waddle back to her dad.

I gasp when I see him; all that growth gone in an instant, it feels like. Just let him run into my arms!

But he is staying put, as always—he is not coming to me. He is smiling at me—why? How?

It would be disingenuous for me to say to you that I went into this conversation with no preferred outcome. I did still love him; if it turned out he had left her, would I have broken and taken him back? I want to say no, but I may have. It is important for me to tell you that. I may have.

But this is not what transpired.

I walk towards him slowly.

"Hi." (Me).

"Hello." (Him).

He is wearing one of his many unfortunate outfits, a terrible pair of long shorts and a hoodie that looks like it was purchased in the shampoo aisle of the supermarket. His curly hair is unkempt. His brows are furrowed, but kind. I used to love these clothes on him; I used to love that look in his eyes.

They both seem a little pathetic to me now, after everything. Buy a decent outfit, Arthur. Change the look in your eyes if you're not going to change your life to match.

"It's good to see you," he says.

"Yes," I say.

Is it good? It's hard, certainly.

We begin to speak as we stand awkwardly on the path, Maisie climbing around her dad's legs, bored and restless. I ask some banal questions, and he takes loop upon loop of time to answer me, mostly in non-answers.

Then he interrupts me, saying in a rush of words, "I've loved you more every day, it won't go away." It feels like he is imploring me, but to do what I do not know.

I deliberate on how to respond to this. I say, evenly, "Arthur, I've always loved you, and you've always known that." I pause. "But I don't know that I can believe you anymore."

He is taken aback by this. He's an honest Abe! That's his thing!

Maisie starts to wander away from us, so he must chase after her and guide her back to where I'm standing. He feels around in his pocket and finds a pen, which he gives her to hold. This keeps her still momentarily.

Attention back on me, he begins again. "I know," he says. "I know, but you *can* believe me." His tone is so pleading. "I keep . . . reading back over all our conversations. I've been trying to understand why I did what I did. I wanted you. I still want you. And I really thought I could end it with Kate. I wasn't lying to you. I never lied to you, never."

I don't know what he wants; what he wants from this conversation. Does he really not appreciate how much he is hurting me, how he's just digging the knife in deeper with every regret he voices and does nothing about?

And a small part of me, a part that flaps about like a tiny bird trapped under my rib, allows myself to wonder, Is this it? Is he telling me he wants me back?

I suppose, when I imagined this conversation happening, I saw it going one of two ways. Either he would tell me he loved me, and he'd left her, and he was begging me to come back to him. Or he'd tell me he hadn't, and wouldn't, and he'd apologise, and it would finally be done.

But he isn't doing either of those things.

He's grasping around at language, he's throwing fizzling grenades. "You know me. I love you; I never wanted to hurt you. It kills me that I'm hurting you. You know me."

All the words seem so trite, so totally unable to do battle with what is happening right now.

He hasn't even said it yet, the truth that seems clearer the more he skirts around it.

"Arthur?"

"Yes?"

I force myself to ask. "Have you left Kate?"

Silence. His face splintering. And for whose benefit are these expressions? I find myself wondering. Is he making these faces for me, to show me that I matter enough to cause him pain? Or are they faces he is performing for himself, so he can convince himself he has a conscience, is a good man still?

"No, I haven't left her."

The final string inside me breaks. That tiny, stupid string I wouldn't allow to snap, the one that's been tethering me to him all this time. The bird beneath my rib cage? It's been shot.

I feel resolve. I feel, for the first time, the red-hot heat of anger. I feel pity and, finally, the pity is not for me.

I say, "This is insane, Arthur." My fists are balled at my sides.

I go on. "It is insane that you made me try to convince you to love me. When you had all my love—and you knew that. You always knew that. And it's insane that you're doing the same thing now. After everything. It's . . . it's so disgusting, Arthur."

I hate saying this, for all the hopes it forecloses, for all that I thought I wanted and could not have. But I must say it.

"You just said you never lied to me. And I think you genuinely believe that?"

Now I've started, I can't stop talking. The words are coming out fast—all the things I've wanted to say: all the things he needs to hear.

"Arthur, you have always told me lies. Because you have *never* told me whole truths. Right now is another classic example. Like, *you* approached *me*; you tell me you still love me, you tell me you want me . . . And it's only when *I* ask that you reveal you haven't left Kate, you're still with her?"

He's staring at me like he wants me to hurt him, like he wants to be whipped.

Maisie begins to wail. He picks her up, he's holding her in his arms, shushing her, bobbing her up and down. I don't stop even for this. I talk louder, over her cries.

"It's like . . . how are you *still* putting me in this position, where I'm hanging on your every word, in case a single fucking one of them gives me hope that you won't be weak anymore?"

He has not left her, and he will not leave me alone, and I feel bile rise in the back of my throat. For the first time, I imagine ending this conversation and then never exchanging another word with him. The prospect is awful and it is miraculous and it is awful.

"Here's the thing, Arthur," I say. "I have only ever loved you honestly. I have always been all in. And you had a chance to be happy, and you didn't take it. Instead, you were weak. And you broke my fucking heart." My voice squeaks here, I'll admit. "And here you are back at it, when you have done *nothing* to change your life. You can't do it again. I won't let you."

He puts Maisie down next to him, and he begins to try to speak, but I cut him off. I will end this.

"You have forgone the future—our future—for a past that you don't even want. And I see it now. I see that you will *never* stop trying to catch my eye, and then have nothing to say when you do. So I'm going to walk away from you now. And I'm not going to look back."

Then an interesting thing happens, before I even have the chance to turn. What happens is that the space behind Arthur on the path—a children's park, with its fake grass green, its swing set—it begins to turn hazy, like heat shimmering on the road in summer. All of a sudden I see Arthur within a frame, a wooden frame at the periphery of my vision. I see Arthur as a painted figure: a painted figure in a painted park. As I stare at him, his figure begins slowly to recede; he is large in the foreground and then he is smaller, further away, merging into the painted set.

He is whispering, "I love you," even as he grows tinier, and tinier, as he fades into the background of the painting of his life.

I can hardly see him anymore; I have to squint to make out where I think he must be, so distant, so far away. Is that him, there, next to that shape that looks like a house? Or is it a tree? It is impossible to tell; it's just a very, very small green smudge on the canvas. So small I lose interest in it. The sun is going down and my eyesight is not that good and, besides, there are other things I want to look at.

I have been staring at the one spot for so long.

ACKNOWLEDGEMENTS

While I wrote this book, I was working as a bookseller at an independent bookstore in Sydney. My colleagues and I were unionising. We won. These colleagues are some of the bravest and strongest (and funniest) people I've ever known. So first, I'd like to thank the OG crew: Tahlia, Stella, Jimmy, Sanjo, Kat, Luca, Carolina, Leona, Emma, Darcy, Reem, Audrey, Ariel, Gin, Lucy, Diana, Bron, Mandy, and everyone at the Retail and Fast Food Workers Union. The workers united will never be defeated. Also ACAB.

Thank you to my family. To Dad, to Isobel, to Helen, to James. I love you.

Thank you, Jen. I hope always to follow your lead. Thank you, Georgie. Making you laugh is my supreme pleasure in life. Thank you, Brendan. You're stunnin. Thank you, Tink, Lily, Georgia, Mik, Kate, Lana. Thank you, Jaclyn; thank you, Young Sun. Thank you, Mikey.

Thank you, Emma and Frances. You are my gals in the trenches.

Thank you, Nell. You said you thought I could write a book, so I did.

Thank you to my agent, Grace Heifetz. We fried the steak. Thank you, Jane Palfreyman, Genevieve Buzo, and Ali Lavau. Thank you, Lettice Franklin. You understood this book sometimes more than I did, I think. Thank you, Caroline Zancan. Thank you, John Ash and Dana Murphy. Thanks to Mary Pender and Kristina Moore.

Finally, thank you to the teachers who've changed my life. Thank you, Suzanne O'Connor, Deborah Moir, Annette Lawlor, Graeme Colman, Jeff Lowndes, Christina Pechey, Matthew Sussman, Adam Guy, and Kaye Mitchell.

ABOUT THE AUTHOR

MADELEINE GRAY is a writer and critic from Sydney. She has written for the *Times Literary Supplement*, the *Guardian*, the BBC, *Electric Literature*, *Sydney Review of Books*, and other publications. In 2019 she was a CA-SRB Emerging Critic, and in 2021 she was a finalist for the Pascall Prize for Arts Criticism, a finalist for the Woollahra Digital Literary Non-Fiction Award, and a recipient of a Neilma Sidney Literary Travel Fund grant. She has an MSt in English from the University of Oxford and is a current doctoral candidate at the University of Manchester. *Green Dot* is her first novel.